For Richard and Taylor, my greatest teachers.
Thank you for showing me the power, potential,
and magic of the teenage years.
My love for you is boundless.

Chapter 1

Today, the old lady is going to talk. I just know it. I woke up knowing it. Okay, it could be desperation, given how Scottie is as weak as I've seen her. Just thinking of her sweet, little tabby legs all wobbly as she crawled up to sleep close to me last night—without a single purr—is killing me. But I don't think that's it. There's a difference between hoping for something and somehow just knowing it. This is definitely in the *somehow just knowing* category.

Anyone sane would say I'm attempting the impossible. Mrs. Ana Quinn, talking? After more than a year of barely coherent babble? It's crazy, I know. But I don't care. It's a chance and I'm taking it. So, yes, today is the day Ana will give me enough information to find…well, whatever it is she has been trying to tell me I have to find if I want to save Scottie.

If…? Want…?

No…*must*.

Scottie has been my best friend, my only sister, my only brother, my mother (so many nights, my mother) and all four of my long-gone grandparents rolled into one. You just can't let that die of unknown causes.

I'm nervous as I reach for the buzzer at the main doors. I shouldn't be. After all, I've spent the majority of my life in old folks' homes. The internationally recognized Sun Heritage Village was probably my first babysitter. Exactly when it was that I started babysitting the elderly residents, instead of the other way around, is hard to say. It was a gradual thing that nobody seemed to notice.

I wait to announce myself, looking forward to the cool blast of air that will rush at me when the door opens. It's not that they don't know me here. But the rules are the rules. It doesn't matter who you are. Even

Dad has to ring the buzzer and remind the person behind the desk that he's the guy who owns the place. He doesn't have to mention that, on last count, he owned forty-five such places across the US, with another few in Mexico and Europe. Everyone who works here learns that on training day.

I look up into the security camera, seeing the red dot blink at me like an accusation. Maybe even a warning. No one knows what I'm up to today. No one could know. Even so, you get paranoid when you are about to bend some pretty important rules.

What's taking them so long?

I know the two women at the front desk are just sitting there, watching me, enjoying their minuscule moment of power. I could stare back, as I often do. But not today. I'll just use my mind to bore an imaginary hole into their brains, keeping my head down and my lying eyes hidden.

While policy states that there must always be two at the desk, it really doesn't matter which two. The same type always applies for the job: Middle-aged women, average intelligence, easily distracted by gossip. The desk is a relatively simple job with decent pay and great benefits. Even so, turnover is high because, you have to admit, the place is pretty depressing, especially over time.

I can just imagine the conversation going on at the desk as they watch me wait. *It's the big boss's daughter again. Third time this week,* I imagine the first one saying.

Indeed, the other will reply. *With the kind of money her dad has, why does she always dress in torn jeans and that old army jacket—in summer no less? And her hair!*

That style is all the rage, the first will say with a barely audible tsk-tsk. *Outrageous, but not cheap. You know how much you have to pay to look like that? Good luck getting ahead in life with that kind of attitude, no matter who your daddy is.* She'll be shaking her head as if what a person wears is the totality of who a person is.

I can't stand imagining it any longer. I throw a big, fake smile into the camera. Not so big my teeth show—they don't deserve a real smile—but a lot bigger than normal. I mentally drill the idea into their skulls: *Just let me in.*

"Can I help you?" the speaker finally blasts, crackling. It makes me jump. I immediately curse myself for letting my nerves show. I've got to keep it cool, like today is no different than any other day.

"Julie Mayden," I drone, speaking the obvious, holding back on rolling the eyes. "I'm here to see Mrs. Quinn."

I jump again, this time to take quick advantage of the buzz that lets me in. Unfortunately, I still have to go to the desk for a nametag and to have my volunteer hours recorded. Dad says there is a grant that matches the hours with funding dollars, so I'm doing him a favor. But from what I can see, it only creates more paperwork, which creates more rules, and then you need more people to enforce them, and on and on it goes. Stuff like that really does make you wonder why you would ever want to grow up at all. Anyway, I play by the rules, if only to keep Dad and everyone else off my back.

Well, except for today.

The unmistakable scent of *nursing home* rushes at me the moment the automatic sliding doors open. It's a combination of bad cafeteria food, old people's drool, pressed face powder (some of it probably left over from the Fifties), and harsh disinfectant—because you just can't have people getting sick and dying in here, now can you? I both hate the smell, for obvious reasons, and love it, because this place is more like home to me than any of the four mini-mansions I've lived in during my short sixteen years.

I smile at the old folks lining the hallway, out for their daily sit. A few recognize me, but most don't. This is the building for the worst off, those who couldn't begin to care for themselves. I remind myself I could go to one of our other buildings, including one where the people sitting in front of the bright red and black checkers boards can actually play the game. But I've always been a bit of an extremist. I go for the hard cases. The supposed lost causes. No idea why.

My mind flashes on Ana Quinn.

Okay, maybe that's why.

"This will be good for my community service hours," I bait the desk ladies. Jenny and Alice are both looking at me like I've come at an inconvenient time, even though signing me in is one of maybe three things they will have to do this morning, at least before the pre-lunch routine gets underway. Then they will have the overwhelmingly strenuous task of getting on the loudspeaker and announcing the menu to people who—let's face it—even if they can understand, just don't care. Low-salt turkey, green beans, wilted lettuce, and applesauce. Hooray!

Did I mention it's depressing around here?

"What did you do wrong to have to complete community service?" Jenny asks, leaning in. Good gossip is a rare commodity and highly prized in this place. Even Alice lifts her suddenly wide eyes over her glasses to look at me more directly.

3

"Fifty hours a year are required to be in the Honor Society at my school," I answer, deadpan, but smiling inside.

I love to shock.

About the only person my attempts at shock value don't work on is my father. He sees me as he has since I was four years old, when I came to live with him full-time, as his perfectly beautiful fairy princess. *Just a little darker these days,* he jokes, and only then when I'm being really obnoxious.

The two women's faces deflate. Honor Society? You can actually see the realization that I might be smart settle in on their faces. Smiles turned downward, eyes gone dull. Not a morsel of indecency to smack their lips over in that kind of community service. They look at each other in disappointment.

Sorry ladies.

My name tag is freshly spit out from the front desk computer, complete with a bad photo of me at about age twelve (still with braces, ugh), and I am sent on. They know I know my way around. If only they knew what I was going to do with that knowledge in just a few minutes.

Talk about an opportunity for gossip.

I keep my head down and my hands in my pockets as I make my way through the squeaky clean halls. I know all of the staff, at least in this wing, and today is not a day to be held up by superficial monotony. Everything has been planned to a tight schedule, and it has to be today. It just has to.

Not that I am sure it will work, I remind myself, feeling the nerves kick into high gear. It borders on insane if I'm honest about it. My own friends would say I'm delusional to try. But a girl is nothing if she won't take a chance on her sweetest feline friend.

Even a really, really dangerous one.

I lift my head only when I've arrived at the door marked *Room 214.* I don't care if I am delusional. You do what you can with what you have, just like Dad always says. And if all I have is a hunched over old lady confined to a wheelchair to help me, that's what I'll work with.

I knock on Ana's door but don't wait for a reply. It would be a long wait. She babbles mostly, at least until she knows it's me. Even then, it's a while before any real words start to form. Taking her to the woods that line the property here always seems to help. I think it relaxes her to get outdoors. Which is why we are going out—way out—today, just as soon as I can get her ready.

I peek through her one, ordinary window that overlooks the huge parking lot. Today's fifty percent chance of rain threatens to kill off every hope I have but, so far, we're fine.

Yes, I'm actually going to do it. I'm going to wheel Ana to the elevator, go to the basement, take her out the side door, down the sidewalk, and then take the paved path that goes through the nearby patch of trees. Once we are as far into the woods as we can get on pavement (this is the part where we officially start breaking rules), I'll leave the path and wheel her deeper into the woods. The further in we go, even on pavement, the more she relaxes. And the more she relaxes, the better she talks.

Anyway, it's happened that way every time so far. And each time, her words have gotten a little clearer. So this time, we'll go even farther. My mouth goes dry as I think of how we could get stuck, especially in the swampy areas. Maybe it will help if I mentally outline my plan for the ten-thousandth time.

So...

We'll take the sidewalk until we are hidden from view, then turn into the woods and go as far in as I can get her wheelchair to go on the dirt. Way, way out of sight. Then I'll lay down the towel I've hidden behind her back and hoist her from her chair to the ground. This will be no easy feat, given the woman is both gargantuan and an invalid. Then I'll put the strange, native-looking leather bag I found in her suitcase around her neck. I swear it changes something about her when she is wearing it. Then finally, *deep breath*, I'll conveniently keep her out to as near to the very end of her medicine cycle as I can and...and...

...see what happens.

Yes, I know it's risky and probably very, very wrong. But I have to do this. I just have to.

Scottie is my life.

Chapter 2

I'm stuck. Not where I should be getting stuck, deep in the woods. But right here on the second floor, hallway B, of the Sun Heritage Village's Pine Crest building. Dr. Garcia stopped me on my way out the door with Ana. Back when she was just a resident here, her daughter Maria was one of my two best friends. It's been a while since I've seen either of them, so I kind of have to talk to her.

My hands are in a sweaty grip on Ana's wheelchair handles. There's a sick feeling in my stomach, and a strong voice inside my head screaming at me: *Turn around! TURN AROUND!* At the same time, my mind is calculating all the possible permutations my plans for today could take. Dr. Garcia could be a witness now. I get a flash image of Ana's normally absent family yanking me into a courtroom for doing something terrible to their feeble old grandmother with Dr. Garcia reluctantly standing up to testify against me. She's weeping, not wanting to speak against me, but what can she do? *Julie was wrong. Very, very wrong,* she'll testify in her still strong Spanish accent.

Then I will be doomed. Completely, totally, and forever.

I forcefully reel my imagination back in.

Just. Stay. Calm.

"I'm glad you still come in to help out, Julie," Dr. Garcia says, looking me over the way every parent looks over their kid's friends. Am I the type who stirs up trouble? Do I get too close to the boys? Will I get into college? *You become like the people you spend time with,* Dad always says. Maybe every parent says.

"I like it here," I admit, using as few words as possible without being rude. This is not even remotely abnormal for me. I'm a watcher, not a talker. Everybody who knows me at all knows that.

I check out the wall clock: 11:32. I have zero minutes to spare, but I can't show it. She's the type to guess something is up and, even more, the type to mention it to Dad. *Is something wrong with Julie these days?*

Ana shifts in her chair as if she knows what's going on and is as impatient as I am. Not likely, but it's nice to think I might not be in this alone.

"I wish I could get Maria to come in with me," Dr. Garcia says in a distinctly fishing tone. "I don't know what keeps her so busy."

Note to all parents: Teenagers are not stupid. We will not throw our friends under the bus, even if those friends no longer have time for us because they are completely consumed by their ever-climbing social status.

I stare blankly and blink like I'm as dumb as Dr. Garcia must think I am.

"I haven't seen Rod around, either," she tries from another angle.

Rod is the third in our trio. Or, what used to be our trio, when all our parents worked here. His dad is still the head of admin, but Rod's way past coming to work on vacation days. That was over by the time we were twelve. Both he and Maria outgrew this place like any normal teenager. Now that he's got that new Mustang convertible, none of us see him much. I'm happy to get a text once every week or so, and only then because he needs something.

"Me neither," I say, glad it's the truth, then quickly add, "Oh look, it's time for Bingo." Actually, there isn't Bingo today, and even if there were, it would not start just before lunch. But Dr. Garcia won't think about that. I'm hoping she's busy enough to appreciate the excuse to get on with her day. She nods, gives the standard *it's always good to see you* and walks on.

I keep my deep sigh of relief to myself. Ana, however, lets out a huge, heaving "Ugh!" Does she know what we are up to? *Could* she know?

No. No way.

I check my watch: 11:35.

If this is going to work, I have exactly three more minutes to get out the door and beyond the part of the path that can be seen from the building. I need enough time for anyone looking to take Ana to the main lunchroom to see my backpack on her bed and assume I've already got her. This alone took significant planning. I set the stage for confusion at lunch half a dozen times before they finally got past the panic of a missing resident. Now they all just assume that if Ana doesn't show in the main lunchroom, it's because I have her, and we are in the guest cafeteria, or the staff lounge, or even all the way down the block talking to some of the more coherent old folks at the Village Grill. I made sure never to go to the same place twice in a row, so there is no obvious second place to look. Even so, if they catch me with her too close to lunch, they'll ask me where, exactly, we'll be today.

That will end it all.

You'd never guess a hallway could be so long. Or a sidewalk. Ana seems all the heavier today, too. A nurse once said she was probably over six feet tall when she was younger. It's hard to tell, what with old people shrinking and the fact that she's pretty significantly bent over. She is also super big boned. Maybe she was fat once, too. It would make sense with all the excess skin she has. Now she just looks like an old gray elephant that you can imagine was once stately, at least before aging took over. Eighty-eight years old, according to her chart. That's seventy-two years older than me. For a second I try to think of myself living another seventy-two years. I just can't imagine it. What do you do with all those years? I'm already bored at sixteen.

Finally, I get to the paved walking trail. "Don't worry, Ana," I say aloud, though she probably can't register it, "we're getting there."

I check out the clouds overhead, which were perfectly cheerful when I walked in the doors today, leaning in our fifty-fifty favor. Now they are starting to loom thick, with the sky getting darker by the minute.

I hope it's not a sign. Not that I'm sure I believe in signs. I mean, I think I do. But I don't have conclusive evidence and anyway, today doesn't seem like the best day to think too much about those kinds of things.

I ask myself for the thousandth time why I'm doing this at all. And for the thousandth time, I remember. I quickly feel for the piece of paper and pen I brought and remind myself I'll need to write down the final details I will need to save Scottie.

"Okay, Ana, I've written down everything that you've said so far, and it is starting to make sense."

Ana grunts, but it could be a total coincidence.

"So you said *Sister help Scottie* about a hundred times one day. And when I asked if you meant Scottie, my cat, you said *Sister magic heals, sister magic heals.*"

I get chills hearing the words aloud, the same way I did that day. The hair stood straight up on the back of my neck, just like it does on Scottie, though she is usually ready for a fight when it happens to her.

"The next week you kept saying *Forest, not governments* and then *Clemmons' Pier.* Then you started repeating *Potter Street and Poplar Drive,* so I checked it all out on Google Earth. There is, in fact, an old Clemmons' Pier, and it's not too far from my house. It's at the edge of a small forest.

And on the other side, at the far opposite corner, there is a Potter Street that curves around into Poplar Drive."

Again Ana grunts.

I get goose bumps, though it might be nothing. It's just that, normally, when I get goose bumps it is something. I try to calm my pounding heart, but fear and excitement are in a race through my veins. I'm not sure if it's helping Ana for me to talk, but it's helping me. The wheelchair isn't getting any easier to push, but really, if I had to, I feel like I could lift a car right now.

"So here's the thing. There's nearly two hundred acres between the pier and Potter Street. I drove by the other day, and it actually is marked as government land. All kinds of *No Trespassing* signs on it. You can't even get to the pier without walking a few miles through the woods or crossing up to your waist in water."

Ana huffs, then coughs, then shakes her head in a kind of bobbling way that might mean something. Or not.

"So I don't know what you're trying to tell me. Does your sister work for the government? Can I find her there on that land? Are you saying she could help my cat? Because Scottie is really sick now. Worse and worse every day. We've been to the vet's office three times, but they never find anything. She's only seven years old, so you know it's not old age."

Even if I am just talking to myself, it feels good to get it out. Anyway, we have arrived at the point where we will leave the beaten path, and there is no way I am turning back now. I look around, though no one from the Village but me ever comes out this far. You see some joggers from the nearby business complex sometimes, but that's about it. Right now, there's not a soul in sight. I look to the soft, mushy ground. We could get seriously stuck, especially if it rains. But for now, the weather is holding. And Scottie is not.

We're only three feet in before the tires start to squish heavily into the earth. I tighten Ana's belt and push on. I want to get her where she can, if nothing else, forget where she lives for a little while. She seems to love it when we come outside, her head bobbling with more of a happy bounce to it.

I'm thinking if we can get far enough away from the Village, and deep into the trees, something new might break loose. I also hope it helps that her meds are running out. We have only a little while until the after-lunch rounds are given. Being at the tail end of the med cycle should be helpful because I Googled her prescription names and, seriously, the stuff they have her on could keep a horse tied into a chair.

Anyway, it might not help, but it can't hurt. Okay, well, it can hurt if something goes wrong, like we get stuck out here and it takes too long to get back, and the meds fully run out, and Ana passes out, falls to the ground, can't get up, and...

No. That won't happen.

Probably.

The wheels are starting to get bogged down. Ana's size isn't making this easy.

"Ethel Mai," she suddenly says.

"What?" I stop to ask, getting the chills, the goose bumps and the hair on the back of my neck rising up, all at once. I go around front and kneel down to see her face. Her normally glassy eyes seem clearer than usual.

"Lillian Luta...Martha Jane...Mary Kelly...Suzanne Mary...Sarah Ashley..." She is speaking carefully as if to enunciate every syllable. Which is completely impossible, at least according to her chart.

"Who are they, Ana?"

"Margaret...Rachel. Sixteen hundred. Ninety..."

"What are you trying to say?" I plead. Her voice is strangely normal. I get a full body shudder, and that never, ever means nothing.

"My medicine bag," she says, lifting her eyes to my own.

Dead. Clear. Lucid.

"I need my medicine bag," she repeats.

"A full sentence!" I nearly shout until I remember where I am. Shivers run all over me now, dance really, around and around and up and down. She's talking! Full sentences!!! I want to scream and have to literally bite my tongue so I don't.

"You have my bag," she insists.

It takes me a second to realize what she means: Her leather bag.

"Yes, yes, Ana, I have it. I hope you don't mind me calling you Ana."

"You always do."

"Whoa! You answered me!" I want to clap and scream and cry, all at once.

She smiles a kind of broken, awkward, jittery smile. It's totally real, but sort of like her mouth has been set the same way too long, and she's just getting used to using it again. But who cares? She answered me! She's talking to me!

Ana of the freakin' Village, near comatose for practically forever, is talking to me!

I quickly find her leather bag, put it around her neck, and watch as she attempts to sit straighter than I've ever seen her. Not straight, but straighter. It makes me all the more curious what's inside the bag. I've never looked because it felt like it would be an invasion of privacy or something, even if she is…was…is….

Well, it just didn't seem like the kind of thing you should look at without permission.

"Farther in," she insists, and even lifts a long, crooked, bony finger to point forward. She has never, ever, *ever* pointed toward something!

My heart is exploding, I swear.

"Whatever you want, Ana," I readily agree, and go back to pushing. It's not hard at all now. In fact, I feel like I could lift two cars, one in each hand, if I had to.

"Ethel Mai, eighteen hundred and ninety-five."

"What's that, Ana?"

"Shhh…Lillian Luta, eighteen hundred and seventy-six. Sarah June, eighteen hundred and fifty-seven. Martha Jane, eighteen hundred and thirty-eight. Mary Kelly, eighteen hundred and two. Suzanne Mary, seventeen hundred and seventy-seven. Sarah Ashley, seventeen hundred and fifty-two. Margaret Cole, seventeen hundred and twelve. Rachel, sixteen hundred and ninety."

Somewhere along her list of names and numbers, I realize what she's doing. She's listing people and dates. Lillian Luta, 1876. Sarah June, 1857. She's going backward in time. Now we are at Rachel, 1690. She's asked me to be quiet, so I just listen. But who are these women?

Her family, I suddenly realize, though I don't know how I could know that. I get another shiver, this time the creepy kind. Because, you know, now I'm *involved* in the weirdness.

"Yes," Ana says.

"Yes, what?"

"Yes, you understand. These are my ancestors. The women who begat me and those who begat them. Repeating their names aloud has Magic in it. It gives me strength."

"Okay, this is freaky, Ana. I don't mean about your ancestors' names and all that. I mean because I didn't say that I thought they were your ancestors' names."

"But you knew."

"Well, I figured it out, but I didn't actually *say* that I figured it out."

"When understanding is present, it can be felt. I felt that you understood."

First her words come out totally, utterly clear. And now she's some kind of mind-reading psychic type as well? I am both completely freaked and totally excited, with excitement winning by a hair. It is possible that

I have never been so happy in all my life.

"This is good," she insists, readying herself by sitting even straighter in her chair. "Now, put me down on the earth."

"I suppose you knew I was going to do that, too?"

"You said so last Monday."

"Wait. *Wait!* You can...you understand me...and you know what day it is, even back there, in your room at the Village?"

Immediately I try to remember all the intimate life details I have shared with her this past year, thinking she was as safe to confide in as Scottie is. You have to wonder, can a person actually die of embarrassment?

"Everything," she says, sounding a little bit sad, "I understand everything."

Her words gut me, but not because of my secrets. Because of her living in there, the way she does. I can't imagine how it must be for her. It's even worse if she understands.

Wait. No. I can't think about that either. Not right now, anyway. There will no doubt be plenty of sleepless nights in my future, thinking about every last bit of this. Right now, there's a plan to get to.

I set her brakes, lay out the towel, untie her belt, and use everything I've learned about lifting an invalid from a wheelchair into a bed. I'm aware it's not a bed, and that there's a significant difference—about a foot from chair to ground. But I'm thinking the same general rules must apply.

It doesn't go well, and I nearly let her fall the last bit of the way. Maybe she understands everything, as she says, but she's had no recent practice in actually using her legs. Despite me practically dumping her down, she doesn't complain, which is amazingly generous. I stretch out her stiff legs and put my jacket under her head as a pillow. She looks to the ground at her left and then her right and starts to cry.

I mean big, sudden, wet-your-wrinkly-face tears.

"What? What's wrong?"

She laughs. "Wrong? What could possibly be wrong?"

"But you're crying."

"I have missed the earth so much. Especially seeing things up close. They took my glasses when I arrived, so I can only see what is immediately in front of me. There is so much beauty I've missed. The vibrant green of moss. The genius of leaves! Oh, and just look at this soil, how beautifully dark and rich it is. Everything is so vivid, so luminous." Her voice shakes, part with age, part with emotion. "I think I might die of joy!"

"You can't die of anything out here, Ana," I insist, instantly terrified. "You're on my watch."

"Yes, yes, we must remember that, mustn't we? It is critical to the plan."

"You have a plan?" I beg to know, hoping desperately that it has something to do with Scottie. Because if Ana herself is a miracle...

"Indeed! Sit down with me," she suggests, reaching to pull me by the hand. "Come close so that I can see your sweet face as I tell you everything."

I get close enough to smell her old woman smell, but I don't mind at all. I want to hear every detail of what she has to say. It's like I've discovered a treasure box in a dusty attic, and now I get to slowly, carefully open it.

Ana takes a moment before she begins, looking at all the nature surrounding us, and then looking carefully, closely at me. I let her take her time, and even smile with my teeth showing, because, let's face it, nobody looks at you like that.

You know, like they see you.

Like they really, *really* see you.

Chapter 3

"You have a boyfriend," Ana says, more of a statement than a question, and frowning as if she doesn't like the idea. Or maybe she's just squinting at the small slug she's got on her finger, pulled up close to her eyes so she can get a good look. Either way, I'm not thrilled to have her bring up the one topic I've been getting more and more worried about.

No, I don't have a boyfriend. In fact, I've never had one. Not even a crush, by me or on me, at least that I know of.

I realize this makes me a bit of a castoff. But in my defense, the vast majority of guys at school are idiots and those who aren't go for girls that are…well, not me. It's not that I don't hover at slightly above average in intelligence and looks. I've done a very honest self-assessment several times. I am confident that I sit squarely in the *okay enough* category in both departments. It's just that virtually every person at my school also checks in at above average, well above average, superior or highly exceptional. It's that kind of school. So fair or not, I am a victim of a skewed personal attribute grading curve.

It's only now I realize I've never spoken about my relationship status to Ana, even when I thought she would never—could never—say a word.

"Not really," is all I can come up with.

"Yet I have seen that brown boy around you," she argues, her thin eyebrows squeezed as she slowly, tenderly, peels the slug off her finger. I start to feel slightly queasy. Slugs are not exactly my thing.

"You mean Rod?" He's the only one I can think of. His dad is black, and his mom is white, so as pure description, it is fair to call him brown. He wouldn't like the boy part, though.

Not. At. All.

Anyway, he's the only guy she might have seen me with. But even that doesn't make sense, given he hasn't visited the Village for years.

"If you say so," she affirms, marveling as she brings up another handful of dirt and moss. "I do not get names clearly. It is amazing how much life there is outdoors. Thank you, dear Mayden, for bringing me here."

I could correct her about Mayden being my last name, not my first, but I want to stay on topic. "But Rod hasn't been at the Village in forever. And you've only been here for a year and a half, right?"

Ana smiles and turns her face to mine. "I did not mean I have seen him with you. I mean I have seen him around you." She waves her hand in the air in circles, like she's conjuring up something hard to describe.

"Oh," I say, feeling another round of creepy wash over me. It's weird enough she's talking and some kind of mind reader. Now she wants me to believe she sees people *around* people? "Anyway, he's a friend, not a boyfriend." Rod as a boyfriend would be totally wrong, like dating a brother. I shudder just thinking of it.

"I see," she says, now smiling, as if Rod as just a friend changes things. But why would she care? I mean, she's eighty-eight, so she could be prejudiced, I guess. But that doesn't seem like her somehow. Anyway, Rod and boyfriends don't matter right now. Only Scottie does.

"So there is a plan?"

"Oh, yes, very much so. Your *friend* Rod will be needed."

"What do we need him for?" Truth be told, I only got as far into my own plan as we are right now. I was hoping something she might say would help me take it the rest of the way.

"My dear, your cat is ill. Very ill."

I feel a thud land in my gut. It's one thing to know your cat is seriously sick, and another to hear it confirmed, especially by someone who claims to see things around things. "But the other day, you said your sister could help."

There is begging in my voice. Even I can hear it.

"Oh, indeed, Bea can help with Scottie. And she will, so long as I am the one sending you to her. She is my twin, and we are very close. You know the location already."

I have to wonder how she can be so attached to a sister who lives nearby yet never visits her, but I decide it's best not to go there.

"The woods by the pier? But that's government land, despite what you said, and…"

Ana laughs. "It is not government land! That is our trick to get people to stay away. Even government people stay away, thinking it is all taken care of by someone else in the government. Bureaucracy at its very best! It was Bea's brilliant plan. I was so delighted you caught on to my meaning, even with my cryptic instructions. What is this Google Earth thing you spoke of?"

"It's a kind of…sort of…Actually, I'll explain it later, if you don't mind. I need to know about Scottie. Is your sister a vet or something? Because we have already been to the vet."

"If anyone can help, my sister can. You can be sure of that. So this is our plan. You will go to the pier. Be sure to cross from the water. I know you could go through the woods, but Bea will find you the moment you step foot on her territory. I do not want your first encounter to happen too close to the public eye. The water between the pier and the land is not deep and it is not too far. I am sure you will be able to cross."

"I know the place, and I don't care about getting wet. So I should take Scottie with me?"

"No!" she cries out a little too loud, and then hushes again. "Not at first. That is why you will need your friend. He will need to keep Scottie for you and wait until you have made your first approach to my sister. You will have to win Bea over. Once she understands that I have sent you, I believe she will make it safe for Scottie to join you."

"Safe? Why wouldn't it be safe?" Suddenly that thud in my stomach is in my throat.

"Things are not what they seem, dear Mayden."

She can't be serious. Like this is supposed to be news? Ana Quinn is talking, knows dates, has made plans and could see if you'd just give her back her glasses, but we are only now getting to the part where things are not what they seem?

Anyway, all craziness aside, this name thing has to stop. "Um, it's Julie, actually. Mayden is my last name."

"No," she replies. I wait for her to explain, but she doesn't.

Again her attention wanders to a handful of tiny, bright blue wildflowers she's brought up close to her face. She giggles in delight and smells the bunch in one huge, long inhale, then lets her breath out with an even longer sigh.

In the back of my mind, I'm already thinking how hard I'm going to have to work to get Rod's help on short notice. I mean, he owes me, but he doesn't keep score unless it's in his favor. Nine times out of ten he doesn't even answer my texts, and when he does it's with nothing more than his signature line, *caught that*.

"How will I find your sister?"

"She will smell you," Ana says matter-of-factly, like that's as normal as everything else happening out here.

"Okay," I start, trying not to be argumentative because I know how adults hate that, "so this is getting a little strange, even for me, and I like strange things. I mean, I can live with 'things are not what they seem,' and all that. And I don't have to know how you can suddenly talk out here in the woods after how you have been for the past year and a half inside. But this is my cat, my very best friend in the world. When it comes to Scottie, I have to know the how, and the why, and the dangers, especially."

"I have always been able to talk. At least, on the days I choose to forgo the pills they attempt to stuff down me. Sometimes I swallow them just to help knock myself out. I like to fly, and the drugs they give make it so easy. The days get long in there, as you might imagine. In any event, I am aware enough to become fully aware whenever I wish. Of course, I have been preparing for this day for some time, and I have been clever enough not to give myself away to anyone before now."

She is smart. Absolutely. But to stay in there like she does? That's just crazy. "But why would you do that? Pretend you're out of it when you're not? And for so long?"

She sighs. "There are things in preparation that you simply could not imagine. It is best that you do not try."

"Okay, so I'm the kind of person who likes to take calculated risks. I mean, I'll take them. You can count on that. But the calculation part is important to me. And to be calculated, you have to know all the elements of the equation."

God, I sound like I'm in geometry class.

"Mayden, dearheart, if I told you everything you would encounter at the water's edge with my sister, you simply would not go. Already you are thinking you might not because I have frightened you. But you also know that you must, because what other option is there for your Scottie?"

She looks at me like she's won our first debate. I guess she has.

I don't even try to mask my incomprehension. I like to think of myself as at least a little hard to read, but she seems to see right through me. "How do you know all that?"

"I have lived a life of Magic," she replies, wistfully, "and my time is nearing an end. But the Magic will live on—must live on—and so we prepare and protect those who will come after us. You have been chosen and, yes, you do have the markings of one that Magic tends to be drawn to. Those things you seem to *just know*? That is Magic trying to reach you."

I have no idea what to say.

Not. A. Clue.

"This much I know," she continues, "You will go to see my sister because you love your Scottie, and also because you trust me, even if you do not know why. But mostly you will go for reasons that reason cannot explain. Reasons that Magic has in mind."

I shudder visibly. What do you say to something like that? I mean, really, what do you say? It doesn't matter. I can't get any words out.

Did she say Magic? And chosen? And markings? And who is "we?" Just Ana and her sister, or others, too? My pulse is racing in surges. At the same time, a horrible sadness rises up in me. That part about her time at an end? That's a kick in the gut.

"I do not know if my sister will accept you right away. Probably not, since she does not know you as I have come to know you. But I can promise this: Whatever her initial welcome when you meet her, you will feel her to be kin. You will also feel more at home on her land than you have felt anywhere on this earth. That may seem hard to believe because I can see that you have crossed the ocean many times. I also see you have not felt at home anywhere. This will change. With Bea, on that land, you will find an entirely new sense and meaning of home. At least, once she lets you in. For that, I must send my signature with you."

Immediately, I'm fumbling for my pen and paper.

"No, Mayden," she says, struggling to sit up, "not that kind."

I help her, steadying my legs in the soft earth and bracing her from behind.

"I'm stable," she assures once she is fully upright. "Now, come around and give me your hands."

I move to kneel in front of her and put my hands up close where she can see them clearly.

"Do you want me to…?"

"Shhh!"

Immediately I hear what she has already noticed—a jogger coming near. My pulse surges yet again, my chest pounding at me. We are far enough into the woods that we won't be seen from the path, but someone could hear us.

It's an interminable minute as we both wait for the plodding footsteps that come and go. Finally, Ana takes my hands in hers again. She cups them, like I'm going to hold something, and brings them close to her face. Slowly, she takes a deep breath, then blows into my palms.

They get hot. Really hot, to the point of near burning.

I have to jerk my hands back. I see a red color glowing at the center, like lit coals that have gotten a blast of oxygen.

"It's all right," she assures, gently guiding my hands back toward her and cupping them again. "This is good fire, carried on air." I don't know what she means, but somehow it seems true. This time, she blows three deep breaths. Each time, the red in my hands glows brighter. It's hot enough that I'm tempted to jerk away again. A fourth blast, and I would have to. But I can take this much. I want to.

When she's done she puts my hands on her forehead, and immediately my palms cool.

"As I suspected," she says in a low mumble, inspecting my hands, which are impossibly unscathed.

"What?" I have to eke out.

"Fire. She likes you."

"What does that mean?"

"Now then," she says, seemingly ignoring my question, "I have put my scent in you."

Like that's normal. Like people have scents, and you can just put them into someone's hand with some ritualistic fire breathing.

"Bea will catch wind of you long before you see her. Stay steady when she approaches, for she is not to be startled. She will not trust you at first, but hold out your hands. Be open. Supplicate. You must be still. And you must stand unafraid, like an animal that is not going to back down but is also not aggressive. Once she has confirmed that I have sent you, I am certain she will help."

"Okay," I say, though it comes out more skeptical than I'd wanted.

"Now, you must return me to my room before you get into trouble."

I sigh, heavy. Just the idea of taking this totally amazing woman and putting her back in that room is plenty sad. It's more than that, though. But what? What? I listen for what I *just know* as hard as I can.

Could I maybe, I don't know, feel her dying? If not now, one day not very far into the future? Or is it her Magic that is dying out somehow? Both ideas grab and twist at my heart.

"I am sure you can understand that there can be no mention of this to anyone," she instructs as I get her chair set in the right direction. "Our plan will keep us safe, but we must remain silent. Fortunate for us, it is in your nature to be quiet. I've noticed that. Also, understand that I only speak of this now to be sure we are clear with each other and not because I do not trust you. You have always been trustworthy as well."

"I get it," I assure her, not sure how to take the compliment, but glad for it. "I can't tell Rod. Or anyone. But does it mean I can't talk to you when we are back at the Village?"

Her already pale face goes especially white. "Without the door closed, absolutely not. Everything is at risk if you let on that I am not as feeble as they think."

I want to ask a thousand questions, a million questions, but I'm not sure I can process any new information. I help her back into her chair, this time a bit more gracefully, and begin to shove her wheels through the mud. Even if she's not dying right away, it kills me to think she'll go back in there, pretending to be some senile invalid. That she'll continue without her glasses or anyone to talk to. It kills me even more to think how long she's been living like that.

I'd go insane. I really would.

It starts to sprinkle and thunder rolls in the distance. There will be total pandemonium among the staff if she comes in wet. I push as fast as I can, wondering about her Magic. I can live with all this being mysterious and everything, and not understanding even two percent of the stuff she has said. But there's one thing I still want to know. Maybe it's selfish—well, it's totally selfish—but maybe I'll never have the chance to ask again. And anyway, she was the one who brought it up.

"Ana?"

"Yes, dear Mayden?"

"With your Magic, um, I mean, do you ever see the future?"

"It happens."

"So...I mean...You said you saw Rod around me. But like I said, he's not my boyfriend. So...do you think...do you see...?"

I'm glad I'm behind her, so she can't see my mouth twisting just to get a few words out.

"A true love?" she asks, a lift in her voice. "For you?"

Hearing her put it like that throws me well beyond any level of embarrassment I have ever felt in my life thus far. I would never have said *love*. And, anyway, this is small. Unimportant. Even so...

"Well, even just a guy that I like, and who likes me, I mean really likes me, would be...well...," I bite my tongue to keep from saying more, like *even though I'm a little bit chubby* (Dad doesn't think so, but he's Dad), and *despite my weird hair* (I can always change that). Dad's Wife #4 says mentioning these things only makes them more obvious to others, which is easy for her to say, perfect little pretty that she is.

"Oh my, yes. Your beloved is right around the corner. At least, if I have anything to do with it, which I intend to. Now, we must shush."

I'm shushing. But I'm also smiling.

Who wouldn't, with a magical old lady and her sister on your side?

Chapter 4

People probably think I don't think much because I don't talk much. If so, they'd be remarkably wrong. I think about everything, from every angle, over and over again. To me, information is a craving, like salt. Days are lifeless without it.

I feel that craving intensely now, waiting for Rod, watching the rain through the screened-in breezeway that attaches the main house to the garage, wondering how high the water will have risen when I cross to the land Ana says her sister lives on.

I cannot help but notice that the fifty-fifty chance of rain went to a hundred percent downpour. I think about Ana and how it's a hundred percent chance of rain every day for her, living in the Village. For some reason, with her, it crushes me, even though I've been around the same scenario my whole life.

Well, not the same scenario. How could anything be like this?

To comfort myself, I purr into Scottie's carrying case, trying to get her to purr back. I got her when I was nine, most likely because I kept asking for a brother, and that was simply not going to happen. Dad said that after my mom, he learned to marry the kind of woman who didn't want kids. I'm not sure he ever stopped to think how that made me feel. Then again, I am not sure he stops to think about much of anything that would indicate a fully developed emotional intelligence. That's not an insult. He's happy-go-lucky, with a lean toward the lucky, and it is not a skill he's needed thus far in life.

Anyway, ever since leaving Ana in her abysmally lifeless room, playing out her hidden identity—dulled eyes, slumped back, and mumbling nonsense like a pro—I've been Rubik's-cubing my brain to try to make sense of each and every detail of what she said, including everything she didn't say.

I swear, I need a spreadsheet for all the questions piling up in my brain.

Small questions, like why doesn't her sister Bea visit her? To mid-sizers like how she knew about my world travels, since that's not something I've talked about. To the biggies, like how does someone smell you coming? I look at my palms, still wondering if they actually turned red-hot with Ana's scent, or if I just imagined it. There's no evidence. No burns or blisters, not even little red marks. So, while I think they turned bright red, and it felt like they did, I can't prove anything.

Anyway, now I'm second-guessing it, which makes me second-guess everything.

I mean, Ana did talk, didn't she?

All this leads to the monster questions, the ones threatening to blow the fuse box that is my brain. Like what is Magic? Is it real? Where does it come from? What can it do? What is it for? And what in the name of crazy does it mean that I have the markings that make me interesting to it? I would toss the idea out completely except that it feels, if not right, at least oddly familiar. Like I knew this day was coming, and I've just been waiting.

"Hey," Rod says out of nowhere, his ultra-polished blue Mustang idling not twenty feet away. It makes me jump a mile.

"Where did you come from?" I frown to cover my embarrassment. I didn't even notice his car come up the drive, even though it's nearly a half-mile long.

"Alabama," he jokes with an exaggerated, cheesy, southern accent. I give him a roll of the eyes. He's not from Alabama. He was born right here in Annapolis, Maryland, same as me.

"What's this about? Is it really a Code Lilly?" I understand his questioning me. When does my life ever have anything worthy of that call, at least these past few years?

Lilly is the code we created back at the Village when we needed each other to do something truly important, usually a cover-up of some mistake or help breaking a rule, without asking questions. It's named after Lilly, the longest running head nurse, who made us crazy with rules that were not important. Rod, Maria, and I all watched out for each other. Like the time I stole my dad's ID to get into his office to see if he actually was talking to a private school in Switzerland, like Wife #3 threatened, just before the divorce papers were served. I never thanked Dad for letting the idea go, but he won some serious fatherly points for it.

"Sorry, can't tell you. That's what makes it a Lilly, remember?"

"Fair play. So what's wrong with Scottie?" he asks, poking a finger into the travel cage. It's not good if someone can see the problem all the way through the mesh door to the back of the cage where Scottie is curled in a ball. Not that I don't know it's not good. I just don't know how to face it not being good, so I keep pretending it can't be that bad, even though it is. And then someone like Ana, and now Rod, reminds me.

"She's sick. That's part of it. I need you to take care of her while I do something."

"What? This is sick cat duty?"

"Hey, when did I last call a Lilly?" I lean into him with my most serious *don't give me shit* expression. "You must owe me at least ten."

"Okay, okay, you're right."

"I'm totally right," I insist, making sure he doesn't think he can slack on the job. This is every bit as risky as taking Ana out this morning, and Rod's not exactly known for being meticulous about his commitments, especially if they don't benefit him directly.

"Okay, I said. Just don't tell anyone I did cat duty."

"Not a problem." When do I talk to his anyones, anyway?

"Where to?"

"You drive, I'll direct," I insist, covering Scottie's cage with a towel.

"It's going to be okay," I whisper to her through her cage door, even though I don't know that. I just know it has to be, somehow. And if it does turn out all right, I'll owe Ana everything. A walk in the woods every day. Maybe even break her out of the Village for good.

Rod's car is spotless inside and out, as usual. I know the idea of a cat, even a caged one, riding in it makes him nervous. Too bad.

I point the way and he drives, starting to give me his most recent updates.

I'm only half listening. Nothing much I don't already know, given it's always about a girl, and if you substitute Linda with Lydia or Latisha or Lori, the story is the same. On and on he goes about how she's hot and totally into him. He's chill with her, interested but not showing it too much. Keeping it low key, which is to say attempting to be the player. He's pretty much a wanna-be in that department, but I have to admit, no one tries harder.

I'd call him on it, saying he's wasting his time, but I prefer to let it slide. *Friendship is like that*, I think as the rain begins to hammer down. If you get close when you're young, you hang with all the crap that comes later and just hope they outgrow the stupid stages they have to go through. After all, Rod outgrew throwing his dirty socks in my face to make me mad. I never told him that I liked that he did it because it made me feel like I had something close to a real brother. Even so, I'm glad he outgrew it, especially because his feet smell like a cow lives in your bathroom.

Anyway, I'm looking for something deeper now, even in a brother.

It makes me wonder again about Ana and Bea, though. Eighty-eight-year-old sisters. Twins, Ana said. They must have gone through a lot together. And now, knowing they will probably die before too long? I mean, wow. Losing each other after all those years? How could you be okay with that? I think if I'd had a sibling, knowing they would die someday, let alone someday soon, would kill me. I wonder if Ana and Bea ever hoped they would get in some crazy car accident together and go at exactly the same time? Not likely with Ana in the nursing home. But they have Magic, right? Then again, if they do have some kind of Magic, why don't they use it to get Ana out, especially if she doesn't need to be there?

Rubik's-cubing again.

Really, I drive myself mad.

"So there's this thing. Kinda big," Rod starts, tentative in that way you are when you don't want to talk about something, but know you have to.

"Yeah?" I say, paying more attention, but still trying to gauge the rain, which keeps going from seriously wet to a sideways holy-hell drench, and back again.

"I don't know, maybe it's not the right time."

"Yeah?" I say again, now looking at him.

"So, my mom and dad are getting a divorce."

Oh. Shit.

In an instant, I feel like I'm pinned to the back of the seat. Like the air bag just burst open and I don't know what came at me. I look more intently at Rod, but he just keeps looking ahead, both his hands in a tight grip on the wheel. First time I have seen him tear up. Ever.

Crap. Crap. Crap.

He's not kidding.

But his dad? And his mom? I know them. They know me. They love me. They're *in* love.

Right?

"They can't do that," I say with what little wind is left in me.

"I know. But they are."

You can see this is killing him. Really, really, killing him. I remember that pain. You never feel like a kid so much as when you hear that news, no matter how old you get. It's not your decision, which means you have zero percent control.

"They love each other," I insist, as if saying it will make it true again. "It's not like my dad. You expect him to get married to cute little gold diggers and then divorce them a few years later. Your parents are different. You're a family."

"I guess not anymore," he says, angry. I can feel it, like a brick through a windshield.

I don't blame him. But I also don't know what to say. I just want this sudden, remarkably big pain in my chest to stop siphoning the life out of me. I just saw his dad last week. Now it's like I didn't see him at all. It had to have been in the works for a while because divorces don't happen overnight. That much I know. But I caught no wind of it. And I catch wind of just this kind of thing all the time, long before most everyone else.

I stare at Rod, who keeps staring at the road. It hits me he's messed up right now, like I've been, even when it was just idiots pulling the rug out from under me. But I know how to deal. That much, you figure out.

"It will be okay," I say, hearing how lame it sounds. "I know it will. You know I know, right?"

He doesn't say anything. Just drives, because really, what else can he do?

I comfort myself as I always have, by remembering that divorced is better than dead. His mom and dad are both still alive. They will still come to his graduation and his wedding and his baby's first birthday. Maybe not together, but they'll both come. I know it's a small comfort, so I don't say that. At least not right now.

"This is it, turn here." I feel my heart take a flying jump into my throat.

"No one's here," he says, pulling into the small, empty, dirt road of a parking lot.

"No one but us," I lie.

I look out at the end of the pier, going straight into the bay water, but with a side leg branching off at the end. This is it, the pier that reaches out to the land Ana spoke of. I look at the fifty-foot span of water I'll have to get across. That, along with the rain, and I'll be one hundred percent soaked.

I take a moment to wonder if an old woman really will be willing to come out in the rain to find me through Ana's scent. And if she doesn't, how far in I'm willing to go to look for her. And what if she can't smell anything but murky seawater? Cause, no doubt, that is what I'm going to smell like by the time I get to her.

It's starting to hit me: Go in there? Suddenly, it's all Hansel-and-Gretel spooky. I'd seriously consider ditching the whole idea, but I have to do what I have to do for Scottie.

Rod seems to get it because he unlocks the doors for me. "Go on."

"Okay, we'll talk more later, though. I promise."

"Sure," he says, but it already sounds like he regrets telling me. I should dive in while I have him cornered, but I can't.

"So I have to cross the water and go into the woods. I'll be back to get Scottie as soon as…well, as soon as I can."

"Why cross by water? It's not like it's an island," he says, sounding worried about me. Which is sweet given what he is going through. Even so, I can't exactly admit it's because an old lady might catch my scent too close to a public road.

"Code Lilly," I remind him, still feeling that sinking, pinned-back feeling, and all the worry about Scottie, too. Rod will make it through the divorce, that much I know for sure. We all do. But Scottie? That's far less certain.

I look into the patch of woods just in time to see a flash of something dark appear a few feet in. One of those creepy chills comes over me. Already someone is watching me. Maybe someone has been waiting.

The one watching is low to the ground. Or maybe it's not someone. Maybe something, like a wild animal. What kinds are out here? I want to slow the adrenaline moving through my entire body but have no idea how.

"Any guidelines?" Rod inquires. "Like *if I don't come out in five minutes* kind of thing?"

I can't think about it that way, or I won't go at all. "No. I'll just be back for Scottie as soon as I can."

I get out of the car and follow the pier out, feeling the water beneath the old wooden boards pulling at me, threatening my footing. Finally at the end of the side leg of the pier, I look down, feeling nothing short of doom. No way to know how deep it is, given the rain and mud. But I can swim if I have to. If I had a handful of leaves, I'd toss them to see how fast the current is going. But it's not been the kind of day where you'd have the brain space you'd need to think to pick up a few leaves on your way out to walk the plank.

I continue to stare at the fifty-foot wide span of water as I take off my jacket to make a small cover for my head. Really, how hard can this be?

It's not like there are riptides at the pier.

Are there?

Finally, I take off my worn flip-flops, put them on top of my jacket overhead, and make my way down the few steps on the wooden ladder. I'm comforted there is a ladder here in the first place. It means that people use this as a platform for swimming, which means it's not like I'm going where no one has ever gone before.

The water is cold for a summer day, and my jeans get heavy as I sink down. I feel for the bottom, and when I find it, I'm in up to my chest. I suck in a huge gulp of air, no doubt a natural, biological, pre-hypothermia response.

"Cut it out, Julie," I whisper to myself through already chattering teeth, "It's summer for God's sake."

Okay, so, good.

Nothing I can't handle.

No, really, this is fine.

It's not long at all before the worries of the water disappear. In their place, the fear of what will or won't be found on land comes upon me with excruciating clarity. The last ten feet across are the hardest, but then the bank appears to rise beneath my feet. My soggy jeans make a strange sucking noise as I rise out of the water. Now firmly on land, I put out my hands as best I can, mentally willing Ana's "scent" to ride the wind.

Do I feel stupid? *Yes.*

Does it matter? *No.*

Maybe all this is total crap. Maybe I am a fool, or I'm in the middle of a super-vivid dream. But maybe not. Maybe something is happening. Something other than what normally happens to normal people on normal summer days.

For some reason, excitement starts to outweigh fear. It's entirely possible that, by nightfall, utter stupidity will have been the big winner as my Feeling Of The Day.

But, for that, we'll just have to see.

Chapter 5

Maybe someone could look a whacked-out crazy woman like this one in the eye right off the bat, but it would be a braver person than me. I wasn't twenty feet in—just past where Rod could see me—and she appeared.

Not a sound, mind you.

Not a twig breaking to warn me.

Stealth personified.

She's wild. Hair sticking out in every direction. Dirty smock of a dress. She moves weird, too, in short, jerky bursts, coming close then backing away. Not like Ana. Not even a tiny bit like Ana. It's like this woman was born wild and lived here, alone, her whole life. Now she's sniffing me like an animal. I'm too freaked to do anything but wait in my soaking wet pants, seriously trying not to pee them. At least I had the presence of mind to put my jacket back on before heading in. Once my mom's, it is a kind of safety blanket for me. Even at sixteen years old, I'm okay with needing that, especially right about now.

I look at the ground while she looks at me. Why am I so afraid? Like full body trembling, weak knees afraid? Maybe because I feel people more than I see them, and she feels totally...wild.

Okay, there must be additional words for her.

But, well, no. I have none.

She's darker skinned than Ana and much, much shorter. A good bit shorter than me, even, and I'm five-foot-seven. Not stooped over like Ana, though, and far more agile. She smells like...what? Goat cheese, maybe? Yeah, that's it—old, moldy, *just-throw-it-out-won't-you-please* goat cheese. Despite my best attempts to contain my fears, I experience a massive, visible shudder.

So now comes the especially insane part. Insane because, as I wait,

I'm beginning to feel what Ana said I would feel out here—like I'm finally home. Yes, there is fear, but something else is slowly taking over. A deeper calm than I've known before. It's like crossing the water washed away who I was as Julie Mayden, and I'm standing here as someone different, or more, or something. It sounds crazy, but I know, I just know, that this new person I am fits in here.

I have this idea that if Rod got worried and came for me now, I'd fight him. I'd scream *you can't take me* and scratch and kick and be a total nutcase about it.

Ana was right. I belong here. I know I do. It's like some alien being dragged me from here long ago, took me to people who are not my people and who behave like everything that doesn't matter does, and everything that does matter doesn't, and now I finally get to return to where I belong. And even though I don't remember it at all, somehow I do.

Okay, so maybe that's a little dramatic. But the feeling is close. Really, really, close.

The old woman (eighty-eight, easily) is taking her time in deciding about me, looking over my body from every angle. It's bizarre, but somehow I know this has to be allowed. Not because of what Ana said, either. It's something deeper. Like instinct. It's important that she do this. I hold my ground, standing tall, willing to be looked over.

Not aggressive, but not backing down.

Another thing I know beyond any doubt is that this old woman is powerful. Seriously, like a blast of something you don't *ever* want to be in the crosswind of. Standing here is like standing in front of someone you never want to disappoint, for a whole lot of reasons.

She prowls now, crouching low. The slight breeze sends her god-awful scent up my nose, but I don't let it sway me. Using all the stretch in me, I turn out my hands even farther, barely moving to wave a bit of Ana's scent her way.

I have to work to drum up the courage to look at her face, but finally do.

I see her but also don't. She's ancient to the point of almost being invisible, as if the feel of her overshadows my capacity to see with my eyes. She looks right into me, or maybe through me. At first she looks confused, then wide-eyed shocked, her mouth hanging open.

But then she smiles. The storm clears. She appears toothless but suddenly not so ugly. Everything has shifted in an instant.

I feel it—*I'm in.*

"You're all right!" she declares. Her deep, crackly, voice seems to ricochet off me, like an echo reverberating back and forth down a long hallway. Only the hallway is inside me, or maybe floating somewhere far away, or even outside of time. I get a long shiver up my spine, starting at my tailbone and shuddering its way up.

"Okay," I whisper, unsure what else to say.

"Come on, then," she says with a curt, satisfied, nod. She turns to start walking farther into the woods.

Only I'm stuck where I stand, caught in a confusing rush of fight-or-flight. I can't seem to make myself take a step. I also notice a bitter taste in my mouth, like metal or something. It's a taste I get at the weirdest times.

"Excuse me, Bea?" I clear my throat because it came out shaky. I ought to use *Mrs. Something*, but her last name may not be Quinn and I don't want to get it wrong.

She turns back in a flash. "How do you know my name?" her eyes narrowing, her smile vanished.

The rush of anger shocks me into moving toward her though I ought to turn and run. "Uh, I know Ana," I stumble, again putting out my hands for her to sniff just in case she didn't get that part.

"Ana?" she demands with nothing short of a roar.

"She lives at the nursing home my dad owns. She sent me."

Now I'm confused. Didn't she recognize me because of the scent Ana put in my palms?

"She *spoke* to you?" Bea seems to find the thought incredible. She looks me over again, up and down and along both sides, as if she is looking for something entirely new now.

"I...yes...she said...well...you see...my cat is sick," I finally spit out. "Scottie. She's back at the car. Ana said you could help. She put her scent in my hands so you would know she sent me and..."

Suddenly, the old hag is laughing. It's a big laugh so that her whole body—which has quite a few layers of rolls around the middle—actually shakes. Yet the tone is oddly pitched. I think it's the strangest sound I've ever heard.

Okay, so she's powerful. But she's also a bit nuts.

Her laughing goes on and on, until she's all-out hooting, bending over in her own delight. Finally, she looks up at me with wet eyes and repeatedly shakes her head, like she just can't believe it. When she does, I see something of Ana in her face. Not much, but maybe enough to peg them as sisters.

"Why is that funny?" I demand, embarrassed to be so far out of my comfort zone.

The woman who is likely Ana's sister clasps my hand. A surge of something like white lightning goes through us. Sort of like what Ana put into my hands, but different, too. And immediate. There's no slow burn here. I'd pull away, but I don't think I can. We're magnets, stuck to each other, at least until she decides to let go.

"Don't be frightened, girlie. I'm just happy. I haven't heard anything firsthand about Ana in so long. It's been too dangerous to be in contact. But maybe things are shifting. You don't know what that means to an old woman like me. Come on, now. You have to tell me everything."

She lets go so that I can follow her, but I don't want to go any farther without Scottie. I have a feeling you could get lost in there, wherever it is we are going, and forget yourself entirely. I don't want to lose track of why I'm here. "Thank you. But could I go back and get my cat first? Scottie's really sick, and I love her so much, and…"

"Sure!" she says, like the whole town would be welcome, though I doubt that would be true. "You go on, and when you come back I'll do a healing and you can tell me all about Ana. I want to know everything."

I sigh the biggest sigh of relief I think I ever have sighed in my whole life. I practically want to cry, and this woman hasn't done a thing to help Scottie yet. But I have this feeling she can, and she will. She doesn't know what *that* means to me.

"Go on," she insists, waving me off, "I'll clear things so you can walk right back in. Don't bring your friend, though, you understand."

I don't know what it means to have her clear things, and I don't see how she could know about Rod, either, unless she was the one watching from the bushes. Anyway, it doesn't matter. Only Scottie matters.

"Yes. Ana said I couldn't let anyone know about you."

"She said that? That clear?" I swear she starts to dance a jig right in front of my eyes, then finally turns and hoots her way deeper into the woods as I turn back toward the water.

The return trip is far easier with the rain stopped. Rod is waiting at the end of the pier with Scottie by the time I reach it.

"Everything okay?" he asks, handing me the cage.

"Sure," I say, noncommittal, wrapping the cage in my jacket to keep Scottie from going suicidal when we cross the water.

"You do get that this is bizzare, right?" His eyes shift between me and the woods and back again.

"Yeah," I say, wishing I could say more. Wishing I could tell him everything. "I don't know how long this will take."

"Just don't dawdle," he mocks, summoning up a private joke from our days together at the old folks home. It's a good sign. It means he's not totally lost, even with the divorce.

It's not three minutes before I'm back on Bea's shore with Scottie, who ought to have gone a little crazy, even with the jacket over her cage. She didn't. Not a single mew. This scares me more than anything. Even her survival instincts are gone.

Walking into the woods, I go toward where Bea met me before and notice there's a narrow trail heading to where she went in, if you look really hard. Finally Scottie lets out a cry, but it's pretty pathetic.

It's okay, we're going to get you well, I send to her in our own little mind-melding way. *This smelly goat woman might be weird, but you have to let her help you.*

Scottie doesn't reply in mind-meld or otherwise.

"Over this way," I hear her voice bellow from a distance, a little to my left. I walk toward it, and sure enough, there she is, standing on the front porch of a house I would never have imagined was out here.

Actually, *house* is a generous word. *Shack* is more like it.

It's rundown, still dripping the last bit of rainwater from its rusty metal roof. It's beyond dirty, with parts that are pure grime, looking like someone has lived here for a hundred years but never thought to push a broom or get out a washrag. Given the junk lying around outside, I can only imagine what it's like inside. Everywhere I look it's overgrown with brush, and there are piles of scrap metal and other mucked-up stuff that probably washed ashore from the bay. I guess it's not surprising, given the woman herself is a mess. Still, the shack is definitely leaning to one side and there are whole floorboards missing on the porch. You'd think someone would say something. Or do something. I mean, an eighty-eight-year-old out here? Shouldn't someone help?

Then again…whoa, wait a minute…whoa, whoa, whoa…

Now that would be some kind of help.

Of all the things I expected to come out of that shack, the very last was a shirtless guy who looks like he just stepped out of an underwear ad.

"Who are you?" he asks, not taking his eyes off me.

He's direct—I'll give him that.

"Our new friend," Bea encourages. "What's your name?"

She pours me a glass of what looks like lemonade and then gently scoops Scottie from her cage. I accept the glass, but there's no way in hell I'm going to drink anything that came from inside that house. I can't begin to imagine what the kitchen sink must look like.

"Mayden," I say, using Ana's name for me. No idea why.

Bea looks at the guy all wide-eyed again. "Jake, this is Mayden.

Mayden, this is Jake. He hasn't seen a girl in quite some time, so forgive him if he's a bit overwhelmed."

I look at Jake, who does not look in the least overwhelmed. In fact, he is looking at me like he likes what he sees, and there is no reason to be shy about it. Which is so very not what I'm used to. Even so, I take it as an invitation to look back, especially since, for some odd reason, I can't get a feel off him.

His face is boyish, even with the blond chin stubble. I'd peg him at exactly my age. He's not dead-on gorgeous, feature wise, but his body makes up for it a hundred times over. It's perfect. As in six-hours-a-day-at-the-gym perfect. While there are lots of good-looking guys at my school, there are exactly zero who are buffed like this one, probably because with our homework load, no one has anything remotely like an extra six hours to put into pumping iron each day. The only other time I've seen a male body chiseled into art like this was in the firefighters charity calendar I got from Aunt Mia for Christmas last year. I remember thinking she didn't know me if she thought I'd swoon over nearly naked firefighters. But there I sat, for several nights in a row, as though I'd been given a personal invitation to gawk. She wrote in the card that she thought it was time I got my motor running. My thank-you note should have mentioned how well it worked, but I couldn't find the words.

Now, looking at Jake, a new thought hits me: Could this be the love that Ana has in mind for me? No. No way. That's far too much to hope for, even if I had a whole bucket full of Magic to toss in his direction.

"Mayden has news of your Great Aunt Ana," Bea says.

Jake circles a small area on the porch like a dog, sits, then looks up at me like I'm about to tell a great story. Without putting on his shirt. Is he unaware of what that can do to a teenage girl? If he hasn't seen other girls in a while, maybe he doesn't get how a body like that has real currency.

I look to Bea, who has taken Scottie onto her arm after wetting her behind the ears with some kind of homemade oil. Now she's put her weak kitty heart in the palm of her hand. I wonder if she'll also put some of that white lightning stuff into Scottie, and if so, whether her sweet little body can take it. It's hard to say, but I have to trust the old lady. She's my very last option.

Bea moves to sit on a barely held together rocking chair, so I pull up a rusted-out lounger and, as covertly as possible, make sure none of the legs are depending on any rotten porch boards. My clothes are getting itchy as they dry, and I realize I'm no more cleaned up than Bea. Jake's the only one looking freshly showered, I just happen to notice.

"Do you know what's wrong with Scottie?"

"Yes, but I'm not gonna say. It would only upset you."

Okay, like throwing that little bomb out there is supposed to make me less upset? "But can you help her?"

"Oh, sure!"

I don't like how she says it, like it's easy. Because if it were easy, wouldn't the vets have figured it out already? I want the crazy old woman to take this seriously.

Scottie, I say in mind-meld, *I love you. Don't be afraid.*

"Now, tell me all about Ana. You said she put her scent in your hands, but I'm afraid she's taken you for a ride on that one, girlie. She does things like that. She'd say she's being cautious. I say we've got no time for that."

"I guess you can't really put your scent in someone's hand?" I laugh a little so as not to look like a fool. Something in me drops, though, like I'm disappointed to find out there's no real Santa.

"Sure you can. But that's not all she did."

"What else did she do?" Already I don't like this.

"She gave you her Magic. Most all she has left from the feel of it. That's why I invited you through the veil, even before I knew it was her that sent you. If I know anything, I know who has Magic. Now that I know it was from my sister, though, I've got a real problem."

"Problem?" I wouldn't have minded her stopping at the "having Ana's Magic" part, even though that's totally selfish of me to want it. Especially if it's all she has left. It's not like Ana doesn't need it herself, right?

"Big one, and that's a fact. Now I've got to think on how I'm going to teach an outsider to use it. We don't even know your elemental nature yet, though the red streaks in your hair are a surefire clue."

"It's natural," I defend, if only because people always ask me where I get my hair done. I'm brunette with a heavy hint of red, same as my mom had, but it's just weird enough that people stare.

"I'm sure it is," Bea says. "Doesn't help with the Magic, though. What claims by fire claims hard. Not exactly easy Magic to work with."

"You're going to teach me Magic? Real Magic?"

Bea gives a half-hearted sigh, then a shrug, then a maybe-sort-of-kind-of nod.

With just that much of a yes, a powerful, heavy…something…runs through my body. It's not a chill. Not a shudder. Not goose bumps. It's like nothing I've ever experienced. Like every part of my body is saying that I was born to learn Magic, even though I never knew it existed before today. Even though I am, in fact, an outsider to these people.

"Maybe you could start with explaining about Ana giving me her Magic," I suggest, my inner control freak jumping out, already wanting to take over, make lists, and highlight precautionary notes. "What does that mean, exactly?"

Jake sits straighter and leans in toward me. "It means you're now one of the three most powerful women in the Quinn Clann." His voice is soft, but there's a bit of grit to it in the background, and his slow-growing smile afterward is one I recognize: This guy likes to shock, just like me.

I look to Bea to confirm or deny what he's said.

She's looking at Scottie, whose ears are perking up for the first time in months. "The other two being myself," she adds casually, not a hint of bragging in her words, "someone who will help you. And Ana's daughter, Helene," she looks at me dead on, "who most assuredly will not."

I look back to Jake again, hoping he'll say more, but he only nods in agreement, like it's obvious. Like everyone knows it. Everyone but me.

Chapter 6

Two things have happened that I'll never be able to explain to anyone.

First, Scottie is up and walking around, curiously checking out Bea's place like she hasn't been truly near death these past few months. *Let it be known right here and now that I thank every god and goddess that ever existed on any planet in any universe at any time in the space-time continuum for Bea saving Scottie's life!* Second is how it came to be that I'm about to get my first lesson in Magic.

It all happened so fast. I told Bea everything about Ana and how I came to find this place and that was that. She fully "agreed" to start teaching me immediately, as if I was the one who asked. Either way, it's not like I'm going to turn it down. I mean, if Magic is real, I most definitely want to learn to use it. It also didn't hurt that Bea was listening to me in a way I've never experienced before. I swear she was listening with her eyes, ears, fingers, and toes. Maybe even her backbone. She got it all on the first take, too. No questions or explanations needed, even though it's not your average, everyday *I ran into your sister* story. She and Jake just kept nodding, like *Yes, yes, absolutely.* It's as if they trust me already. Or maybe they are just confident that they would know if I was lying? All I know is that somewhere along the line, I started trusting them.

For me, that's big.

When I was done talking, and a playful Scottie was set down with a *that oughta do it,* Bea stood up and said we should get on with seeing how well I take to Magic. Even though it was gifted to me, she said it wasn't a sure thing that I would be any good at actually using it. She explained it was like the difference between talent and skill. The first you could be blessed with but, even then, the second is critical.

So here I am, ready and willing, even though my insides are curling around themselves in trepidation. After all, Ana's blowing fire into my palm was pretty intense, and she's spent the last year plus in a wheelchair. What must Bea's Magic be like?

"What exactly is Magic?" I ask, still trying to get a handle on it.

Bea appears not to hear me, seemingly off in her own world as she works out her thought process with her feet. Three steps forward, two back, four forward, one back—it's almost like she's trying to find exactly the right spot on which to speak me.

"Come on over here and start with your posture," she instructs, seemingly satisfied.

I come over, but I'm not sure if she means for me to stand up straight, like Dad's Wife #2 always used to say, or throw out my chest, like Wife #3 nagged during my formidable, barely-pubescent years. I do a little of both, which only makes Jake laugh. I shoot him a look that says, *Oh, thanks, you are such a help.* He smiles back at me with a set of perfect white teeth. I don't know how long he's been out here living this shack-in-the-woods life, but I know teeth that have been through the torture of braces when I see them. It can't have been that long.

"Pay attention!" my new teacher scolds, using a twisted vine-like walking stick to move my left foot a little more left. "Feet shoulder width apart. Shoulders tucked into your back pocket. Knees slightly bent."

I do as I'm told, but it's more than a little weird having Jake watch. Gawk, rather. He keeps looking at me like I'm some combo of a rapturous goddess and lunch. I'm torn between wishing I could have my lesson in private and being glad for every chance I can steal a glance at him. I know for sure I'll be able to ride the possibilities inherent in this attention for quite some time, even if absolutely nothing else happens with a guy all year.

"Now, tilt your pelvis forward. No, no. Tuck your butt in." She puts one hand on the small of my back and pushes forward, and the other on my stomach to make sure it doesn't move. The lightning goes through me, making me tremble. Scottie meows as if delighted. A rush of joy surges through me at the thought that Scottie is going to be okay. Or was it from her hands on me? Either way, I'll do anything Bea tells me to, purely out of gratitude.

"Now your spine is straight so you're in a solid, grounded position."

"For what?"

"To pull up the energy of the earth!" She looks at me like I'm dumb not to know at least this much.

"And why do I want the energy of the earth?" This is probably one of the more annoying quirks I have. I'll go days without talking to anyone in the hall or cafeteria at school, yet ask a billion questions in class.

"So you can blow the hell out of anything you want!" she says, cackling, then hooting.

You have to wonder, is Bea is a good witch or a bad witch?

"Na, we're not destroyers," she responds to my unspoken thought.

Reading my mind? Given Ana's abilities, it wouldn't exactly be surprising. I remind myself how insane that sounds, but also that context is everything. This isn't the strangest thing to happen today. Not by a long shot. Even so, I'm back to having that unsettled, spooky feeling.

"We're not to be pushed around either, though. Say Jake here is bothering you. You know, pestering you like a little brother."

Jake growls. I mean, literally growls, which makes Scottie perk up in concern.

"Or maybe someone else is giving you trouble. You want the power to handle that, right?"

"Sure," I reply, adding, "someone else, I mean" to comfort Jake. You can tell he wants to impress me. I want to assure him that there's not exactly a line of guys at my door. But I'm thinking it's best to avoid directly addressing the vibes between us, brotherly or otherwise.

"Now, start breathing in from the earth," she instructs, breathing with her own huge, heaving, chest to show me. "Deep, deep, from inside the soles of your feet. Like the arches in your soles are lungs, and the air you're pulling in is pure energy. If you use your real breathing to keep the rhythm up at the same time, it's easier to imagine. And when it comes to Magic, you've got to imagine it, or it flat out won't work."

I try to imagine breathing through my feet in time to my pumping lungs without feeling totally stupid. I look to Jake to see if Bea is just pulling one over on me. He nods as if to say, *Go on, she's right.*

"Don't get distracted girlie, or the energy will spill out all over the place! That's one surefire way to make a mess. You want it all to go directly into your belly. Here." She smacks my stomach so that it naturally tightens. I think I can feel some kind of energy jump in. Without trying, I begin to imagine I can see lines running from the center of my feet to my stomach and then something—not sure what—running up the lines. I swear, I've never in my life imagined such a thing. And yet, it's strange, like I also sort of know this stuff. Like I'm remembering something, not learning it new.

"Now pull the Magic in."

"What Magic?"

"Same Magic that makes seeds sprout in the dark of the earth! That makes gardens grow and fruit pop out of a tree! Isn't that Magic?"

"I've never thought about it that way."

"Well, think about it that way!" she sends back with a snort, smacking my gut again.

I don't feel an ounce of Magic coming in through my feet. Not that I know what it's supposed to feel like. But I do sort of see the lines, and there is something moving around inside my stomach. That should count for something.

"Okay, that's enough for today," she says, thumping her twisted stick on the ground three times. Like that, the lines disappear from my imagination. I'm left with one part of me feeling like a fool for even attempting to suck in Magic, and another part surer than ever that these old ladies have something real going on.

"That's all?"

Bea laughs. "Just see for yourself if *that's all* the next time you get mad at someone. Do that breathing often enough, filling up your belly with power each time, and between that and what Ana gave you, you'll find you are a real force to reckon with. It's hard to tell how much of your own magic you'll naturally add to it. For that, we've got to wait and see. But this method will work for anyone with even a hint of talent for Magic, given enough practice and time."

"Is that how you healed Scottie? With the earth through your feet?"

She answers with what sounds like metered out patience: "Girlie, it takes years to learn and perfect such healing techniques. What I just showed you with the earth is potent, sure. But that's just the rudimentary basics of the basics. We're only testing things out. Don't go expecting to use it to change the world just yet."

"I'm in total agreement on that one," I assure her. "But can you at least tell me what it means that Ana gave me her Magic? I mean, she needs it herself, if she's going to get out of there, right?"

Bea sighs, her eyes going dim. "You might as well forget about that, at least so long as Helene's on the warpath."

I get that Helene's the villain here, at least according to just about everyone. Even so, how do you just give up on a sister like that? I can't say that, given what Bea just did for Scottie. But I want to. "Why would her own daughter want her in a nursing home if she doesn't need to be there? That's so absolutely, utterly cruel." The idea makes me even more angry, now that I know about Magic. I don't know if it has anything to do with the thing we just did with my feet, but it feels like I could do something with the power I just took in.

What, I don't know.

But something.

She looks me over as if trying to decide what to say. "You ever heard of a dysfunctional family?"

She's kidding, right? "I probably have the equivalent of an honorary PhD in the topic."

"Then you understand how little things can become big things, even in normal families, when something is not sitting right between members."

"Sure," I say. Completely. Totally. One hundred and ten percent understood.

"So think of that, then add Magic. On top of Magic, add layers and levels and lifetimes of attempts at deceit, betrayal, jealousy, and power. Now add twelve hundred years of countries and continents, mythologies and cultures, religions and rebellions and fortunes won and lost. Add everything else you can imagine to complicate a family line."

Epic, I think, but do not say.

"Epic is right. But despite all that, goodness has always prevailed for the Quinn Clann, at least until now. Now our very own Helene's taken it upon herself to upend this great and true history, wasting all the good Magic that flows through our line in the name of what she wants for herself and her own legacy. She's nearly unstoppable now that she's learned to turn lead into gold. In this world, that gets you anything money can buy. That includes all the right—and wrong—people you need to help you out."

I try to take it all in, but her words land hard. Am I just trading my personal dysfunctional family for a fully dysfunctional dynasty?

"Ana is where she is, and must stay where she is, to protect our only hope of properly continuing the work of the Quinn Clann—finding the right woman to take over as our Keeper of Magic. Jake and Michael are with us and they'll do their part, but it will take more than these two to set things right again."

She looks at me like this should mean something to me, if not now, then soon.

I look to Jake, but he's looking away.

"I'll bet your friend at the pier is losing patience," she adds, nodding back toward the beach.

Rod! How long has it been?

I want to ask who Michael is, but even if Rod isn't getting ticked off as he waits, which I'm sure he is, I get that this is my invitation to be heading out. I'd ask about coming back, but I want to talk to Ana before I do. It would be good to know more about what I'm getting myself into here.

A lot more.

"Well then, thank you, especially for Scottie," I say, but Bea has already turned to walk into her house. She lifts a hand to wave without turning back. Probably thinks time is too short to waste on insignificant pleasantries.

I scoop up Scottie to put her back in the cage, then I remember I still don't know what made her sick.

"Wait! Bea?"

"Don't bother," Jake says, looking like he's going to join me in the short walk back to the beach. "She can't hear."

"What do you mean?" I ask, suddenly nervous to have him standing so close.

"She's deaf."

"I don't understand."

"She doesn't hear," he says, mocking deafness with dramatic sweeps of sign language.

"But we just talked. She heard everything I said."

He shrugs. "That's her Magic. She hears what she wants when she wants. But she is deaf."

"You do realize how insane that sounds, right?"

He laughs and shrugs. "I guess I'm used to things like that."

I stop and turn to him, catching a whiff of the musky male wow coming off his body. I will attempt to pretend I'm not affected by it, but it won't be easy.

"What else are you used to, Jake? What's going on out here? And while you are at it, what in the context of the Quinn Clann is Magic?"

"I wondered when you were going to get around to asking me instead of her." He steps even nearer, like he's the one I should be warming up to. Normally I would not be opposed, but there's too much going on, and anyway, I still can't seem to get the feel of him. More to talk to Ana about.

"That doesn't answer anything." I step back, but this only allows me a better look at his bare upper body, all bright and shining in the sun. I wonder if he got those abs from that breathing into the gut thing? It would definitely make it worth practicing.

Like every five minutes.

"Ana's my great grandaunt and Bea is my great grandmother. We are here, at least partially, because I started learning Magic when I was young—everyone says too young—and some things got messed up. Between that and what happened with Gran Ana, everyone agreed it was best we move out here. At least for now."

"Messed up?" I probe.

"That, and because Michael and I are the last ones to carry on the family Magic."

A thousand questions I could ask. A hundred thousand. "So, this Michael. Who is he?"

"Another long story," he replies, moving a step closer again, but offering no more detail.

I get a weird feeling about Michael. A good-bad weird, which is even weirder.

"Okay. So then back to the Magic. I mean, what kind of Magic? Are you like witches and warlocks? Because I have to say, that would just be too much for me to really, you know, believe in or anything."

"It's not like anything you think you know. It's not to believe in. It just is. Our Magic is real, Mayden. Real and powerful. It's only a small line within the Great Magic that runs the world. Even so, a small line can change a lot. The only thing is…"

He waits for me to dive in. "Yes?"

"You have to be sure you want to know more. Are you sure?" His voice drops, making him sound about ten years older and a hundred times sexier. "Because knowing things will change things. What you learn does stuff to you, even if you don't want it to. And once it starts, you can't stop it." He moves in yet another step. "You come in, you're in. All the way."

It sure does do something to you. Something like jellyfish swimming in your knees. Only you like it, even though you shouldn't. And you…

Wait, no, I will not be sucked in.

Just because I've never had a boyfriend, and…

No. This is too important.

I have to go slow here. I have to consider.

Wait, what was the question?

"See," he says, backing off, "you're not ready."

"How do you know?" I defend, suddenly clearer. Who is he to tell me anything?

"Because I live it, Mayden. I live our Magic. You get power, sure. But that doesn't make things easier. Not even close to easier."

His words hit me. I stare at him, wondering. What could it mean that you *live* Magic, and have since you were little? At first I thought he might be a bit slow or something, living out here in the backwoods, and staring at me like he did at first. But now I get that he's far from slow. He's got things going for him I can't even imagine. I'm sure of it.

I start walking away, needing time to think on my own. Get some real perspective. That's how I work things out for myself. And I do work it out, given enough time.

"I will tell you this," he says, following me, then gently touching my arm and turning me back toward him. A jolt goes through me, like Ana's and Bea's, but also uniquely his own.

Finally, I can feel him. God, I can feel him.

My stomach stirs the way galaxies might if they had been disturbed by a foreign star. Again I get the sense I know this stuff, and these people, from some time or place that's maybe a million light years away. It's more than liking Jake because he's so…whatever.

"I want to know," I say, though I just told myself I'd take my time.

"You can trust GranBea completely," he jumps in, as if not wanting to give me time to change my mind, "as far as good intentions go. But she's not always herself, and when she's not, she's not reliable. Sometimes, she's even dangerous. And you will never know when those times will be."

I nod, remembering Ana said coming here could be dangerous. "Good to know."

"As far as Scottie?" He lowers his voice as if someone might hear. "You asked why she got sick. It's the cook at your house."

"What?"

"Your cook. Keep Scottie away from her."

"Mrs. Hamilton?" Already I'm wondering how he even knows we have a cook.

"Your cook is poisoning Scottie. *Intentionally.*"

No way. Then again, Mrs. Hamilton always has hated Scottie. But poison her? "How do you know this?"

"My Magic lets me see things. When Bea was doing the work on Scottie, I saw your cook. You live in a very big house, right?"

I nod slowly, warily.

"I saw that. And that your cook is poisoning Scottie when she feeds her. By the way, you can test me on what I know anytime. In fact, you should. If you're going to learn Magic, the most important thing to know is who you can trust."

I stare at him, wondering how you sort all this family stuff out. For the first time ever, I feel like I've lived a simple, sheltered life.

"As well as who you can't," he adds in a decidedly ominous tone. Our eyes lock on each other and something happens. I don't know what. I have no experience in these things. But something.

The silence seems to last forever.

"Welcome to the family, Mayden," he finally says, then moves to brush his face against mine softly. Not a kiss, not with his lips, but also not *not* a kiss. It's almost like a nuzzle from Scottie, so close, so sweet, so pure.

I don't know what to say, and so I don't say anything. I don't move toward him or move away. All I can think, all I know for sure, is that this is the most divine human touch I've ever felt, and it would be completely and totally okay with me if it never stops.

Chapter 7

I don't know if Bea's lesson actually put Magic into my stomach. But I'm more than sure Jake put a fireball of furious loathing into my heart—for Mrs. Hamilton. I've been imagining her poisoning Scottie ever since he told me about it. I tried to be reasonable in the off chance he was wrong. But he did know I had a cook and a big house. With that much in his favor, and the fact that something had to be making Scottie sick, his Magical intuition didn't seem overly far-fetched. I even asked Rod on the ride home—after he got past giving me the silent treatment for making him wait so long—if he thought someone who worked for your family could be capable of such a thing. He's never met Mrs. Hamilton, but said sure, that people are always capable of stupid acts of grotesque horror when acting in their own petty self-interests. That wasn't really what I was looking for, but it did tell me his frame of mind was no more reliable than mine. So I just shut up, hugged Scottie in sweet relief, and tried to ward off the fire that was heating up inside me.

It didn't work.

Once we got home, I promised Rod I'd call him and come over to help clean up the soggy mess I made of his car, but he just said it was fine and that he'd be busy anyway. In other words, it will be weeks before I see him again. Maybe months, given what he's going through. He's the type that hides when things get rough. Not much you can do about it but wait it out.

Then I snuck in the back door of our house, locked Scottie safely in my room, and came back out so that I could make a real entrance through the formal front door. It's easy to make yourself known when you come through it, and not only because of the echoing marble foyer. The door itself is gigantic—doublewide and as thick as three normal front doors. Which means that when you slam it, the entire house feels like a bomb dropped. Even the six-foot wide entryway chandelier, set a good thirty feet high, swings from side to side. It is impossible to slam the door accidentally, so if it blows, you know someone means business. Usually, it's Dad making the dramatic display. I only get away with the gesture when it is used exceedingly sparingly. Fortunately, it's been half a year, at least.

I take a whiff of myself, still wet but no longer dripping, noting that I smell like a mix of sludge and day-old clams. I must look ten times worse than I smell. *Good.* I want to appear every bit as haggard as I feel. I step inside and give the door the biggest shove I can. It slams so hard even I jump, and I knew it was coming. I then follow it with my very best, most serious and demanding, *"Daaad!"*

"Upstairs," he yells back casually, like he's half-listening. It only makes me more determined that we are going to deal with Mrs. Hamilton.

Right. Now.

The blare of the game (who knows which one, who cares?) comes from the upstairs theater. It's smaller than the full theater in the basement, with room for only one big screen and four leather chairs, all facing forward. The setup means it will be practically impossible to pull his attention away from the game. The screen is just too in-your-face. I storm the steps three at a time. When I reach him, I realize Sally, a.k.a. Wife #4, has already poked her head out of her office and started to clickity-clack her stilettos down the hallway to see what is up.

Lovely. Just lovely.

"Dad, you have to fire Mrs. Hamilton!" I insist from the theater room doorway. If he ignores me, I can always step in front of his line of view. But that's a drastic measure, even for me. It should be used only in case of an emergency. Which this is. But you have to start and build up with Dad.

"Why?" he says, not looking up.

"Dad!" I stomp on the buffed-clean hardwood floors. My shoes squish. He looks a little more alert, probably because I'm not supposed to wear shoes in the house at all. He gets as much crap from Wife #4 as I do when I break the rule.

"What?" Dad asks, now giving one full eye to me.

"Mrs. Hamilton is poisoning Scottie. That's why she's been so sick. I want her fired. Today. *Now.*"

"I hired her," Sally interjects, whining, her eyes all willowy, her mouth all pout.

No mention of how terrible for Scottie, mind you. Not a word of comfort or outrage.

"Wait," Dad says, standing and looking as if he is only now realizing what he's in the middle of. "That's a strong accusation, sweetheart."

It would be a good time to be smart. To say something like *Yes, Daddy, I am your sweetheart, and I completely understand it's a strong accusation. But you see a witch-like hag across the river told me of this horrific crime at the hands of our cook, or rather her great-grandson told me because he's psychic that way, and...*

Actually, that would be completely stupid, now that I walk it through my brain. Anyway, it doesn't matter, because I can feel that the Magic that came up into my feet and traveled to my stomach has become some kind of raging wildfire, the kind that could light up a thousand acres during a Colorado summer.

"Get rid of her!" is all I can muster without outright exploding through my skin.

"Julie!" Dad insists, his volume a perfect match to my own. He's a master at verbal challenge. But I'm nothing if not my father's daughter, at least when I have to be.

"I mean it. Fire Mrs. Hamilton. She has been trying to kill Scottie and I will not live in the same house with any human being who would..."

"But...but," Sally whines, "I need a cook who understands my dietary concerns."

I am speechless. Speechless!

I stare at this woman barely more than a decade older than me. I mean, really, dietary needs? Mrs. Hamilton is killing my cat, and all she can say is that she needs a cook who understands her lactose intolerance and desperate need for a thigh gap?

This is everything that is wrong with this family, right here.

"Julie," Dad says in a forced calm, the avid sailor in him taking a politically correct tack, "I understand how you'd feel this way if something like that were true, but we don't know that."

"It. Is. True!" I spit the words out like three rusty nails.

I can almost see Dad's mind whirling, as if thinking that, as teens go, I'm usually pretty reasonable. "Do you have proof?"

My answer comes to me quickly, spilling out. "Yes. I can't reveal my source. But it is a reliable source. And that source has helped Scottie get well. She's well, Dad!" Now I'm pleading. It makes me sound pathetic, but I don't care. "I cannot risk her getting sick again."

I'd swear Sally looks disappointed at the news of Scottie's recovery. I'm telling you, if she has anything to do with this, I will draw up and sign their divorce papers myself.

As can always be expected at the most important moments of my life, Dad's cell rings. If he answers, I will know, finally and for sure, that I am merely an orphan with a father on the side. I rock in my fury as I watch him contemplate.

He hesitates. I'll grant him that. But then he takes it.

Of course, he takes it.

"Dad!" I yell. I mean, right at him, with the phone answered and all. This is so very not what he expects of me.

"Excuse me a moment, Helene," he says into the phone, totally calm.

"Julie," he returns to me, "This is Helene Quinn. I have to take this call."

"Who?" I demand, shaking my head, because something is tumbling around in the back of my brain. Something that doesn't fully compute.

"My silent business partner," he says, his hand over the microphone. He looks at me like I should know this. Like he has told me before. And he probably has during one of his long, boring, *can't-I-go-now-please?* talks. But when have I ever taken notes on anyone he does business with, silent or otherwise?

I can almost hear the dominoes clicking in my brain as one nugget of understanding topples into another. *Won't you please pay a little extra attention to Mrs. Quinn?* I recall him saying before I began to take Ana for walks. Something else, too, about her daughter and the business. The next domino crashes as I recall Bea saying Helene can turn lead into gold and that she does so to buy people. I hate to admit it, but if there is one thing I know for sure, my father can be bought.

"Dad!" I say one more time, though he has turned away. Wife #4 is just looking at me with a satisfied smile, like I got what I deserved. Just like Wife #2 and #3 would have. I want to say: *You, too, can be fired. Just wait. It always happens.* But that would really be asking for it.

Without waiting for Dad's attention to return, which could take eons, I bound down the stairs, my legs on some kind of supercharged firepower. I go through the formal dining room, the main kitchen, down another set of stairs into the pantry kitchen and abruptly come face-to-face with Mrs. Hamilton. I don't know if it's only my imagination or some kind of vision like Jake said, but I can sort of see her spooning some evil concoction into Scottie's food dish. It's like a movie screen in the front of my forehead, the same one where I saw those lines running up from my feet during Bea's lesson in Magic. Again, I get a metallic taste in my mouth. Can Magic make you taste things as well as see them?

Fury rises in and through me. Fury like I've never known before.

I enter Mrs. Hamilton's personal space so fast she doesn't know what to do. There's a strong force-like feeling in me, so much that I think I could shove her with just the power in my belly. She'd be no match for it.

"You poisoned Scottie!" That's all I say. It's all I need to say. I can see that it's true. Her dark, dilated, fast-blinking eyes give her away.

Thing is, I don't know what else to do.

I just stare, wishing the Magic could do something.

Anything.

Out of nowhere, I hear a kind of crack, then a crash. We both turn to look at a glass bowl on the other side of the room that has—what? Spontaneously combusted? Large hunks of glass are broken off around the bread bowl she uses each day. From the looks of it, a loaf had been rising. If not for the towel over the bowl, and the dough inside, it might have shot glass daggers across the room.

Now Mrs. Hamilton is scared. I am too, but I'm not going to waste this moment. I make my eyes big, lean in and wordlessly say, *Yeah, I did that, and you'd better watch out.* What I actually say is, "Do you know that we have hidden cameras throughout the house?"

It is true, though not in the kitchen. But she doesn't know that.

Mrs. Hamilton is speechless, backing herself into a corner. Or maybe I'm the one backing her into it, all because this fire in me will not let up.

"Julie!" Dad bellows from behind me. I turn to see him and Wife #4. She's come along to watch, no doubt gleeful for the ringside seat.

"I know what Mrs. Hamilton is doing to Scottie," I insist through clenched teeth. "I *know* it."

"Are you on drugs?" Dad both asks and accuses at the same time.

My mouth drops open in disbelief.

"No, Dad," I sputter, "I am not on drugs. I don't even smoke cigarettes. I don't drink, either, in case you were wondering. And while we are having this ever so private heart-to-heart, you will be glad to know I've never had sex. But I am NOT going to be a good girl and pretend I don't know something I do when this woman has been trying to Kill. My. Cat!"

"Mrs. Hamilton," Dad inquires in a strained calm, "is there anything you can think of that might have led to this misunderstanding?"

I'd love to say Mrs. Hamilton turned to look at Wife #4 and their locked eyes confirmed a long planned and utterly devious plot. But they don't. Sally looks as baffled as Dad. And with all that energy spent on the bowl and confronting Mrs. Hamilton, not to mention all this standing up to Dad, I suddenly feel my magical strength quickly spiral down and out of me.

"Nothing at all," Mrs. Hamilton insists, bursting red in the face, "but if you have cameras on me, I'm not sure I want to work here."

"We don't have cameras in the kitchen," Dad assures.

"Because I don't like being spied on," she adds, nervously balling up her hands in her apron.

"Understandably," Dad replies, looking at me like I'm the bad guy here.

Me!

So, well, there you have it. I can see that this is going to land as it always does. Everything will be my fault and, just wait, Dad will even expect an apology. A few minutes ago, I might have had a more sustained strength and courage. But now my power is seeping out of my feet and into an invisible puddle on the floor. Honestly, I can barely stand without leaning on something.

"Okay, here's the deal," I lay out, using the last wattage of energy in me. "You are all going to make this my fault, so why don't we just chalk it up to me being a hormonal teenager? Then everyone can go back to their life like nothing happened, and I'll just be the fool."

"I think an apology is also in order," Dad pushes.

I pretend I don't hear him, because there is no way, ever, ever, in a million years, anyone is getting an apology on this. "But from here on out, nobody feeds, nobody pets, nobody even *looks* at Scottie but me. She stays in my bedroom suite, and it is totally off limits. I'll clean it myself so that no one—no one—is in there but me. As in, one hundred percent of the time. Got it?"

I look at each of them with hard eyes, expecting full agreement.

It seems like they are going to take the deal, if only to have the whole incident put behind us. Nobody says anything but, eventually, everyone nods. I send a quick squinty glare toward the bowl and then Mrs. Hamilton, just to make sure she doesn't forget who she is dealing with, and then leave with a growl. It's all the final statement I can muster at the moment.

Making my way up the stairs, my legs feel like they are nothing more than burnt charcoal, especially from the knees down. Tomorrow, when I've had a good night's sleep with Scottie purring happily next to me, I'll outline a long list of questions and go see Ana. Given she knows all about dysfunctional families, as well as the Magic that can break bread bowls from across a room, she will surely know what I'm supposed to do next.

Chapter 8

I close Ana's door behind me. It's too close to lunch to take her out, thanks to a long and involved post-family apocalypse text chat with Rod. I can't wait one more minute to tell her all that's happened. I'm not supposed to shut the door with a resident, but it's not a huge rule. With the door closed, no one will hear a thing. They built this place with the intention that patients don't hear each other moaning and groaning, especially at night.

"It's me," I say, kneeling in front of Ana's chair. I plan to get her a pair of drugstore glasses, even if she can only wear them when we are alone in the woods. Her head is dropped and she has a slight pulse to her upper body, moving her frame just an inch forward and back. Nothing I haven't seen before, but now I know better. Her eyes are open, but she won't make contact with mine.

"Ana, I have to talk to you."

Nothing. She doesn't even look up. But she can hear and understand. That much she made perfectly clear.

"I found Bea. And Jake. And Bea helped Scottie!"

Again, nothing. I sigh. What must it be like to know what I'm saying and not be able to respond? The idea tortures me. Seriously. Stick a dozen steak knives in my feet and twist them a little bit every day before this happens to me, please.

I turn to get her medicine bag, then put it on her lap.

She doesn't even pick it up.

"Ana," I plead, with growing insistence. "I made a bowl break with Magic. Bea showed me how to get power and then it exploded because our cook is poisoning Scottie. But it was a huge mess with my Dad, and now I have to…"

As if out of nowhere, yet right next to us, I hear a toilet flush. I look to Ana's closed bathroom door, my mouth dropped open in horror, ready to shoot myself for not checking. I hear the water faucet come on.

No, no, no!

My gut takes a flying leap. You can hear through the thin bathroom door just fine. I should have looked. But when does anyone else ever use Ana's bathroom?

She catches my eye with what I can imagine is a stern look. I give her a look back that says, *Sorry, I get it now.* I'm confident she understands, but that doesn't mean she'll forgive me.

Immediately, I'm ready to tell a lie: *I just talk to Mrs. Quinn like I talk to my cat, Scottie. I've been looking for some friends, and I found them and I wanted to tell someone about it, but everyone else is too busy to listen to my teenage angst. It's nothing important. Mrs. Quinn is a great listener, even if she sometimes drools. Yes, I know she can't understand me, but...*

The door begins to open. My mind races through the options. A nurse? Dr. Garcia? My stomach drops at the next thought...Helene?

Please, please, please, no.

I watch to see the door open fully, revealing none of the above. It's a guy.

Wait, a guy? In here?

Yes, confirmed, a guy. About my age. Dark curls, bright blue eyes, tall and thin, with a face that is so perfect it appears slightly awkward. He's dressed kind of odd, too, especially for this place: Off-white button-down with a striped blue scarf and pure white skinny jeans. Blue leather shoes—the expensive kind, like Dad gets in Europe.

Wannabe New York model type, I'm thinking. I only know the look because we have a few guys just like him at school.

"Hi," I say, unsteady as I attempt to stand and back away from Ana at the same time.

"Hi," he replies, noncommittal, looking at me, then at Ana, then back at me.

Damn.

"I'm Julie. I volunteer to take care of Ana...I mean Mrs. Quinn...sometimes. She listens to my problems. Kind of lame I know, but..."

My words taper off. I wasn't expecting to lie to a guy my age. It's harder.

"That's nice of you," he says. No introduction. No handshake. No smile. In fact, he looks nervous. And seriously attractive. I wouldn't notice, at least at a time like this, but he's the kind of good-looking you can't help but take note of. It's like a fact that stares you in the face, taking your breath away just a little, so that you can't *not* think about it. Not even when you've just betrayed the most amazing woman in the world and she's bobbing her head in a wheelchair right next to you.

"So, you know Mrs. Quinn?" I ask, like it's small talk.

Lame again. I mean, why else would he be in here?

"Sort of," he says, still uncommitted. He's looking at me, but also around me, like Bea did when I first met her. "Does she ever talk back?" he asks, looking at the medicine bag in her lap, then right into my eyes.

Now, I'm really in it. I have to outright lie.

"She babbles a lot," I say, looking away and shrugging it off. "Sometimes there's something that seems like words, repeating things, stuff like that. But nobody pays any attention. How do you know her?"

His eyes are staring deeply into mine now. Would it be too dramatic to call the stare *penetrating*?

No, not really.

"I'm wondering if we could talk somewhere?" he asks, clearly avoiding the question. "Get lunch, maybe? Not here, though."

"I guess," I reply, thinking if there were anything significant enough to delay my talk with Ana, it would be this. "I was going to take her to lunch, but the staff can do that. I can walk with her later. Not like she's going anywhere, right?"

I half laugh and roll my eyes, but inwardly kick myself. I mean, Ana knows what I'm saying, even if she can't respond. It's got to land pretty hard when you just helped save someone's cat and she starts joking about your life plight right in front of you, even if it is to make a lie more convincing.

"I could walk with you both," he suggests tentatively, "after we go to lunch."

Well, there goes my talk with Ana. I can't exactly admit I want to talk to her alone. "I'm sure she'd like that." I put a happy pitch in my voice and then throw a patronizing spin on it, like everyone does when they are talking to the patients here. "Wouldn't you, Mrs. Quinn?"

She offers no reply. Not even a grunt or a bobble. Later, I will profusely apologize, begging on my knees, and offer up every expression of regret I can think of. I can only hope it will be enough. I don't want to lose her, especially so soon after finding the real her.

"We can go sign out," I suggest.

"Actually," the guy says, all jumpy about it, "I was going to do a quick stop in to see someone else, so why don't I just meet you outside the front door?" He looks at his overly elegant watch. "Give me five minutes?"

Okay, so now he's lying. You can just tell. But why?

Immediately it comes to me: He doesn't want to sign out because he never signed in. I would not burn at the stake over the sudden jolt of intuition, but I would definitely place a hefty bet.

"Sounds good," I reply, and watch him quietly open and then slip out the heavy door.

It isn't until he's gone that it comes to me who he is: Michael. The idea just lands on me. I could be wrong, but I don't think so. I bend down to get close to Ana.

"Can you talk now?" I make sure to whisper.

Again she does not speak, just pulses, her head hung low.

"I know you can hear me. I'm sorry about that. I didn't think about the bathroom. I'll be more careful next time, I swear." She says nothing. She doesn't even attempt to look me in the eye. Pure guilt floods every cell of my body. Could there be any creature on earth that is lower than me at this moment?

No, there could not.

"That was Michael, wasn't it?" I ask, thinking she might at least confirm this. "Your great-grandson?"

Again, nothing.

"Look, I have to talk to you. I found Bea!"

Ana shoots me a sudden look of warning, her eyes widening with punctuation.

"I'll just wait," I quickly agree. "I guess we'll be back for a walk after lunch."

"Comealone comealone comealone comealone," she blurts out in a sudden spurt, her babbling keeping pace with her head, which has gone from a pulse to a full-out bob.

"Okay, I can ditch him. I'll work it out." That much I can surely do. I would try to get more from her in the three minutes we have left, but the door is opening again.

"Julie!" Nurse Edna scolds. "You know this door isn't supposed to be closed in the daytime unless Mrs. Quinn is being attended to by the staff."

"Oh, sorry," I say, slipping Ana's medicine bag into my pocket so the nurse won't see. "It must have closed behind me."

Nurse Edna looks at the entryway, knowing full well these doors do not close on their own. "Just watch it in the future, okay? We don't want Mrs. Quinn to need us and not have a way for us to know about it."

She's talking down to me, same way I was just talking down to Ana. Like I couldn't get a nurse if there was a problem, given I am right here in the room? But now more than ever, I have to let things like that slide.

"Sure. Sorry. Okay, I have to go. Lunch date. Sort of. I'll be back later, to take Mrs. Quinn for a walk." I let my voice trail off, knowing that offering up the lunch date as gossip will likely come back to haunt me. But it's a small price to pay if it distracts her enough to forget the door issue.

My plan works. After enduring a long story—which I already knew—about how her first date with her now-husband was also a lunch date, I hurry to the main desk to sign out and then practically run out the door to meet Michael. He's waiting for me as promised.

"I have a car, assuming you don't mind riding with a stranger." He says, smiling. Actually, that was probably more than smiling. It might even have been flirting, not that I'm an expert. I mean, it might not have been, but it could have been. Despite the uncertainty, my stomach does a happy little flip-flop, which it shouldn't, given what just went on with Ana.

This is serious, Julie Mayden, I reprimand myself.

Despite everything I have been told about not taking a ride from strangers, and everything I know about date rape and a thousand other things that could go wrong given Ana's concern about him, I find myself nodding in agreement. I'm far less worried about Michael than Ana, I realize as the guilt piles up. Stacks and stacks of it. There's no amount of penance I could do before I, myself, am eighty-eight years old that would make up for what I just did. I can only hope I don't add to the blunder over lunch.

He doesn't say anything, which makes the walk take forever. Apparently he parked at the far, far end of the lot. But why?

"I think you know who I am," he finally says.

"Michael?" I make it sound like a guess, even though it doesn't feel like one.

"Yes," he nods, solemn around the eyes.

"I'm Julie," I offer back, just as we arrive at his car.

"Hello, Julie," he offers, getting my door for me.

It's only now I realize it's a Jaguar. Hunter green with a polish that says either he washes it daily or there are no more than thirty-one miles on it. I keep my groan to myself. Yep, this one is going to be just like the other hot little rich guys at school. It's disappointing because, being Ana's great-grandson, there was a chance he might have been nice.

Not now. This guy is a player. For sure. Absolutely. No way around it.

Despite a thousand inner warning bells, which are at this very moment at war with my salt-craving compulsion to discover what this guy is all about, I slide in.

Nice seats. Nice smell. Sort of like sliding into a perfectly fitting leather glove.

He gets in and gives me a nervous smile but doesn't say anything as he drives. I take his lead and keep to myself, looking at him only from the corner of my eye. Now that I know who he is, it's easy to see how he's Ana's great-grandson, with the same strong bones in the face. Not built, like Jake is. Still, pretty much pitch-perfect as looks go. Kind of hard to imagine which type is further out of my reach.

We're a strange pair—me in my grungy army jacket and jeans, and him in all white. His thin body looks even thinner sitting down, accentuated by his sockless, bony ankles. I notice his legs have just the right amount of hair. Not that I know what the right amount is. It's just not offensively dense or scraggly. The shoes must be in the five-hundred dollar range—no way they are knock-offs. I think I heard a bit of an accent in his voice, too, but I can't make where it's from.

I turn to look out my window to keep my focus as the questions start their typical avalanche in my brain: How clearly could he hear me in Ana's room? Does he know about Bea and Jake? He must, if he is Michael. But how much about them did I give away? I was so stunned that anyone was there, I can't recall. So many questions, none of which I should be asking.

Really, I should wait. Let him make the first conversational move. Only I can't.

Info craving has kicked in.

"Exactly how much did you overhear when you were in the bathroom?"

He looks at me with these insanely blue eyes. I mean, seriously, you could probably swim laps in them.

"Everything. I wouldn't have come out of hiding if you hadn't mentioned Bea and Jake."

His honesty surprises me. "Hiding?"

He looks at me cautiously, like he wonders if he can trust me. He puts his eyes back on the road. "I couldn't sign in. My grandmother Helene doesn't know I've discovered where GranAna is. She can't know I visited today."

"*I'm* not going to tell her," I assure. I feel for him, though I don't know why. Either way, it's an easy promise for me to make. I've never even met Helene. I hope I never do.

"Thank you." He sounds like he means it.

Gorgeous guy, fancy clothes, mega car and, yet, sincere? Doesn't add up. Not in my world.

"But really," I offer, carefully probing, "if you wanted to go unnoticed, don't you think dressing a little more like a normal teenager would be smart?"

He keeps his eyes on the road. "I find that the more different you appear, as long as you are well-dressed, the more people will assume you know exactly what you are doing. A typical teenage guy would be out of place in a nursing home. Yet one dressed as I am is so unusual, it confuses more than it raises suspicion. As such, I am left to walk freely about."

I never thought of that, but he might be right. Interesting guy. Smart, too. But who uses *as such* in conversation these days?

"So you know about the family...dysfunction?" I'm probing, maybe even baiting, to see where he takes it.

He laughs. It's actually a nice sound, like a river rolling over rocks. I guess that's pretty gushy. But, honestly, that's how it sounds. "Most likely, I *am* the family dysfunction."

"I'm not sure what that means." More probing. Can't help it.

"It means I'm probably the reason my great-grandmother is in that place," he says, his voice dropping. "I think she's protecting me and Jake, somehow. Maybe GranBea, too, though she's never been the type to need it. As least, that's the closest understanding I've been able to come to on my own."

It sounds like he knows pretty much everything I do and then some. But I have to be sure. I don't want Ana or Bea saying I'm the one who gave too much away.

"Protecting you from what?"

He soundlessly swerves into the drive of the North Waters restaurant. I know it because I've been a few times with Dad for dinner, mostly for business entertaining when families are expected. I didn't know they had a lunch menu. Bringing me here goes right along with the clothes and the car, though. He puts the car in park, undoes his seat belt, but then turns to face me without turning off the engine. A cool, steady stream of air keeps things slightly frigid.

"I don't know," he finally says. "But I think you do."

My mind goes off in twelve directions at once, like I'm in front of a chessboard, but have no idea how to make the next move. There are too many ways for this to unravel, too many ways for me to really mess up.

Again.

I can see Michael is asking for help. But am I supposed to help him?

Or not help him? Should I throw nails behind his wheels so that when he backs onto them, his pretty car takes a hit? I have no idea what Ana, Bea, or Jake would want, or even if any of them would want the same thing. He's family, but then, so is Helene.

I continue to hesitate, starting to talk, then stopping. I want to help. I really do. I generally want to help anyone so long as they are good people. But I also feel I owe it to Ana to not discuss any details.

"I think it would be best if you do the talking," I finally offer.

He takes his own moment to think about it. "And then you'll go to the others to see what's okay to tell me?"

"Something like that."

He pauses, nods his agreement, then turns off the engine and gets out of the car. Before I've figured out how to unlatch my seatbelt, he's come around and opened my door. He leans over to unbuckle me (what is that crazy beautiful smell he's wearing, sweet and light, or maybe he just emanates that all by himself?) He offers me his hand like a guy on a date might. It unnerves me, but in a good way. Or, a bad way. I am not sure yet. He smiles bigger this time. Perfect teeth, like Jake, I think, feeling slightly guilty to be out on a date with someone besides Jake, crazy as that is. I don't take Michael's hand.

Players play, I remind myself.

Even so, I consider something that three days ago I would never, ever have thought possible. Somehow, this just might end up being the best summer of my life.

Chapter 9

"There's no one here," I say to Michael, looking at the huge restaurant full of empty tables. Some are fully set with a formal place setting, but others don't even have tablecloths. Chairs are scattered like someone left in the middle of vacuuming. If not for the full wall of windows, there would be no light in the room.

"It's not open for lunch."

I stop. "Then why did we come?"

He laughs in that rolling river way again. It makes me think of Ireland. Maybe that's the accent? "It's okay. I own the place. At least I will next year, when I turn eighteen." As if to prove it, he goes for the hidden set of light switches and the room comes alive.

Owner? Of this place? Ugh!

I don't care how much his laugh sounds like the Irish countryside. Rich, cute boys are not fun to play with. And really rich, really gorgeous guys are abysmal, even as acquaintances. I've been forced to meet enough of his type at Dad's social events to know that. They think they don't have to be decent human beings, because, well, they've got everything that everyone else supposedly wants.

Everyone but me, anyway.

It's not very sexy, but when it comes to real dollars, the truth is that someday I'll inherit a hefty number of nursing home complexes. That, on top of the substantial inheritance from my mom, and I'm probably as financially set up as he is. Maybe more so.

I just don't toss it around as social currency, thankyouverymuch.

"I wanted to talk in private," he says, gently leading me by the elbow to the back corner of the room. I can feel his Magic shoot into my arm. It's like the kind I get from the others in his family, yet, at the same time, totally unique. It feels warm, and even kind, which sort of throws me.

"Besides, it's the best organic food in town."

Organic? He's a health nut? Okay, just shoot me now.

I swear, if his phone rings and he…

His phone rings. How did I know?

Strike three if you take that call, I think but don't say. I don't care how important you are in your own little world. Manners are manners.

"I'm sorry, but I have to take this. I've been waiting all morning."

"No problem," I say flatly. It's plenty problematic, but you're not going to hear me take him down over it. Anyway, I get to listen in on his conversation, which is like gold. You can learn a lot about a person that way.

"Hello? Yes, sir, it is. Thank you for calling, sir." Pause. "That's very kind of you, sir." He pauses again, sending a dramatic *sooo sorry* look my way. "Yes, sir, I'll look forward to meeting her. Six o'clock. Yes, sir. Thank you, sir."

Three strikes with the phone, four for being a total suck-up. How many times can you say "sir" in two minutes?

"I'm sorry," he says, making sure to show me he is turning the phone completely off. Seems he picked up on my attitude. Not that anyone even halfway awake could have missed it.

A boyish waif of a waiter comes over and greets us in what must be off-duty clothes. Only an apron covers his trendy cut white t-shirt and slim-fit jeans. He'd be more attractive without the dyed blond streak running through the left side of his jet black hair. It's a small deduction, though, especially because I give extra points for originality, no matter how well it actually works for someone. I try not to notice him too much, given things are already complex, but Ana's prediction for my love life could be around any corner. I don't want to be looking the other way when he finally arrives.

The waiter offers Michael the bro hug of a good friend and then offers me a proper hand to shake. "I'm Gerry."

"Hi," I say, omitting my name. I don't mean to be rude, but Michael didn't introduce us, and I have a feeling he'd rather not. Either that or he has already forgotten my name.

Gerry smiles with a near-grin, seeming genuinely glad to meet me. Again it throws me. These are not my people. Well, not that I actually have people. But if I did have people, they would not be these people.

After a few updates about mutual friends, I learn that Gerry is more than happy to whip up something amazing for us to eat. Apparently it doesn't matter that they are closed. Not when you own the place, or almost do.

"Anything at all," Gerry insists.

Michael orders organic greens with sun-dried tomatoes and some warmed goat cheese, plus a mini-loaf of their signature ancient grain bread, lightly toasted. What kind of guy doesn't order at least a hearty free-range burger? No wonder he's so thin.

I can't think without a menu in front of me, so I say I'll take the same, making sure to ask for butter with the bread. I'm all for salad, but I like my butter, and I'm not going to forgo it for a guy who answers his phone at the table. Not a chance.

"Are you sure?" Gerry asks. "Your imagination is the limit."

Yes, he's youngish and cute, but he also has a sophisticated feel to him. Not so far off from Michael's, actually.

I try to imagine Gerry is *the one* for me.

Nope. Just can't.

"I'm good with the salad," I reply, a little more curt than I had intended.

You can probably feel the chip on my shoulder, but it's only there because I'm so out of my element. I try to remember what Jake said about me being one of the three most powerful women in their family. It's impossible to believe, so it doesn't help. Here, with two guys staring at me, in this setting? I just feel awkward.

Gerry nods, either unaware of my attitude or accustomed to it given the clientele of this place, and says he'll whip up a few amazing flavors of butter for me to sample. One hundred percent pure Vermont maple syrup and sea salt is his signature, he boasts with genuine foodie passion, but he's done some fun things lately with raspberry, fennel, and a hint of caramel.

"Naturally, we use Irish butter," he adds with a knowing smile to Michael.

You have to wonder, what's wrong with plain old American butter?

"Gerry is our sous-chef," Michael informs me when he leaves. "One day he'll be head chef if I can keep him from moving to New York. He's already got offers. We went to school together. He was two years ahead of me but bored senseless with the academics. I guess because he already knew what his dream was. He's a real genius in the kitchen."

"Nice," I say, non-committal, though I am slightly more excited about the butter.

"On to my dysfunctional family?" Michael offers. His voice is quiet, even though we are alone again, and well away from the kitchen.

"Go for it."

"It's hard to know where to start. I don't understand how you got involved with my family…" He trails off, no doubt hoping I'll chime in with a little something more to go on.

I don't reply. He considers me again.

"Look, I'm sure it must seem like I'm just some spoiled rich kid. But all this? The car? The clothes? It's a game. I'm playing it full-tilt, but I am completely aware of it, and there's a good reason."

This would be hopeful, if true. "What kind of game?"

"I guess I have to start at the beginning," he says with a sigh. "Maybe you know my mother died when I was young?"

Immediately, my heart seizes up. I mean, that's as big a bomb to drop as any I know. Because I do know. It takes a minute to sink in. I want to say that I'm sorry, because I am. But I always hate it when people say that to me.

"I didn't know," I finally manage.

"This means I'm not only Helene's grandson. I'm also her legal charge. And, at least according to her, her only hope. I'm the end of her line, just like Jake is the end of GranBea's line. Jake doesn't have a mother or a grandmother. It's just him and GranBea."

I take a deep, sharp breath. Jake, too? I mean, what are the odds? And what is wrong with their family that so many women die young? It's not exactly a winning advertisement for signing on to their Magic. Suddenly I'm more drawn to both Jake and Michael, only for terrible reasons. I begin to get an image of them as kids, left standing at the curb like I was. It probably didn't happen that way, but I could see it, and it kills me.

Don't go there Julie Mayden. Just don't.

I force myself to shut my empathy off. I need to remember why I'm here. I'll process this bomb later, like when I have an extra two years on my hands.

"GranBea?" I manage to ask, getting confused again about who is what to whom.

"Yeah, I know. She's not my gran, and GranAna's not Jake's. They are both great-grandmothers, though, so everyone in the family calls them GranAna and GranBea." He gives a short, sarcastic laugh. "Except Helene. And by the way, if you ever meet her, just call her Helene. No one dares use any form of *Gran* in front of her name."

"You have an interesting family," I respond, which is about a tenth of what I could say.

"It became even more so after my mom died." He says it like he is a bit sad, but it's not ripping his heart out. Not like it does mine. I still can't speak the words *mom* and *died* out loud in the same sentence, and it's been twelve years. "Helene sent me across the ocean to go to school, insisting she had to protect me from the rest of the family. I was only nine."

I can't help but do the math. He got five more years with his mom than I did with mine. What I wouldn't give for just five more hours.

"What's so bad about the rest of the family?" I'm trying to stay on topic, even though the ground is sort of swaying under my chair.

"She said Bea and Jake were unsophisticated and too wild. Unfit to carry on the Quinn name. And trust me, Helene is all about carrying on our name. It consumes her. She wants it to consume me, too. I do what she says because it's best to have her think I'm on board with her agenda. If I didn't, I have a feeling all of our lives would become even more hellish than they already are. Especially GranAna's."

"Why do you think that?" I lead, dying, dying, dying to ask a billion specific questions on this topic alone. I don't, because questions give you away every bit as much as answers.

Michael looks at me for a long time, his face cocked to the side as if doing some hefty pondering. Finally, he clears the table space in front of him. He puts one spoon in the cleared area, looks over his shoulder to make sure Gerry is not in eyesight, and then puts his hand over the spoon. He sort of bounces his hand above it, then takes a finger and— I swear—without touching it, it starts to spin.

Seriously.

He is not touching it.

At all.

I look up at him. He looks back, intent, but the spoon keeps spinning. His eyes seem achingly hopeful that I understand. Which I do.

"You have Magic," I say. Not a question, an obvious fact. My whole body lights up in truth-telling response.

He nods and stops the spinning, but then lifts the spoon higher— still without touching it—and starts to move it toward me. I back up even more in my chair. It's impossible, but undeniable. The spoon hovers in the air, then comes right toward me.

Without. Michael. Touching. It.

Next to this, making a bread bowl break is kid stuff. I'd assume it was a chump magic show trick if I didn't feel the same energy around the spoon that I used on the bread bowl with Mrs. Hamilton. It's a palpable sensation, something I can almost see, like the waves that appear in a mirage. I tilt back in my chair, balancing on only two legs. I'm not afraid, but, well, this is just way bigger than what I did. Way, way bigger.

This is *controlled*.

"Keep talking," I say. At least I think I said it out loud.

He lets the spoon drop in my lap. It's hot, like Ana's Magic when it went into my hands. With the drop, I feel a release of my own tension. I set my chair back on all fours. A small bit of nausea stirs inside me. Some of that buttered bread would be great right about now.

"From what I've been able to figure out, what you call 'Magic' runs in the family. I remember there were arguments, lots of them when I was little, between Helene and GranAna and GranBea. Then Mom died, and they made some kind of agreement. I was promptly shipped off to boarding school without a goodbye." He looks at me, his eyes practically begging me to understand.

"That's amazing," I barely manage to reply.

"I'm guessing that there are parts of this Magic that just come naturally," he continues, both explaining and asking, "like the spoons, plus a few other things I can do. Anyway, that is what I've pieced together."

I notice the hair standing straight up on my arms. He's got his story right. I can feel it. Even so, I try not to give anything away. No matter how much I feel for him, my first allegiance has to be to Ana.

He leans in toward me again and lowers his voice even further. "GranAna's not out of it, is she? That's why you were talking to her about Jake and GranBea—and by the way, neither of them have been seen by anyone in the family for more than a year, ever since GranAna was admitted to the nursing home. It's made Helene furious because, even with all her resources, she can't find them. I'm thinking either GranAna's being punished or she's protecting us. Maybe both?"

I can't say anything. I just can't.

He resets his place setting like nothing ever happened, then sits back and stares at me. "I heard you tell GranAna you've seen Bea and Jake. Since I can't ask her, I have to ask you: Where are they? Why did they go into hiding? What, if anything, does it have to do with me? And what is this Magic that our family has?"

Again I say nothing, though it is starting to kill me. I feel a straining pull on my heart and my lungs feel like an elephant stepped on them.

"Can you tell me if I am even warm on all this?" He is honestly pleading.

I want to reply, if only so we can start figuring it all out together. His pieces do fit with my pieces, at least mostly. But I still don't have a full picture, or permission to try to make sense of it with him. Thankfully, Gerry brings the bread with three small cups of butter and explains my options in excruciating detail.

Michael thanks him, but his eyes never leave me. He's waiting for answers that I can't give.

"Okay, you don't have to confirm or deny anything," he says once a slightly deflated Gerry has taken the hint and left again. "But I have something I would like you to tell GranAna, assuming—as I do—that you have a way to get through to her. Tell her I already have this Magic thing. You've seen it, and it's how I found her at that place, with you there. They don't have to wait to teach me, if that is the agreement, because I'm already teaching myself. GranAna once told me we would all spend time together when I was older—her, me, GranBea, and Jake. She said she would teach us wonderful, magical things, but that I had to grow up first. It was a long time ago, but I never forgot."

"I wouldn't forget either," I offer, noncommittal but at least a little compassionate.

"I've missed them," he admits, looking far more like a little boy some trendy New York runway model. "All of them. They are my family. And now, seeing GranAna like that? I mean, a promise just can't be that important, can it?" His eyes grow darker with a kind of frustrated panic. The same way I have felt when I've thought about Ana trapped in there. "They need to know I'm ready. I can play the game with Helene and learn without her knowing. I swear I can. Believe me, I'm a master of secrets. No one else knows about what I can do. No one but you."

His eyes are begging me to help him. No kidding, this guy is desperate. It's hard to hold anything against someone like that. And he's trusted me. That's big.

I am so very tempted to tell him he's right, at least about the parts I know. I'd love to say that Jake is also learning Magic, and I'm starting to as well. I'd confirm that, yes, they totally plan to teach him when he turns eighteen. That they have said he's in line for the Magic to continue, just like Jake. But if what he's saying is true, maybe they don't want him to know any more than he does, at least not yet. I wonder, though—would that change if they knew he already has their Magic?

I swear, my head is ready to explode on me, right here on the table. I have to say something. He deserves some kind of reply. But it has to be exactly right, for Ana's sake.

"I get it," I offer, careful. "I want you to know that I heard every word you said. Really. But I have promised some people that I know that I won't say anything to anyone. So I think it's best if I take Ana out on a walk this afternoon. Alone."

I realize I have given something up, just in those few words. But I had to. I'm not heartless.

He nods his understanding slowly, intently, like it's an agreement between us. Like we're on the same side.

"You have an accent," I divert, going for the most promising dish of butter, and hopefully calming my stomach as I lead our conversation in another direction. One that helps me but doesn't help him.

"I go to boarding school in Ireland. It's an all-male school in the middle of god-forsaken-nowhere. I'm supposed to return in August. I'm hoping something happens before then so that I don't have to."

I like being right about the Irish accent, but I feel for him with the whole boarding school scenario. I wonder who I'd be if Dad had boarded me out to Switzerland. I hate to even think about it.

"Is this your first time back to the US?" I probe, thinking that, as butter goes, this is nothing short of amazing.

He nods. "I've spent years convincing Helene that I'm completely on board with the career track she has for me, so she's finally seen the wisdom in my starting to build my pre-college resume here in the states. She's enrolled me in a top-level soccer camp."

I raise my eyebrows to that. It makes him laugh, like he knows how all this just doesn't add up.

"Like I said, I know what this looks like. When I got here a week ago she handed me the keys to my new car and gave me a credit card, supposedly with no limit. She knows I like good food, so she promised me this place. She even gave Gerry the job before I got here. I came in for the first time the day I arrived. Pretty much haven't left since."

"She hired Gerry on your say-so?"

"She doesn't do anything on my say-so. I think she just wanted to see firsthand if I'm totally enrolled in her world or not, so she's set up a series of tests. Gerry is here for me to prove I can be a boss, even to my own friends. This whole visit is all about showing her that I'm exactly who she wants me to be, a few thousand dollars at a pop."

I have no idea what to say. But he's given me a ton of insight into a whole lot of things. I'm grateful, even if I can't admit it.

"Isn't Europe a better place for soccer?"

"Definitely. I've played for years. But she wants me to consider a career in the Navy. The Naval Academy has an elite-level soccer camp. She said it's an entry point."

This guy? The Naval Academy? I know the type that becomes a midshipman because Dad serves as a sponsor father for a new cadet each year. They come over for a respite from not being able to take their feet off the floor from morning till night. I have to say I can't see it in

Michael. Not for a second.

"So she'll be watching you like a hawk?"

"From behind the scenes. She knows I'll be on my best behavior when I'm with her, so she's leaving me to my own devices, at least partially. She'll be traveling for work, so she's hooked me up with someone who will no doubt report back to her on what kind of man I'm becoming. That was what the call was about. I'm staying in her business partner's guesthouse. He's got a teenage daughter, so no doubt Helene's also trying to see if I have any interest in her. I wouldn't put it past her to arrange my marriage if she could figure out a way to get away with it."

Casual news for him. An earthquake for me.

My body gets all tingly-shaky-excited-nervous. I mean, from head to toe.

It could be a different business partner and another teenage daughter that he is going to be living with for a few weeks. But Dad asked me to be home for a young dinner guest tonight at six, so I don't think so. Despite myself, I think about watching him go off to soccer camp in those cute long shorts every morning and come home with sore muscles and grass stains every evening. Which is just, so...

Really, Julie? Ana is trapped in the Village, and all you can think about is...that kind of thing?

I get a hold of myself and regroup. Even so, I wonder where the boring, impossible life I was leading just two days ago has gone. It's like the world did a quick spin and tilt, and then threw me out into someone else's reality. A better reality, mind you. But nothing like what I've known up to now.

"I have to meet them for dinner tonight at six," he goes on, "but I'm sure I can slip out and meet you after, if you text me where."

"You might like the daughter," I toss out casually.

"I am not here to like anyone's daughter," he says flatly, completely unaware he's also flattened every last one of my tinglies. "How could I be with GranAna drugged up like that? She's my first priority. I have to get her out of there. Nothing is worse than that, especially if she is aware of what's going on. It's got to be a living hell, you know?"

Now I feel even more like a jerk. How many times is that today?

"So could you meet me after?" he asks anxiously.

Once again, there are too many variables in this to know what to do. But at least this I can play straight: "No. But I'll see you at six tonight."

"I'm sorry, like I just said, I have a dinner."

"With me. I'm Julie Mayden. Your grandmother's business partner's teenage daughter."

Chapter 10

"There are two reasons you must never let this medicine bag leave my possession," Ana insists, her voice as clear as the blue sky filtering through the treetops. My heart cringes in on itself as I prepare to learn all about my screw up #356. Not that I don't know exactly what I did wrong. After the nurse came in, I hid Ana's medicine bag in my pocket and then forgot and took it with me.

Not only cruel, dumb as well.

While I do want to hear about the two reasons, and maybe learn something about Magic in the process, we've got all of thirteen minutes, sixteen at the outer limits, to talk here in the woods. I have a feeling the whole Michael thing needs every second of it.

"First, it holds precious meaning to me. Second, if you travel with it and go anywhere near Bea, the resonance it will create with her medicine bag will be enough to lead Helene straight to my sister's hiding place. That must not happen."

"It won't. Not ever again. I'll also be exponentially careful that no one is in your room. Like Michael."

I hope she takes the hint and gets on topic. I have to figure him out—fast. Especially because, by the time I stepped out of his car after lunch, I realized that I like him. I don't want to, but I do. I don't know that I *like him*, like him. But for sure I like him. And that could be a mistake.

"Well and good," she says, forgiving me far too readily. "I understand you want to talk about Michael. Indeed, we must. But first, tell me about your meeting with Bea and how things are with Scottie. Please, I want every detail."

I try to shorten the *every detail* part, but she won't let me. She insists I go through every single thing, from Rod to Scottie to Jake, to my lesson in Magic, to Mrs. Hamilton and the bowl breaking. Her responses include snorting, sighing, chuckling, and outright laughter, but she doesn't interrupt. "So then I came to see you this morning and found Michael here."

She considers what I've said as I look at my watch. Fourteen minutes in.

"My dear, we have come to a moment of truth," she declares, veering off topic yet again. "I invited you into our world, at least in part, because I do see the potential for Magic in you. Even so, you are at this moment an outsider. While we desperately need our Clann to continue, there are many risks to you and us. Therefore, I will have to ask you to decide, here and now, if you are called to take these risks."

I start to say *yes, absolutely*, but she's barreling on.

"You accepted my Magic because you wanted help for your beloved Scottie. But you would have done anything, given your love for her. What I am asking of you now is more. Far more. It must be decided in this moment because it has implications not only for your future, but also ours."

She looks at me straight on to be sure I understand. I nod that I do. Nods take less time than words.

"I realize it is a great leap to agree to a future without knowing what you are agreeing to, yet I can reveal no more until you do. It is classic to our ways, and the ways of all Magic, to take such leaps of faith. Of course, you would not know that. I can only ask you, therefore, to trust in your heart."

I nod again. This time it's more definitive.

"It is natural to be afraid. Do not let that stop you. Fear is always with us. We can only learn when to heed it and when to move past it. What it comes to is this: If you are pulled to say yes, say yes. If you are repelled, say no. Choosing one over the other is as simple and profound as that. That is the best wisdom I can give you in this monumental, life-altering, and permanent decision."

I was a hundred percent ready to go with it, but her last words jam in my brain. A monumental, life-altering decision is fine. Intense, but fine. But a *permanent* decision? Right now, with zero minutes on the clock?

I mean, what are the risks? What are the rewards?

Well, the rewards at least I feel clear on. It has to be something amazing to be one of the three most powerful women in the Quinn Clann. And I loved being able to break that bread bowl. But it's more than just having the power. Being in the Clann, not just hanging out with them, means something. At least to me. I mean having Ana, Bea, Jake, Michael—all of them—as something like family?

Even dealing with Helene would be worth that.

Probably.

Suddenly, like a meteor has just landed in my gut, I realize there is only one risk I would not take. "Are you asking me to sell my soul?"

"Never!" she insists, her hand grasping mine. Her electricity jolts through us so that it feels as if our hands are glued together by a centrifugal force. "Any kind of Magic which asks you for that—and there are many forms that will—is not our Magic. In the Quinn Clann, your ultimate power is in your soul's freedom. There will be sacrifices, yes. Many and great sacrifices. But we will never ask you to put the power of your life force in a cage and certainly never to hand it over to another. This should have been your first instruction in Magic and I do intend to take it up with Bea that it was not!"

"Then I agree." I hear the words roll out of my mouth. They ring true. I guess you could call that a pulling. Sure wasn't a repelling.

"Good then," she replies, as though she knew the answer all along and was just waiting for it to be official. "Now, I must clarify a few things."

I steal a glance at my phone to check the time, my nerves pinching at the perimeter of my stomach.

"The idea that I would give you all of my Magic and thus be left with too little is ridiculous."

My heart sinks a bit, though it shouldn't. I mean, it's just plain greedy to want it all, right? "I'm sure you need a lot of it."

"Need it?" she scoffs. "Seriously, dear, when you sneeze on someone and pass on your cold, does that mean you lose it? Bea was being dramatic, and I assure you, that is just her style." She says this as if she's upset with Bea, but a small smile gives her away. She misses her sister. A lot.

"As for your first Magic lesson, she should never have taught you to take in earth energy without giving you some guidance on control and protection. Especially since it had to be clear to her that fire will claim you, and I had already empowered you with my air."

Fire? Air? For the sake of time, I let it go.

"You will have to tell Bea that I fully disapprove of her methods. Not that it will matter to her what I say. I have never been able to tell her anything she did not want to hear. You will just have to insist out of your own sense of integrity that she teach you about protection, lest you break something more than a bread bowl. It's lucky your Mrs. Hamilton did not get an eye put out, as furious as you must have been with her!"

"I will insist," I agree, though I like the idea of Mrs. Hamilton with an eye out, not to mention more Magic lessons, especially if Jake is around for them.

The thought of Jake makes me remember when his cheek touched mine. I feel my face go warm.

"Yes, yes, we can speak of Jake," she offers, even though I didn't say anything out loud. "And Michael, too. One cannot explain Jake without explaining Michael, can one? You see, dear Mayden, our family is a complex web of…"

I try to steal another quick, hidden glance at my phone clock, already dreading what I will see. While I desperately want to hear every word she has to say, especially about Jake and Michael, I am terrified to lose the chance to take her out again tomorrow, and the next day, and the day after that.

"Oh, do stop worrying about the time, dear. It is ever so malleable. I am sure I still have it in me to shapeshift an hour, anyway. Now, as I was about to say, our family is complex, and our history goes back twelve hundred years."

I try to drop the mountain of questions that arise from her one word, *shapeshift*, if only because this is the first history lesson in my life that I'm actually eager to listen to. I guess I'll just have to trust her on the time issue—along with about a hundred thousand other things.

"The story of our most current troubles began with my father, which is saying a lot, given we are a feminine tradition of Magic. There are five generations from my father to Jake and Michael, and five is always a challenging number in any family."

I nod like I agree, even though I know absolutely zero about fives in families.

"Try not to let this offend you, but the fact of the matter is that Bea and I are not traditional twins. Yes, we were born on the same day, and within minutes of each other." She takes a deep breath, as if bracing herself to hear her own words. "However, while we did share the same father, we were born of different mothers."

I notice her eyebrows are pulled together into a rare frown as if she is worried about my reaction. Only I don't have one. I make a mental note that this technically makes Ana and Bea half sisters, not twins. But why would that offend me?

Oh, wait, she's old. It's probably about decency and family honor and all that. I want to tell her that, these days, it's practically normal to have a dad that gets around, at least in my experience.

71

"It is also possible," she continues cautiously, "but not certain, that we have a third sister from yet another mother. Are we triplets? We never knew for sure, as Father always kept from positively confirming it. But we sensed a third sister in the same way Bea and I sensed each other's existence long before we laid eyes upon each other."

"How old were you when you and Bea first met?"

"Eighteen. We were not allowed to meet before then. The Magic between us would have been too powerful, according to my father. But was that true? Or was he simply controlling us? You see, he was as secretive as he was brilliant, and our mothers were both gone, leaving little protection from him.

Both mothers gone?

"It is hard to say if he was more good or bad, he did so much that called upon each quality. He was not our Keeper of Magic—could not be, being male—and I think that ate away at him. What is one to do when one has a huge aptitude and yet no role?"

I nod like I understand.

"In any event, it would seem I inherited his goodness, while Bea got an equal measure of both his good and his bad. She has channeled her darker aspects well, though, to her credit. Mostly she is just mischievous, and there is no real harm in that. For example, giving you just enough magical instruction to break a bowl. I am sure she is still cackling over it."

It's not hard to imagine.

At all.

"You understand, I hope," she adds, trying to lean up on one elbow, "that this is not pride speaking, saying I'm good, and she is both good and bad. It is a matter of the essential, inborn traits we bear, like the color of your hair, or being of a quiet or loud nature. I am not proud to be good. I am just good. Do you understand?"

"You mean being good or bad is inherited?"

"Think of it as a soul trait, one that develops as a path of energy within you and gets expressed as you make choices throughout your life. No one is perfectly good or perfectly bad, of course. The world would be annihilated should that be the case. It is a world of up and down, left and right, after all. Most people are a balanced mixture. Some cling a little more to the positive; others are drawn a little more to the negative. If you are mostly positive in both virtues and choices, we would still call that good. Those who lean more toward the negative and base, we would consider bad. Whenever predominance of one over the other is evident, or when one leans a little too far one way or the other, there is always trouble. Always."

"Am I good or bad?" I blurt out. "I mean, can you see that?"

"Oh, dear," she says, sounding surprised, "I see it so very clearly. But you can, and should, learn the answer for yourself. Simply feel for the pulse, good or bad, that runs through you. You may try to fool yourself or cover up your true nature at times. But if you feel for that pulse, you will know."

"I'm mostly good," I admit after feeling for it for a second. "But I want to be more interesting, so I pretend I'm bad."

Ana nods like it's a reasonable assessment. "And what does this pretending do for you?"

I shrug. "I don't know. Good is kind of boring, I guess."

"True enough," she says with a light laugh, "and completely out of vogue today. But you have yet to see what good can do and the unique Magic it contains. Good is no small thing, I assure you. You will be amazed at what is possible when good is applied with skill."

"You're not going to tell anyone? About me being good, I mean, right?"

"Your goodness is safe with me."

"So what about Michael? Is he good? Or bad? And Jake? Because I might, you know, sort of..."

"Fancy one of them? Yes, that does make knowing one's temperament rather important, doesn't it? Again, it all goes back to our history."

I try to remember we are shapeshifting time and settle in, but it's hard. Getting caught would be decidedly problematic.

"I am afraid I married bad. It is a classic pitfall for those of us who are good. We seek what we are missing. My daughter, Helene, takes after her father. I tried not to see it. She fooled me just long enough so that I would hand her my role as Keeper of Magic on her thirtieth birthday. Bea warned me, but I did not listen. We all suffer to this day from my mistake."

Wait! What? Ana has been the Keeper of Magic? I swear, she just grew ten feet taller in my eyes. But then she just gave the role to Helene? I can't imagine feeling that guilty.

"It's true," she says with a sigh, "I could not help but love my daughter and try to see the best in her, no matter her prevailing nature. But we cannot pretend things are other than what they are. Not any more. I learned that most assuredly, and perhaps too late for us all."

"I don't get it," I admit, only now noticing how honest I feel I can be with Ana. "How do you love someone, even your own kid, who puts you away in a place like the Village, especially when you don't need to be there? I mean, there's bad and there's vile."

She doesn't argue with me. "It is true. Yet Bea lost far more to my mistake than I did. You see, Jake's grandmother, Emilia, died giving birth to Jake's mother, Georgia. And then we lost Georgia, too."

I add these names to my patchy understanding of the Quinn family tree as provided by Michael and try to create a mental outline. There's Jake, his mother Georgia (DY, for deceased young), her mother Emilia (DY), and then Bea. Then there's Michael, his mother (DY), his grandmother Helene, and then Ana. Looking at all the DY's, then adding both Ana's and Bea's moms, one can only conclude that it sucks to be a female member of the Quinn Clann, feminine tradition or not. Then again, with only a father and one aunt in my own family tree, who am I to talk? I try to figure out who I feel for most and, for some reason, maybe just intuition, it's Jake.

"How did Jake's mom die?" I ask softly.

"It was the drugs. And, I must admit, also Helene."

My eyes beg her to explain, even though I am not sure I want to know.

"Growing up without a mother, Georgia was always lonely. We tried to care for her, but the ache went deep. She naturally turned to her Aunt Helene as a mother figure. When Jake was born prematurely, Helene suggested that Magic had shown her that the baby would not live. Georgia overdosed with poor little Jake still hooked up to a dozen tubes. As if history was bent on repeating itself, he never knew his mother."

God. God. God.

"I might as well mention it now. Magic doesn't take well to drugs."

"What happens?" Not that I'm into drugs. I always felt weird about losing control. Like life's not hard enough to manage straight up sober?

"Nothing. Nothing happens because Magic has nothing to work with. Even when desperately needed, it simply passes the recipient by. This is not a judgment. There is simply not enough of the soul-self present to be helped. Getting into drugs, Georgia was left to live an ordinary life with no hope of the Magic she saw working for everyone else around her. Spiraling down, it became a daily battle. Truth be told, she was lost to us years before she died. Helene simply gave her that last push."

To my aching horror, I can imagine it all. It makes me want to nuzzle Jake and say *I'm sorry,* only without words.

"It was Bea's remarkable generosity and forgiveness that allowed our families to remain bonded. The Quinn Clann continued on without splitting into factions. Goodness prevailed, to my sister's immense credit."

"But Jake is good, right? Even with his mom turning out like that?"

Ana smiles. "Mostly good and a little, shall we say, damaged? He pays the price for her self-destruction even now, poor child."

Damaged? That's harsh.

"What do you mean? Exactly?" Now I want details, no matter how long it takes.

"Let it suffice to say that Jake would have also been lost, had Bea and I not intervened. We started teaching him Magic very young, which was and still is a great risk. Even so, we felt the risk of beginning his magical education was far less than the risk of growing up without hope. From the very first day, he has devoted himself to the path."

"And Michael?"

She takes a deep breath, and then lets it out, long and slow. "Michael. Flesh of my flesh. Do you know I have not been allowed to see him since he was a child? As much as he should not have come here today, I cannot be upset that he did. He is beautiful, isn't he?"

"Yes," I agree, because he really is.

"But you see, this is the problem. Michael is as good as he is beautiful, which is too good. Helene has tempted him with riches and the power of darkness both, I am sure. In doing so, she has likely tempered him. At least it seemed so to me, today. We cannot know how much balance he has found. Hopefully, just enough. As I have said, an excess of either good or bad is dangerous, especially when you are powerfully Magical, as he will be."

"Not will be," I blurt out, "already is. He can spin spoons without touching them and move them toward you. I saw him do it at lunch. And he found you here, without Helene knowing."

She laughs quietly, almost to herself. "Then it is as I have suspected. This is exactly why we need you, Mayden." She looks directly into my eyes. "Do you recall asking me if I saw a boyfriend for you?"

My head starts to buzz. I feel a pink embarrassment rush into my face.

"I must admit, it was Jake I had in mind for you. But with Michael back, perhaps Magic will want a say in who you are to be with."

Tell me she didn't just say that.

Crazy. Impossible. Weirder than Magic itself.

"Magic wants a say in my first-ever boyfriend?" I have to choke the words out.

"You will have the freedom to choose," she assures.

Like this is normal. Like a near-dynasty is not potentially resting on my shoulders with Magic—*Magic*—having an opinion on the matter!

As if changing course, Ana laughs me off. "Now, now, we are getting ahead of ourselves here. You are young. You will not be expected to choose a helpmeet for a while."

Helpmeet? Helpmeet!!

"Are you saying I will have to choose between Michael and Jake as my...?"

"Not today," she quickly assures.

This is not happening.

Simply. Not. Possible.

Two days ago, I had no prospects for a boyfriend. Not even a prayer of a prospect. Now I'm choosing between the supposedly ultra-good, beautiful Michael and the damaged-but-hot nuzzler Jake? It's beyond what the brain can imagine.

Beyond what it can imagine imagining.

"Perhaps we should be getting back now," she suggests.

I nearly leap up, realizing I finally forgot about the time. I'm amazed we haven't heard sirens blaring and had a search team combing the place. In fact, until this moment, I forgot where we were. I haven't noticed a single bird chirp, or a bug or a breeze or anything.

I think that's Ana's doing, but right now, it doesn't matter.

"We have to go," I insist, because while I don't have any idea how to make sense of all this, I sure as hell don't want to lose all my future chances to find out.

"It will be fine, as I have assured you."

Even so, I hurry her into an upright position, and then hoist her into her chair. We nearly fly back through the woods and finally into the building. I'm sweating like crazy and my heart is jumping like a badly played game of ping-pong. I can barely gather the courage to check the wall clock, terrified to see what's coming.

But...But...It can't be.

I look again.

We were gone for a total of...five minutes?

"Itoldyou, Itoldyou, Itoldyou," Ana mumbles.

Impossible! I still have a few hours before my dinner with Michael.

Crap! Dinner with Michael!

"Wait! Wait!" I whisper, close to her ear, "I still don't know what to say to Michael!"

Ana smiles with her eyes, her head now bobbing wildly: "Welcomehome, welcomehome, welcomehome, welcomehome."

Chapter 11

No trail. No shack. Nothing. It's like Jake and Bea are not here. Like they never were here. But they have to be. I still don't know what to do with Michael, and dinner at the house is less than two hours away. They've got to tell me what I can and can't say, and do, and everything.

I pry my soaking wet pants from my legs. It's not easy after crossing that creek again. They're nearly suctioned to me. The water line is lower than yesterday, and it's thick with mud. I wouldn't be surprised if a dozen leeches were waging war on my calves right now. But I can't think about that. I need to find Bea, or at least Jake. Apparently, they have vanished.

As in gone. Poof.

Nobody home.

Not even a home.

"Hellooooo?" I whisper as loud as a whispering voice can project. I want to keep their hiding place a secret, but I also want to talk to them.

Need to talk to them. Now.

Already I'm kicking myself for not asking when I could come back, not to mention how to get back. But the shack was only a few feet in, wasn't it? I also recall Jake saying Bea is deaf—another thing I was going to ask Ana about, had she not gone so deep into the family saga. So Bea may not hear me, no matter how loudly I call.

Unless she wants to, which is just so...

"What do you want?" a harsh voice from behind me barks, making me jump clean out of my skin.

I turn, instantly face-to-face with Bea. "You scared me," I sputter.

"You again! You didn't announce yourself. When you come, come slow, so we can smell you."

I want to ask why, but she doesn't look like she's in the mood for questions. "I'm sorry. But I have to tell you something. I mean ask you something. Because Ana didn't tell me what to do about…"

"You saw her today? How is she?"

"She's good. I mean, about the same. I wasn't able to talk because…"

"Her vitality was faint for several hours around lunchtime. I feel it when something is off with her."

"Oh, that. That's my fault. I took her leather bag when I went to lunch with…"

"You what?" she growls. I mean, truly growls. Like an animal.

"I didn't know it was a problem. This nurse was going to see it and…"

"You don't have it with you now, do you?" She blurts out with big, terrified eyes.

"No, no. Ana told me about the power when her bag is near yours and all that. But you see…"

After interrupting practically every sentence, now she ignores me, abruptly turning to go deeper into the woods. She indicates that I follow her with that one-armed, insistent wave. Within ten seconds, we're on her property again, standing next to the fire pit, with the shack just a stone's throw away. I'd swear I was right here just a few minutes ago.

And it wasn't.

I start to look around for some clue, then stop dead in my tracks. I'd scream, but my mouth won't move.

"What…what…what's…that?" I finally manage to ask, quiet so as not to disturb the, the, the…

"That? That's Jake," she says, pointing toward a spotted leopard panting near the fire pit.

A spotted leopard? In Maryland? Without a cage?

What? *What!!??*

It can't be.

But it is. A real, live, living, breathing leopard. Big, though I've nothing to compare it to. Meaty. And by the way it is looking at me, hungry. I don't dare get close, so I just laser focus my eyes to get a better look.

I mean, yeah, this is the real thing. It's sort of mangled, though. Two legs are shriveled up a bit, and the back quarters sort of sit funny. So maybe this is a pet? A kickback from the zoo?

"What's wrong with it?"

"I told you," she insists, "It is Jake."

"Jake? You mean *Jake*-Jake? You turned Jake into a leopard?"

He said she could be unstable, but this is insane. I mean, Magic is Magic, and breaking bowls is fine. But turning people into animals?

Come. On.

"Certainly not," she says, looking at me like I am truly dense. "He did it himself. What good is it if I do it for him?"

She has to be kidding. She just has to be. Yet there it is.

I slowly inch toward it, trying to get close enough to see the breath laboring in and out, and get a better whiff of its husky scent. It's far more pungent than me, even in my smelly river pants. I look more closely at the deformed legs. The front right and the hind left are both sort of withered. On the right side, the bone looks like it's drawn up into the ribs and there is hardly a paw. More like a flipper.

"What's wrong with it? I mean, him?"

"He's not very good at it yet," Bea explains dryly, as if that should be obvious.

I take another step, but the leopard-supposedly-Jake bares his teeth at me and growls—not entirely unlike Bea was growling at me just moments ago.

Suddenly everything starts to come clear. Growls. Nuzzling cheeks. Is this…Can it possibly be…their *Magic*?

I take another step forward, thinking if I go slow, Jake will let me approach. He seemed to like me before, anyway.

"I wouldn't do that. He's not fully aware he's Jake right now. He'll do what animals do if he feels threatened."

"Can you do this, too?" I ask, thinking things could get pretty wild, if not downright dangerous, if she can. I recall Jake saying she had good intentions but isn't always herself. This would most definitely qualify. Funny he didn't mention anything about himself.

"Depends what you mean," she says, starting to gather wood, like this is just another day at the shack. Though I guess for her, it is. "Can I turn myself into a spotted leopard? No."

I feel a deep sigh of relief and move to help with the fire, but my hands are shaking so much it's not easy to grasp even the larger sticks.

I make sure not to get too close to…*Jake*.

I try to get the idea to lock in my brain. I mean, how can you even take it seriously? It's in the realm of pure fantasy. Then again, there is a leopard in easy pouncing distance from me right this very moment, and despite his legs, I'm guessing his teeth work just fine. That would be in the realm of pure fact.

"My true nature is akin to the black panther, so that's what I shapeshift into."

That word again: *Shapeshift.*

I look at her like she must be joking. But then she looks at me hard, and I see a flash of something. Something dark and primitive. It's like she is showing me a side of her that's normally hidden. It's so primal, so animal-like. I feel I have no choice but to take her at her word. "And Ana?"

"I don't know if she can shapeshift anymore."

"She told me she was going to shapeshift time with me today, and I think she did. She made what seemed like half an hour, maybe an hour, fit into about five minutes."

My magical teacher smiles half-heartedly, like she is both sad and pleased to hear it.

I want to ask if I'm going to be able to turn into some kind of animal as well when I learn their Magic. I'm definitely curious about what my nature is akin to. Even so, that can wait. For now, I'll tuck it and this whole Jake thing away in the *Probably Impossible* category of my brain, which I notice has been getting pretty crowded these past few days.

Suddenly, the great cat begins to move. He stands up shakily, then limps himself off into the woods.

"It's about privacy," Bea offers in explanation, though it explains nothing to me.

"What about Ana? What is she? I mean, if she could still shapeshift, what would she turn into?"

"A mountain lion. Surely you can see that in her?"

I suppose if Bea is a black panther, and Jake a spotted leopard, then Ana could be a mountain lion. Sort of like in standardized tests where as A is to B, so C is to D.

Or something like that.

"It's hard to know what anyone will become until they make the leap for the first time," she continues, moving toward the fire pit, dumping her load of logs and sticks, then dousing the pile with lighter fluid.

I feel a bit disappointed. Somehow I expected her to rub the two sticks together or wave her hands to conjure up fire. Lighter fluid feels like cheating.

"But once you've shown your colors, that's it. You'll never be anything but what you are. Except when you're nothing." She cackles at what must be an inside joke.

Don't even try to make sense of this, Julie Mayden.

Almost immediately, there is a solid fire going. I worry about outside people seeing it and finding us here, then remember I just spent a decent amount of time looking for this whole place, only to find it was right where I had been looking.

Another thing for the *Probably Impossible* file.

"I know you're wondering," she continues, feeding the fire and talking over her shoulder, "so I'll tell you right off. There's no guarantee that you'll be able to do it. But, yes, I believe you are meant to be taught Magic and to at least try to shapeshift into the animal that you truly are."

First thought: *Oh. My. God.*

Second thought: *Yes.*

"Is it hard to learn?" I wish I could conjure up a more intelligent question right now. Surely there are a gazillion out there.

"Sometimes. Sometimes not. Okay, fire's set. Now dry yourself, and while you're at it, tell me what you're here for so I can get back to my life. Hardly a moment's peace with a visitor two days in a row."

"I met Michael today."

The old woman spins around. Deaf or not, the look of shock on her face says she heard me just fine. "How? Where?"

"He was hiding in Ana's bathroom. The door was closed, but he still heard me talking about you and Jake…"

"He was there? And he heard you?" Again she growls, which I now know must be the growl of a black panther, even if it is filtered through a human set of vocal chords.

"I didn't give anything specific about you away, I promise. Ana played her role perfectly. He suspects a lot, but doesn't know anything for sure. That's why I came to ask you what to do. He's staying at my house for a few weeks. He wanted me to tell Ana that he already has Magic."

She raises her eyebrows but otherwise seems to be calming down.

"He's not kidding. I saw it. He was able to spin a spoon without touching it."

"Tell me, what did Ana have to say today?"

I'm not sure if she's changing the subject or just needs context. Either way, I'm guessing it's best not to tell her about Ana's views on the breaking bowl and how that was the wrong thing to have taught me to do right away, even if I did promise to. Save that for next time. Or never.

"She didn't help much with Michael, which is why I'm here. Mostly she told me about your family history. About your dad being bad, and her being good, and Michael being too good."

"Poppycock! She can't be going on about that with you! Child, you're not to pay a whit of attention to her. Makes me wish she really were losing her mind right about now. It's all we need, her teaching you that kind of thing."

"So you don't agree? I mean that we are good or bad, or that I'll have to choose between Jake and Michael to see who gets to be my..."

I can't even say it out loud.

Besides, she is now nearly doubled over laughing. She goes on and on until Jake—the real, human Jake—walks in from the woods. He's rubbing his head and staggering a bit.

"Mayden!" he says, like he didn't just see me here three minutes ago. Well, maybe he didn't. Maybe he wasn't a spotted leopard. In fact, maybe both Bea and Ana are as loony as it gets. Maybe I've been suckered in. Totally snowed.

"What's funny?" he asks Bea, who is still whooping and hopping from foot to foot, looking like it's all she can do not to pee her pants right here.

Clearly the woman is easily humored.

"Tell him," she manages to get out.

"I saw Ana again today. She was telling me about how there were good and bad people, inherently, sort of like genetics or something."

I don't go into detail about me and him or Michael. I'm not stupid.

He chuckles. "They have differing opinions on the matter."

"Clearly," I reply, huffy. But I mean, really, what do you expect when no one is giving me straightforward information? It would be insane enough even if they all agreed.

"Don't be upset. There's some truth to it."

"Truth?" Bea mocks, losing the laugh. "Not the way Ana tells it! Honestly, you can't explain away life like that."

"You know that's not what she's doing," he defends somewhat cautiously.

I smile at him. At least he has a mind of his own. He smiles back.

"I know exactly what she means," Bea says, "and Ana is going off the deep end to try to teach a novice anything about good and bad. It's master-level material, and there's no way Mayden here is going to take it right."

"I'm confused," I admit, the way a person admits total defeat.

"Not surprising," Bea says, poking at the fire. "You probably think good is helping an old lady cross the street, and bad is playing with matches."

Now I'm offended. "I think I can consider good and evil at a slightly deeper level than that."

"Let's hope. Now, tell me about Michael."

"Michael?" Jake says, instantly standing straight. If he were a spotted leopard right now, I'd bet the farm his fur would be raised up along his spine.

"He's here from Ireland," I offer.

"And he's already found Ana," Bea explains. Her eyebrows rise in an unspoken communication that he seems to understand.

"He is staying with my family for a few weeks. So I sort of need to know what to do."

"Staying with you?" he demands.

He's clearly upset, but I have no time to think about what the implications of that are. Right now I need to get home. "He told me to tell Ana he's already doing Magic. Helene doesn't know, but he's figured out a lot about what is going on here, or at least he has some pretty clear ideas about it all."

"Magic *on his own*," she says to Jake, again with raised eyebrows.

"Things like spinning spoons and making them move through the air," I explain.

"Easy stuff," he grunts, immediately glum.

"Michael thinks you don't want to teach him until he's older, but he's ready now. I'm sort of stuck in the middle, not sure what to say, and what not to say."

Bea nods, sympathetic but firm. "He has it right about his coming of age. It's not that we don't want to teach him, though. It's that we can't."

I'd tell her that's what Ana said when she went into the family history, but I don't want to risk hearing about something else they disagree on. I like thinking of them as beloved old sisters, not antagonistic ones.

"So what do I do? Tell him no? Pretend I don't know you? Bring him here?"

Bea stops playing with the fire and goes to sit on her front porch rocker.

"Hey!" I say, pointing at a snake underneath one of the rocker blades.

"Python," she scolds, "get out from under there!"

"Python?" I ask, though I should leave it. I really should.

"Friend of the family," she says as the snake moves out of the way.

I remind myself that things like this don't happen in real life—you know, just in case there's still a sliver of sanity left in me.

"I'll have to think on this," she mumbles to no one in particular. "Magic is surely on the move, if Mayden has found us, and Michael has found her. But what does it want?" She looks contemplative as she pulls out a pipe, stuffs it with tobacco, and lights up.

Why does this not surprise me?

"Why is he staying with Mayden? And what is Helene up to? What does she know?"

She sounds like me when I go at my own infinity of questions.

Even though I know she's not talking to me, I feel compelled to answer. "Michael thinks she's testing him, but the official word is she's traveling. Since he has to stay with someone, and Dad loves to host guests, it probably just worked out that way. She doesn't know I know Ana, at least the way I do now."

"It would be hard to say what Helene knows and what she doesn't." She's still not talking to me so much as to think air. "Most times, she's several steps ahead of us. We can know, though, that Magic is moving quickly. If Magic is moving quickly, we must as well."

She looks around, blinking as she again focuses on me. "All right then. You'll need to find out when she'll be traveling. When she is actually on a plane and in the air, to be precise. It's the safest time for Earth Magic with the likes of her. Then I'll meet with Michael at your house. I've wanted to have a heart-to-heart with your Mrs. Hamilton, anyway."

"You're coming over?" The idea splits my brain into tiny little fractions.

Bea looks up like it's yet another question that ought to be obvious. "I need to meet your cook. She tried to poison Scottie, a member of our family. That cannot go without retribution."

She leans toward me, removes her pipe, and winks: "You see, I'm as bad as Ana says."

Chapter 12

I don't know if Michael is extra good the way Ana says, but he sure is smooth.

A shapeshifter like his family, only he turns into a total player. He hooked Dad with sports talk and an intelligent argument on the potential worth of an MBA, even if you already have a business of your own. There are now plans for the two of them to pal around with some of Dad's colleagues to help Michael explore his options when expanding his restaurant business to other cities which, clearly, Michael could not be more grateful for.

He got Sally too with the organic food thing, even promising he'd try to find a visiting chef for the next two weeks since dad gave the "understandably upset" Mrs. Hamilton a two-week vacation starting Monday. Apparently Michael knows a few brilliant chefs who cook organic that he's been dying to try out at the restaurant. Why not have one of them cook for us for two weeks as an audition? He was sure they could keep Sally's nutritional needs a priority in the planning. It's the least he could do to repay his stay in our guesthouse.

I could almost hear Wife #4's heart fluttering in adoration.

And then there's me. After witnessing all that, I wasn't going to be taken in by him again. No way. Not going to happen. But then he started petting Scottie after dinner when I brought her out to relieve her cabin fever. And he kept at it for a whole half an hour—not just a *nice little kitty, now scoot* like most people. He kept looking at me as if we share something important, like we know the score and the rest is just a game. It was so, I don't know...?

Seductive?

Yes, seductive.

And so there you have it: Despite myself, he got right back in.

The real problem, though, is not his smooth inner chameleon. It's his looks. I try not to go on and on about it in my head, because it's just so shallow to think like that, but it's like ignoring Michelangelo's David when he's standing right there in the middle of your psychic living room. He's not attractive if he's your type. He's attractive no matter what your type is. And I just don't know what to do with that. Especially with what Ana said about him and Jake and me. I've heard of girls melting with a look and always assumed it was just a combination of ignorance, stupidity, and a low tolerance for flattery. But there I was at dinner, melting whenever he glanced my way, just like any ignorant, stupid, flattered girl. I think I visibly winced when I heard his schedule, which is totally packed these next few weeks. I have no idea when he plans to actually spend time with Ana or Bea, should they open their arms to him, let alone me.

"You looked uncomfortable in there," he says, slowly walking the gardens of the backyard. I don't have a fancy parasol, but otherwise, we look ridiculously similar to how they looked in the old days when a boy courted a girl. It's adding a weird if not bizarre icing to the already crazy cake that is my life.

"You swept us all off our feet, like any good salesman."

"I was authentic with them both, I thought," he defends, sounding hurt, or maybe just confused.

I have to think about that. Is it possible? Could he have been authentic with all three of us?

Boggles the mind.

"I just hate them sometimes. They're so phony. It seems weird that anyone my age would like them. I mean, I love them. At least, Dad. But you seemed like you actually liked them. I just don't get how that could be real."

He shrugs good-naturedly. "I like people as a general rule. Always have. You can find something good in anyone, so I figure why not look for that and connect through it? The world would be a better place if we all did that."

I think about the world being a better place, and what kind of guy talks like that, or even thinks like that. "So you really did like them?"

"I don't know them well enough to like them or not like them. But if I'm going to be a guest here, I want to get along with them well enough to have them trust me, especially with you. And I also need them to send good reports back to Helene. It would be relational suicide to dislike them right off the bat, wouldn't it?"

"Then you *are* snowing them."

And me, I think but don't add.

"No. I'm just taking them at face value and letting that be the starting point of the conversation. I didn't suck up to your dad by saying I might want an MBA. I think I actually might. And I could see by the way Sally was picking at her food that it was a pretty important part of her life. It's smart, not manipulative. Why do you hate them?"

I sigh. "I don't *hate them*, hate them. They are just so, I don't know, like I said, superficial. All they care about is the stuff they buy, and it's always so over the top. For Valentine's Day, I got a watch. No problem, except it was diamond-studded and made of titanium. It was sitting there on my breakfast plate. And that's for Valentine's Day. Now imagine what Christmas is like around here."

We get to one end of the far backyard and settle in on a two-seater bench near our big clay chiminea. Not too close, but close enough that I notice it.

"I get it," he says, "because I grew up rich and alone, like you did. I understand how all that can feel like it's killing you. But I also know there's no such thing as a simple person. Everyone hurts."

I stare at him, pondering, at first thinking he did not grow up even remotely like I did, but then thinking maybe he actually could understand, at least some of it, given his own history. It seems fair to give him the benefit of the doubt.

"Have you given Sally a chance? She's got some good ideas about the business she's starting."

He's losing me again. Fast.

"Wife #2 used up most of the step-mom chances," I spit out, knowing I sound ugly, but unable to help myself, "and Wife #3 overdrew them by a mile. Wife #4 gets no chances. Nada. Zip."

"I suppose it's reasonable to be mad he's on his fourth wife. Even so, hate will limit you if you hold on to it. You'll end up just like them if you don't figure out a way to deal with it."

"You don't want an MBA. You want to be a shrink. Or a saint."

He doesn't laugh. "I want a life of Magic, just like you. I won't say any more about them because I can see you don't want me to. But think about it. They can only get to you if you let them."

I try not to roll my eyes at his wisdom, if only because he might be right.

"So what about GranAna? Will she see me?"

I'm enormously relieved to be off the topic of my family, yet not so sure I'm ready to talk about his. "I don't know. When I mentioned your name she just babbled "welcomehome, welcomehome, welcomehome.""

"That's something, isn't it?" he asks, though you can see he wanted more.

A lot more.

"So I went to see your GranBea to ask her about it."

He jumps to standing in a single second. "GranBea! You saw her?"

"She said she will meet with you. Here, at my house. It needs to be when your Aunt Helene is flying, though, as in actually *in* the airplane."

"Okay, sure! Why when she's flying?"

"Something about it being safest when using Earth Magic. Oh, and she wants to meet Mrs. Hamilton, our cook, so we'd better make it quick now that I know she's leaving for vacation next week."

"This is amazing! Thank you!" He spontaneously leans down to hug me. I give him a half hug and pat, unsure about how to be that close to his body.

It's like a live wire, I swear.

"Glad to help," I say, moving things along. "But how do we figure out when Helene is going to be on a plane?"

"Easy. I can get on her computer through the cloud. I'm sure she's got the whole itinerary there. Everything else is."

"You hacked your own grandmother?"

"More like I found her password."

"Found?"

"Okay, since you are intent on semantics, I felt for it in her psychic field and then tried it. As usual, I was right. That's how I found out where GranAna is. I felt where Helene kept the information in a hidden file and went to look. That's how I find out a lot. Feel for it psychically first, then check."

Maybe I'll just leave that tiny bomb alone for a bit. "And you hack your way in?"

He shrugs a pair of large, bony shoulders. "I don't like it, but there's a lot about Helene no one likes. If I can keep up with her, I figure it's probably all the better for everyone."

I'll have to think about that. But anyway, I'm hardly one to judge. Not with the mile-long history of Lillies I've called in over the years.

"Can you guess my password?" I challenge. It would be good to know now, upfront.

He looks at me with a totally serious face. "I didn't come here to spy on you, Julie."

"Call me Mayden, at least when Dad or Sally aren't around. Ana and Bea call me that, like a family name. I sort of got used to it."

"Mayden, it is."

"So can you?"

"Is this a test?" he asks, only slightly flirty.

"Sure. Why not?" I slightly flirt back. Jake said to test everyone. Might as well start with his rival.

"Stand up," he instructs, then comes around behind me and puts his face right up in my hair. "It's easier this way."

Maybe so, but come on, like he did this with Helene to hack into her computer? I don't think so. I can feel his breath on my neck. Not entirely unlike Jake's cheek against mine. It feels different in essence, though. He's not as into it, I can tell. But then, they are two totally different guys. As different as Ana and Bea are to each other, so I guess it makes sense.

"Think of your password," he instructs, his voice all low and rumbly. I get shivers up and down my spine. If only to distract myself, I think my password over and over, the way Ana babbles.

Scottiegirl. Scottiegirl. Scottiegirl.

After an entire minute of deep inhales and exhales, he steps away. "Scottiegirl."

I jump a full mile, I swear. "That's all you have to do? Stand up close to someone and listen in?"

"I don't have to stand close," he admits as he comes around to face me, smiling with his eyes.

"Then why did you?" I demand, stepping away. I beg the entire universe of gods and goddesses to help me if this is about him gaming me, because I'm completely unprepared for a player of his stature.

"I wanted to see what your hair smelled like. I was thinking strawberries, but it's not. What is it?"

"I call bullshit," I say, angry. Or scared. Or something.

"Okay. Truth then?"

"Always." Well, maybe not always, at least on my end.

"Everyone has some kind of Magic. When you get close to them, you can feel it. I wanted to feel what yours felt like. You don't let me very close, so I thought I'd try this."

"I thought you didn't want anything to do with someone's daughter this summer?" I'm frustrated with the way this is confusing me.

"It's not about that. And you're not just someone's daughter, anyway," he says, oh so slick. Or maybe not. I honestly can't tell.

"Who am I, then?"

"You're someone who gets Magic. That is beyond rare to find. I want to be friends with you, Mayden. Real friends."

"Don't mess with me."

"I'm not. I was honest, wasn't I, about the password?"

"Like I hadn't already figured that out."

"Look, I come in peace. Why all this resentment?"

"I don't want a boyfriend," I blurt out, though I have no idea why. "In specific, I don't want you for a boyfriend. Okay?"

He looks at me like he's considering whether I'm serious or not.

Poker face, please, please, please do not betray me now.

I do not want to get hurt by this guy. Not even a tiny little bit.

"Sure," he agrees. "That works for me. We are friends, though, right?"

"Possibly," I say, feeling myself finally take a full breath.

"Good enough." He starts to talk, then stops, then finally starts again. "Is it because you're with Jake? It's fine if you are. I'm just wondering."

Ana's words about choosing between the two great-grandsons jump back into my memory. "No," I say, unsure if I am lying now or not.

"Okay," he says again, nodding, but you can almost see his mind clicking away, trying to figure things out.

"Good. So when can you get Helene's schedule?"

"Let's head back and I can jump on my laptop in the guest house. She syncs everything in real time. Last I looked, it seemed like she was going to meetings in different cities every day this week. So we'll have options. You want to come with me?"

"I don't think I should. There's something in the Magic that is more powerful when magical people are together. Probably not so great when you're stealing someone's personal itinerary."

"Good thought. I didn't know about the two people together. Anything else? Like how the family uses Magic? And what for?"

"I've asked the same questions myself. But I've probably said more than I was supposed to already."

"But Ana said *welcomehome*, so she must be glad I'm here. And Bea must be okay with me knowing she is close by if she said she's going to come see me."

"This would be easier if you were a little more stupid," I joke, feeling a tiny bit lighter again.

"I'll work on it," he returns, matching my tone.

I leave it there. But if I could, I'd tell him about the shapeshifting of time and also into animals. About his family line and the twelve hundred-year-old tradition. It would sound crazy, but I think it would comfort him to know he's not too far off base with it all.

"What are you thinking?" he asks. "You'll have to tell me because I've already decided I won't look into your field again without permission."

"Nothing," I say, realizing only now that I've been smiling to myself.

"Well, I like how you look when you are thinking about nothing, Julie Mayden. And I am very glad to meet you."

Chapter 13

"**M**ichael," I whisper as loudly as I can without drawing attention to the fact that I'm out at the guesthouse early in the morning. I tap on the bedroom window, though he might have crashed on the couch.

He can't be half as exhausted as I am, given I was texting with Rod again, this time until almost three am, helping him get more of the family drama out of his system. The endnote was pretty much the same as the start: Divorce sucks, and there's nothing you can do about it until it's your turn to not get divorced. Maybe not even then.

"Michael!" If he doesn't respond soon, I'm going to let myself in. Bea and Mrs. Hamilton are alone in our kitchen, and it can't be pretty in there. If it's ugly, I don't want to miss a thing. Okay, so I am bad, right along with the best of them. But really, seeing Mrs. Hamilton get hers directly from Bea? Who wouldn't want a ringside seat for that?

I hear stirring, then see the door open.

"Yeah?" he says, groggy, his tall, thin frame standing in the doorway in only white cotton pajama bottoms. What's with these shirtless Quinn boys? I shouldn't, but I immediately compare him to Jake. Michael is far prettier, but Jake has the body of a god, especially in comparison.

Focus, Julie!

"Get dressed right now. She's here."

"Who?" he asks, looking around with squinting eyes. "What time is it?"

I push past him, not wanting to get caught on his doorstep at God-o'clock in the morning. Dad might get the wrong idea. "Early. Bea is already here. In the kitchen. With our cook."

"Here?" He immediately shifts into hurry mode, hopping around trying to get socks and a shirt on. I guess the pants could pass as tropical casual or something. He grabs a pair of hippy hemp-type sandals, just to complete the look.

How is it this guy keeps surprising me?

"I don't know why she came so early," I muse, finally having a half a second to do so. "She said we needed to find out when Helene was going to be in the air, but then she just went ahead and showed up at the kitchen door at quarter to seven."

He messes with his hair, like that matters. "Did you say it's seven?"

"Right at."

"So get this—according to Helene's schedule, she's in the air right now. Left fifteen minutes ago."

"Somehow Bea knew," I say, grinning.

"That's GranBea for you," he agrees, grinning back. "She always knew stuff."

"She said you had to put this on." I hand him a medicine bag. It's not fancy like Ana's. Just plain brown and heavy. "She said to wear it when you come in, and to not come any closer than eight feet to her. I'm guessing it's the too-powerful-together thing."

He starts to look inside it, but I stop him. "She said don't look inside."

"Lots of rules for seven in the morning," he complains, a morning gruff in his throat. Which is kind of cute.

He takes the bag from me and tucks it under his shirt. I guess he doesn't balk at rules the way I do. I'd have probably at least given it a good squeeze. Well, actually, I did. Hard to tell what's inside, but if someone told me it was a big, thick chunk of lead, I wouldn't argue.

"I have to warn you about something," I say as we head out across the lawn, making our way from the guest cottage to the main house, hoping beyond hope that Dad or Sally won't be looking. It's not like I can't explain I'm with him out here because someone is waiting in the kitchen for him. But it would be better not to put doubts in their mind about our being alone together. I want them to trust me. If they do, they'll let me hang out without needing to look over my shoulder, just because he's a boy. For the most part, they don't notice what I do or don't do. But this would be over the top, even for them.

"Warn away."

"There's something going on, I mean, already. You see, Mrs. Hamilton was poisoning Scottie, my cat, at least Jake said that is who he psychically saw it was."

"He saw it using Magic?" He stops walking.

I nudge him along. "Can't confirm or deny. But I already did some Magic with Mrs. Hamilton myself, so I'm thinking it could get a little strange in there."

"*You* did Magic? What kind?"

"It was just one lesson."

"They're teaching you and not me?"

"Don't worry, I probably have no real talent. I just broke a bowl without even knowing how. But I think Mrs. Hamilton got the drift. Then Bea hinted that we might see her bad side today."

"Ought to be interesting," he replies. It comes out deflated, if not downright depressed. I feel for him, but now's not the time to get into it.

We approach the kitchen door and step inside to see Bea leaning over Mrs. Hamilton. I walk toward them slowly, while Michael hangs back a good twenty feet. Only eight were instructed, but I'm glad he's not taking chances.

"I found Michael," I say tentatively, trying to break the mud-thick tension with a cheerful tone.

"Goodness gracious," Bea says, turning to me with an over-the-top worried look, completely ignoring that Michael is behind me. "Did you know Mrs. Hamilton is allergic to cats?"

Now Mrs. Hamilton turns toward me. Her eyes are red and practically pouring tears, and her face is hugely swollen. It is all I can do not to laugh. Isn't Bea supposed to turn into a black panther when she shapeshifts? That would be one big cat. Still, I don't dare say anything. Mrs. Hamilton is falling apart. I don't want to give anything away by being outwardly glad about it.

"Ith's neva behn thith bad," Mrs. Hamilton says through a thick tongue, looking bewildered.

"Poor dear, you're getting worse. You should see a doctor right away." She is speaking as if she were the most compassionate person in the world, only looking out for Mrs. Hamilton's wellbeing.

Right.

Our murderous cook doesn't have to be told twice. She reaches for her purse. "Tell yar dad I'm goin on vacathon early. Ih be back in two weekth."

"This kind of reaction could last much longer," Bea warns with dramatically furrowed eyebrows, shaking her head. "You might need a series of shots or something."

Mrs. Hamilton's fear is palpable.

Yippee, hooray and *hallelujah* are all screaming in my head.

"In fact," she goes on, her tone getting stronger, "you might not want to work here at all."

Then—I swear this on the graves of a hundred thousand saintly people—Bea's head changes into that of a black panther. Not all of her, just her head. It lasts only a few seconds, but that is long enough to look from Mrs. Hamilton to me, and then beyond me to Michael.

I check myself. A black panther head?

Yes. Totally. Completely. Unmistakable.

And then it's over. It happened so fast, you could almost think it didn't. But it did, and we all know it. Mrs. Hamilton is in a complete state of shock, no doubt wondering if her watery eyes are playing tricks on her. A perfectly straight-faced Bea helps usher her to the dining room door, which is opposite the door Michael is standing in, and tells her to hurry on to the doctor now.

"Bye-bye, Mrs. Hamilton," I say in mock, unable to help myself. I add "forever" once she's out the door.

"Well now," Bea says, returning to look past me at Michael, "how is my long lost great-nephew?"

"Hi, GranBea," he says, still shocked, but smiling this huge, adorable smile.

"I'm sorry you can't come closer. I've wanted to give you a great big GranBea hug for so many years now." At last, she sounds like her genuine self, maybe even a little nicer. I think there are tears rimming her eyes.

He nods without moving closer. I'd swear he had water in his eyes, too. "I understand. You can't right now."

"Do you understand? How much?" she probes.

"I have Magic," he offers. "Not like what you just did. That was unbelievable. But I can do some things."

"Show me," she insists, and takes a seat at the far window table.

"Can I have a spoon?" he asks me, moving to our butcher-block island, which is still a dozen feet from Bea. I give him one, and he begins to bob his hand over it, just like he did with me in the restaurant. Only this time, it doesn't spin. It doesn't do anything. Well, maybe it wobbles a bit in place.

Maybe.

"I don't know what's wrong," he says, turning red. Anger or embarrassment? Most likely both.

"I saw him do it yesterday," I offer in his defense.

She waits as he tries again, but nothing happens.

"I don't get it," he complains, trying harder.

"Don't worry. I know you can do it. You were doing that as a toddler. You wouldn't remember—because that is how we planned it. You were not supposed to have learned this again. Not yet. I confess we have been blocking you to the best of our ability for years. It seems you've gotten around that."

"Blocking me? Why?" He sounds one part confused, two parts crushed.

"It is not time for you to learn yet."

"But I'm ready!" he bursts, not exactly raising his voice, but definitely straining it.

"Even if you are. We all swore an oath you would not be taught until you became of legal age. Your eighteenth birthday, and not a day sooner. A great deal rides on that agreement, or we would never have made it."

"But—and I say this respectfully, GranBea—as Mayden has seen, it's already happening. Only I don't know what to do with it. I feel like I don't even know who we are as a family. And what you just did? What was that? How can I know who I am if I don't know who we are?"

You can see Bea doesn't like this any more than Michael. She's struggling with what to say and how to say it. But it's also clear she's not a woman to back down. She considers for a time, looking him over carefully, much the way she looked me over that first day, albeit from a greater distance.

"It's one thing to be able to spin spoons," she finally says, "when there is nothing working against you. It's another when someone, or something, blocks the way. The smart magician seeks to discover what is blocking him and how to dissipate the interruption."

There is a silence, but also an unspoken invitation to read into her words.

Is she teaching him without teaching him? Was that just a lesson she supposedly didn't give?

"Who are you?" Sally comes out of nowhere and demands to know, scaring the living daylights out of me.

Bea is instantly on her feet. "Ah, the lady of the house!" she says, her voice totally different, though I can't say how. It's only now I notice she's dressed in the white coat of a chef. Her hair is nicely done and netted back in a knot. She's even got a full set of teeth in. "I've come to cook for you, dearie. I'll arrive daily at two and be gone by eight."

Michael and I look at each other: *How does she know about the cooking job?*

"Oh, right!" Sally says, instantly stepping into her I'm-the-boss persona. "You're the chef that Michael wants to audition while Mrs. Hamilton is away. That was fast."

"Indeed," Bea says, approaching her gregariously, pumping her hand as they shake in greeting. "You may call me Finola."

Again, Michael and I offer each other quick glances. *Finola?* Well, I guess she can't use her real name. Word would get back to Helene pretty quick.

"I'm Sally," she says, looking Bea over, no doubt wondering how an older woman is going to handle the workload at a large restaurant. But then a *not my problem* look comes over her.

So very, very, Wife #4.

"Perhaps we should find a time to go over my dietary requirements before our cook leaves us for vacation on Monday."

"Actually," I chime in, "Mrs. Hamilton left for vacation already. She was having an allergic reaction to something. Said to tell you."

Sally frowns at me, instantly suspicious.

"I'd be thrilled to start today!" our new Finola insists. "I'm sure we can all discover a great deal in two weeks."

I feel a surge of glee rush through me and notice it registers on Michael's face as well. Bea, here with us, for two weeks? That's more than we could have dreamed.

"I must be upfront, though," Bea says, feigning concern, "I'm deaf as a doornail. It makes things look odd every so often. You'll have to be right in front of me when you speak to me. I hope that is not what these young folks call a deal-breaker?"

Sally wavers. She doesn't like handicaps of any variety. Makes her nervous.

"Not at all," Michael jumps in. "You mentioned that on your application, and you come with brilliant references. You're a master, from what I hear. We can work around that without a problem, can't we, Sally?"

The way he says it, who could deny him?

"What about payment?" she replies, no doubt looking for a loophole. "My husband will want to know about rates."

She doesn't care about rates. Not if you hit the right buttons.

"I've got it covered through the restaurant," Michael assures. "It's only fair since I want to try her out without our current chef getting wind of it. You won't say anything to anyone about this, though, will you, Sally? Especially to my Aunt Helene. I'm dying to show her that I'm a true entrepreneur, just like you! I know she'll have to give the go-ahead eventually. But in the meantime, you'd be helping me prove myself. And you'll be able to say you helped bring a top new chef to town!"

Sally hesitates again, but you can see Michael hit those buttons. Finally, she nods in agreement. It's the bragging rights that got her, for sure. It will make for a wonderfully self-important story to tell her friends when they go out.

"We won't say a word, will we, Julie?" she says pointedly, indicating it's not really a question. "I'll let my husband know, too. He likes a young man with initiative."

"Just one more thing," Bea offers, smiling wide. Everyone seems to be holding their breath. "I'll need some basic assistance. Julie, dear, you seem like you could be a fine young helper. Would you be willing?"

Immediately Sally is looking at me like I'd better say yes. Like I'm not doing anything else this summer, or any summer, and I'd better not be rude and selfish.

This is just too good.

Too, too good.

"No problem. I'd love to," I deliver at a hundred percent deadpan. I want to high-five myself as Sally's face registers the exact note of shock I intended. It delights me, but I know that's not the big win here. My own teacher of Magic, right here in my house, every day?

Really, that just hits it out of the park.

Chapter 14

"**D**o you think she can cook?" I ask Michael, now that Bea has left and Sally went back upstairs to get ready for work.

"She said *it's one thing to be able to spin spoons when there is nothing working against you*," Michael repeats, distracted. He tries again to bob and spin the spoon. "*But another when someone or something is in the way.*"

It's still not working. I'm sure he knows he needs to head out to his soccer camp soon, but it's obvious he doesn't want to leave the kitchen before he masters this. "*A smart magician learns what is blocking him and how to dissipate the interruption.* Do you know what that could mean?"

"Not really."

"Me neither. But I am sure she was giving me a clue. At first, I thought I was blocked because I was so close to her, but it's still not working, so that's not it."

Again and again, he attempts to bob and spin, but the spoon just won't play along.

"Hungry?" I suggest, starting to look around for something to eat. I'd just eat nachos, the only warm food I ever make for breakfast, lunch or dinner, but Michael is into organic food. It's hard to know what that means for his first meal of the day.

"Sure. It's not you, either, because it worked with you at the restaurant. It could be GranBea's energy is still in the room."

"She has a lot of that. But more important, at least for the moment, can she cook?"

"What?" He finally looks up at me.

"Can Bea cook? She's going to be playing the part of a famed chef starting at two o'clock today, remember?"

"Oh. Didn't think of that. Probably. But I can get Gerry to make something at the restaurant and send it over if she's not that great. That's the easy part."

"What's the hard part?"

"Hello? Did you see what she did to Mrs. Hamilton? And what she changed into? You did see it, right? It wasn't just me?"

"Oh, I saw it. It's called shapeshifting. That's part of your family's Magic." I feel confident I'm not giving anything substantial away. Bea would be solidly to blame for that.

"You've seen her do this before?" He sounds as freshly astounded as I was yesterday. It is amazing, though, you have to give it that, and totally impossible to believe if you have not actually seen it for yourself. Then, once you do, it is real and you just have to make that work in your tiny little head.

I want to answer, but still have to think about every one of his questions. This is getting into the territory of giving away stuff he doesn't know. Where exactly is the line to be drawn? And anyway, why should I be taught when he isn't? In an attempt to slightly level the playing field for him, I offer the truth: "Not her. But I saw Jake do it. And more than just the head was involved."

"They're teaching him that kind of thing already?" he nearly shouts, standing up and shoving the spoon away in defeat.

Okay, maybe not such a good move on my part. "He sort of mangled it, though."

"They'll teach him but not me. He's five days younger than me!"

"I think they're worried about him having started too soon. It might be what's messing things up."

"He shouldn't be learning before me," he insists.

Michael might be good, but he's also competitive. I never thought about whether you could be both, but I'll spend some time pondering it when I get a chance. You know, like in ten years or something.

"What's with the big rivalry between you guys?" I ask, pretending not to care as I load some peanut butter, banana, and honey onto some rice cakes. It's healthy, even if all the ingredients are not exactly organic. "You want some of this?"

"Sure. And it's complicated."

"How unusual. Honey good?"

He nods without enthusiasm. "Jake was always a loose cannon as a kid. No real self-control. Kind of all over the place, like ADD, but also a little lost. I was told to look after him, even though we were so close in age, and he hated that. But he also sort of looked up to me, too. Besides, we have some messed up karma between us."

"Karma? You believe in that?"

"Hard not to believe when I've seen who I was in a past life. And who he was."

"Wait? What? Who was he? Who were you?" This seems so out in left field. Then again, considering his family, is anything?

"I've been having past life visions since I was little. It's another skill I've been developing, like the spoons. The most vivid life with Jake was shown to me when were only six or seven. Playing war. One day I saw it all unfold."

"What do you mean, *saw?*"

"I don't know. Things just changed, so that I saw what was in front of me, but also this scene, like from a movie. We were soldiers together, but not for play. For real. Adults, not kids. I'm not sure where, or when, but we had guns and uniforms. I was his superior and I led the way onto the field. He lost a leg and an arm. I carried him back, but he just kept saying I should leave him, just please leave him." He shakes his head as if to rid himself of the memory.

"It sounds terrible." Images of Jake's mangled animal legs flash in my mind. Can that kind of thing carry over from one lifetime to another? "So you think we've all had past lives?"

He nods like it's no big deal, then reaches over to put extra peanut butter on the rice cakes I've given him, which makes me feel a little better about his energy levels holding up for a long day of soccer. Not that I'm his mother or anything. Though I guess I could have been, if past lives are real.

"Many of the world's religions include past lives as a central belief. I'm not saying it's true. How can you know for sure? I'm just saying the images show themselves to me, and they sure feel real."

I have no idea how to think about this, and so I choose not to.

"Okay, so what next? Soccer camp, right?"

He looks at his watch. "In about an hour. It's from ten to five, every day but Sunday. That gives us some time together in the early mornings, then some time with GranBea before dinner, I hope. Then there is after dinner with you, if you don't have plans, that is."

I listen for how he says "plans," trying to get a clue about how he feels. It might sound a little flirty. Or not.

"No plans tonight," I confirm, not flirty. Well, mostly not flirty.

"Okay. We can take it day by day. I also want to talk to Ana. Maybe Sunday?"

"We'll see if that works," I reply, still not ready to admit too much.

"You know," he says, reaching out to touch my shoulder, "you don't have to be so wary of me. I'm being straight with you. Can't you feel that?"

I pull away, trying not to show the shiver that came from his touch. Spoons or not, he's got some kind of Magic going for him. "I don't know."

It hits me that it was just three days ago that I was taking Ana for a walk, helping her come to life out in the woods. Now here we are, this far in.

"Why not?"

"Because I just met you and learned about Magic, and all this. I'm in what feels like a whole new world. I'm not sure I'm able to assimilate it all that fast."

"Okay," he says as if it really is, "but try not to take it out on me. I'm …"

"Michael! Julie!" Dad comes around the corner, practically singing in his I-can-sell-the-world-anything-cause-it's-a-bright-and-shining-new-day voice. "I hear we have a new guest cook!"

I offer Dad a cheek as he comes to give me my good morning kiss. It's one of the few father/daughter rituals we still have. I think it means there is a bridge between us, even if it's hard to see.

"Hmm," he says, "breakfast looks a little lean for a soccer player. Maybe we need to hire a day cook as well, at least while you're here."

"I can make eggs," Sally says, rounding the corner after him.

She can't make eggs.

Not even close.

Michael has already stood to shake Dad's hand. "No, sir, this is wonderful. I like to eat light before hitting the field. I stopped by the grocery last night to pick up some high-protein drinks to add to my lunches, and you can bet with Finola on board we will all eat magnificently at dinner!"

"Finola," Dad repeats. "Sally says if she works out, it will be a nice surprise for your grandmother. I like that. Shows entrepreneurial spirit. Speaking of which, I've invited a few friends for after-dinner drinks tonight to meet with you. Naval Academy grads from way back. I'm sure they'll be able to offer you some excellent advice. We won't keep you up too late, though. Soccer is hard work!"

I see Michael's face drop a bit at the mention of an after-dinner talk, but return to normal again in a split second. "That would be wonderful, sir. Very kind of you."

He shoots me a look as if to say *we'll find a way*.

I shoot him back a small shrug.

"Not at all, son," Dad says, then notices Michael's leather pouch. "What's this?"

For once, Michael seems caught off guard. He hems and haws as he holds on to the pouch, trying to think.

"I gave it to him," I step in. "It's for good luck with his soccer."

Michael smiles the exactly right smile, like it's a weird gift, but what can he do?

"Where did you get it?" Dad queries me, frowning. Great, all I need is another *I just don't know enough about your life, Julie* lecture.

"A nurse's aid at the Village gave it to me," I say, shrugging it off. "To thank me for helping her out. She said it had good juju."

Dad laughs nervously, obviously embarrassed. "Sounds sort of wacky to me. Just don't go getting too strange on us, okay?"

"How else will I find ways to embarrass you, Dad?" I challenge in a jest. Michael is not the only one who can play an adult.

"Alright then," he says, no doubt glad to move on, "I'll take some eggs. But let's go out, Sally. I'm feeling like pancakes and bacon, too."

And decent cooking, I think, but don't say. Sally looks hurt, but agrees. She knows bacon and pancakes are well beyond her skill set.

"As for tonight," Dad turns to Michael, "you're not going to have our new cook go too fancy on us, are you? I'm a hungry man come dinnertime. Tiny plates drive me crazy."

"I'll be sure to have Finola go over the menu with your beautiful wife," he replies, giving Sally a look as if he'd be indebted to her if she would.

It works.

Of course, it works.

And so it is settled. In three short days we've gone from a totally boring summer to being shot out of a cannon in a pop-up circus. Michael and I will have breakfasts and dinner and late evenings together. In the mornings I will take walks with Ana, and in the afternoons I'll learn Magic from Bea. Maybe somewhere in there, I'll see Jake again.

A surge of feeling comes up, like the tinglies, only inside, and all over. It's hard to define, but I'm guessing it's something like happiness. It takes me a minute to realize why it's so hard for me to define: I haven't felt this good since I was four years old.

Chapter 15

Ana has been moved.

They could have told me that at the desk. They could have led with something like *there's something we need to tell you...*Instead, they just nodded when I said I was here to take Mrs. Quinn for a walk and let me find her empty room.

Not just empty of her, but cleared out and scrubbed down. *White-washed* is what we call it. It means all traces of the person having ever lived in the room are gone, floor to ceiling. Not a germ in sight. You never get used to it. Usually, there's only a sudden white-wash when someone dies. So, naturally, I started screaming. At least until the aide who came running told me what had happened.

Apparently, Ana was upset.

Apparently, she had to be restrained.

Apparently, it had to do with a visit from her daughter late last night.

Apparently, the room was torn apart by the time anyone realized something was wrong.

Apparently, it was decided that Ana was the one who created the mess.

As could be expected, no one thought to question Helene, even though Ana is confined to a wheelchair and completely incapable of tearing up anything, let alone a whole room. Likewise, it made perfect sense to everyone to punish Ana by IV sedating her, putting her in wrist restraints, and moving her to the most terrible wing in the building.

Idiots. Total, complete idiots.

But they're not the only ones. I'm an idiot, too. It appears that life is still wholly, completely, and ridiculously unfair. I was kidding myself to think anything had changed, even with Magic. I feel like a deer sliced open by an expert; my useless innards left on the ground to rot.

At least Ana is alive—if you can call it that.

"Ana," I whisper, "can you hear me?"

I take her hand, cruelly cuffed to her bed, and feel nothing. No Magic. No centrifugal force. Not even a deep, knowing connection. But, most of all, no response. It's not surprising, given the IV in her arm and the kind of crap that goes into it. Even so, I am surprised, if only because everything was going so amazingly well.

I want to cry, but force myself to hold it together. I've got a lot of thinking to do.

I look around. The new room is pretty much like her old one, only more sterile and with a lot more equipment. Everything is set up, just waiting for that one bad moment that will end it all.

Her medicine bag, I suddenly think, irrationally afraid.

I search her suitcase and every drawer in the room, but it's gone. Somehow I knew it would be. The one thing she cannot bear to be without is the one thing that's gone. Someone probably tossed it without a thought.

Idiots!

I swear, it's like Helene reached out from her dark, magical abyss, grabbed my heart with strong, gnarly hands and started twisting. The mind games start in on me, too: Is this my fault? Does Helene know about me? Did she figure out about the hacking and do this just before flying out this morning, knowing exactly what she was leaving in her wake? You can't comprehend that Magic is real, even if you've seen a deformed spotted leopard and the head of a black panther with your very own eyes, until an IV and restraining cuffs tell you just how real things can get.

"What do you want me to do?" I whisper, making sure not a living soul hears. If I didn't know Helene was on a plane this morning, I would be utterly terrified for us both right now. I lay my head down on her bedside, completely confused about every last thing.

"You seem like you were close to Mrs. Quinn," a nurse says, surprising me. She must be new in this section because I've never met her. It doesn't matter. She's an idiot, too. You don't use *were* until it's *were.*

"She doesn't need to be restrained," I insist as the tears finally start to stream. I can't help it—bottled rage eventually undoes me every time. "She is totally harmless. Everyone knows that."

"The cuffs don't hurt. They're well padded, as you can see, and they are there for her safety. If she were to pull out her IV, she could hurt herself. We wouldn't want that, now would we?"

You think the cuffs don't hurt? What about freedom? What about a lack of dignity?

The nurse checks Ana's vital signs, moves meaningless things around, and adds medicine to the IV. I say nothing, but refuse to let go of my teacher's hand.

"Are you sure you're going to be okay?" she asks me, though it comes out more as a warning. "We need to keep Mrs. Quinn calm. These people can sense things, even if you think they can't."

These people? These People??? This is Ana! My Ana! Ana Quinn, Magician of the highest order, you insensitive freak of human nature.

"I'm fine."

"It is nice to see someone care so much," the idiot replies, a patronizing attempt at comforting me. But she can't comfort me. Not now. The only thing left now is strategy. I have to get Ana out of here. I owe her that and a thousand times more.

"Do you think her daughter will come back soon?" I ask, attempting to flat-line my tone. I have to know what I am up against. How much time I have.

"I don't think so. She travels a lot." This is standard nursing home speak for the countless adult children who supposedly love their parents, but never come to see them. I could say it's actually true in this case, but don't. Silence is power, and right now my power is in precious low supply.

"How long before she can move back to her old room?"

"I think it's safe to assume this is her home now," she replies, feigning cheerfulness, like we'll just decorate the walls a bit and all will be well.

I've never heard the sound of a jail door closing, but I can imagine it sounds just like *this is her home now.*

"I'll be back," I say to Ana. "Every day. I promise."

"You're a good friend."

"No," I insist. "I'm not any kind of good. Mrs. Quinn is the good one."

The nurse doesn't understand. Who could?

Only Ana.

I walk the long hall to check out and start the drive home. Everything echoes empty. Everything's gone dark. Everything's lost without Ana.

I could use several hours alone with a spreadsheet to make a plan for what to do next, but somehow I know I won't get the chance. Bea will be back at the house. She'll know something is up. But what words do I use to tell her about Ana? And what will she do? Will it break her heart the way it's breaking mine?

I ask myself this a hundred times over, and in as many different ways, until I'm standing in the kitchen with Bea busy unpacking groceries. Two pots are boiling and the house would smell divine, if you were in any kind of mood to eat.

"What are you making?" I ask, easing into the conversation, peering into a pan and doing my best to appear interested.

"Fried onions in butter as our start," she says, like I ought to know at least that much.

"Um, fried?" I try not to sound alarmed. "Did you talk to Sally about that? Because we don't do fried anything here, ever. I mean, never ever." I've seen Wife #4 go wild for a good half-hour over something fried instead of baked.

Bea huffs. "What she doesn't know won't kill her—and what she does know may well. That stepmother of yours is thin as a chicken in the dead of winter! No wonder. I've seen what's in that refrigerator. Low fat this. Reduced calorie that. Fake food and pesticide-ridden vegetables. It's a wonder you're alive, girlie!"

I don't like the "girlie," but the stepmother comment makes me cringe. I stopped having stepmothers after the first one. Now I just see them for what they are—Dad's temporary playmates. I'm not going to say that to Bea because it would make me sound like I'm a difficult teen on top of being the primary reason her beloved sister is in a near coma. Besides, for her to remain our cook, I need her to trust me on this one.

"I agree with you. But Sally will know first thing tomorrow morning when she steps on the scale. It's this huge digital monster that measures to the ounce. She won't drink a sip of water before weighing in. And if she's gained, it's the cook who hears about it."

Bea stops stirring the onions long enough to really look at me. At first, she has a blank face, like she just can't imagine it. Then she rolls her eyes, like that is even more ridiculous than what is in the fridge.

What can I say? It's true.

"Well then, we will have to enlist the help of the onions, the butter, the iron skillet and—most important—the flame."

Okay, not exactly what I expected. Not that I am ever going to know what to expect from Bea.

"How do you enlist help?" I ask, watching her continue to nearly dance between her tasks—stirring the frying pan, putting away the groceries, making a note on the chalkboard, and turning on another pot to boil. She seems to know the place as well as Mrs. Hamilton ever did.

"We shall call upon Magic!"

"Are you going to teach me Magic here at the house, too?" I ask, feeling tingly all over. Yesterday, I would have wanted to scream to the entire neighborhood "I've got a teacher! She's teaching me Magic!" But it's hard to get too excited when you know what little good it can actually do when it comes to the most important things. Like Ana.

Crap. The moment I start to forget the full cost of my magical education, her practically lifeless body strapped to that bed flashes before my eyes.

Bea harrumphs. "I'm surely not here to take care of Sally's waistline, I can tell you that! Now that I think of it, we could skip the cooking Magic and just give her a bad case of the runs. But that wouldn't be good for our intentions, and our intentions are what matter most."

I have to laugh, at least a little, because it's completely delightful to think of Sally getting the runs. Bea laughs with me. Giggles, really. Seriously, you just can't know what to expect out of this woman from one moment to the next.

"Alright, then. We'll need to ask Magic for help. You've got to get the spirits on your side, or there's no reason bothering with Magic in the first place. The spirit of earth, that's the mother of the onion. The spirits of the animal kingdom, they get thanked for the cow that gifted us the butter. I buy only the good stuff—that means from cattle that have had a free range of the farm, and no hormones to make them uncomfortably productive. If you don't have this kind of goodness to start, it's a long road to getting Magic to see things your way. We have to do our part. Never forget that."

I nod, amazed at how many things she talks about that I've never even considered. The earth as the mother of the onion? Magic wanting us to do our part? As for the cow, do hormones really make you uncomfortable? I guess they could. They get blamed for every feminine bad mood in this house.

"The iron in the pan will be of enormous help," she goes on, flipping the heavy skillet in one hand like it weighs nothing. "It's a base element. Makes your blood strong. That's power. The iron alone could do the trick for us today, but why leave anything out? You're asking for jealousy amongst elements, and then you have to do even more Magic to smooth that over. Better to invite everyone to the table from the start."

"Okay," I say, though I don't get it. An onion jealous of the iron a pan is made out of? This Magic stuff is complicated. It makes me wonder, though, could Helene be jealous of her own mother? Can that be what this is about?

I flash for a moment on my mother. I could never have been jealous of her even though she was a hundred times more beautiful and talented than I will ever be.

"Can't you just cast a spell or something?" I ask, pulling my mind from where I can't afford it to go. Not today, with Ana. There's only so much loss a girl can bear to consider at one time.

"Never!" Bea insists, instantly losing all humor. "We are the Quinn Clann. Magicians of the highest order. We do not manipulate. We request. We make agreements. We solicit so that goodness may prevail. We always, always give of ourselves in the process."

"Sorry," I say. But really, how am I supposed to know this stuff, at least before she teaches me?

"As our final element, we enlist the support of the flame, for it is the flame within that burns the calories, is it not?" To emphasize her point, she cranks all six of the gas burners on the stove and drops a cup of water to sizzle into a hot skillet. Steam rises. "Up, up, up Sally goes in flames of skinny glory!"

How that's not a spell, I'm not sure, but it's not like I'm going to say that out loud. I watch as Bea moves herself, and the ingredients, with such ease. I'd have a hard time imagining her fifty years old right now, let alone eighty-eight. I really and truly hope no one comes in and sees this, not only because it is fascinatingly strange, but because I don't want it to stop.

Bea puts her hands over two of the open flames just like Michael put his over the spoon yesterday, bouncing the flames up and down. They leap to her touch without her adjusting the dials. It makes my stomach flip with excitement.

"Pay attention, girlie!"

I'm half afraid she'll burn down the house, not to mention toast her hands off. But if she's right, it's worth the risk. Because if it works on Sally, I bet it will work on other things. And if it works on other things, I'll figure out a way to use it to spring Ana from the Village for good.

Your life isn't over yet, Ana. Just you wait and see.

Chapter 16

Bea seems to be nearly purring into the flames, tossing the onions like the gourmet chef she's supposed to be. She's even pulled out her gnarly old cane and started incorporating it into some kind of cosmic cooking dance. Every one of the six burners are taking part.

I don't know where Magic comes from, but it's here, for sure.

I can feel it.

Suddenly, she's done. She comes back down from her tippy toes onto sure footing, taps her stick on the floor three times, turns down the burners, and gets on with the cooking like nothing has happened.

No explanation, either.

"So now Sally won't gain weight?" I ask, once Bea turns to face me.

"Not an ounce. Might even lose some—too bad for her."

"Will you do that every time? I mean, with every meal?"

She looks at me like I can't possibly be that dense. "Do you think we have time for this every day? No, that'll cover my full stay here. Not an ounce of weight will be gained, I promise you that. Anything I cook here will be under the Magical Caloric Assistance Program. Think of it as an umbrella policy—covers every food cooked every which way. Even ice cream. It goes for everyone, too. Your dad could stand to benefit, I happened to notice."

"Oh," I say, disappointed. Not that none of us will gain weight— that's awesome. I mean, if you could bottle that you'd be set for life. It's just that I don't know how I am going to learn Magic if we only do things one time. I'm not all that quick a learner, and as my freshman math teacher was fond of saying, *repetition is your friend.*

"What a silly thing to worry about! There are a thousand chances a day for Magic, especially in the kitchen. Have you ever spoken to an egg?"

"I don't think so," I admit, wondering and worrying about when, exactly, to tell her about Ana. I should have the moment I walked in. Now it just keeps getting harder.

"Well, that's your first mistake then, girlie. Because the egg is the whole of it. You've heard folks say it's a question of which came first, the chicken or the egg?"

I nod.

"There's no answer to that, now is there?" She waves her wooden spoon in the air, then turns it into a question mark she dots at the bottom.

I shake my head no.

"Indeed there is not! Because the egg is the beginning of it, and the continuation of it, and the end of it. So you'll want the blessing of the whole egg. You know, in the ancient times, having egg on your face was a good thing. Like most things—Friday the thirteenth, Halloween—they twisted it all around and made it scary. Magic isn't scary. It's just power put to your dreams."

"You're suggesting we put egg on Sally's face?" I relish the thought, especially if we can sell her on the amazing health benefits of getting egg-faced. I'll hold that over her for as long as she lasts as Wife #4.

"It's a fine facial cleanser, especially with oatmeal and a little lemon. But that's for another day. Tonight, it's a caramelized onion and shiitake mushroom frittata with a Burgundy wine glaze. That'll start things off right, get everyone balanced in the whole of things."

"It sounds great," I say, even if I don't know what that means.

Maybe I can ask Ana once I get her out of that place.

Bea looks at me square on. "Alright, what's hammering at the back of your mind? Something about Ana."

"Um," I say, still not sure how to tell her. "Well, yes. I mean…"

"Out with it, girlie!" She leans in toward my face so that it feels like she is pulling at the words through my tongue.

"Did you notice something off today?" I ask. "Psychically, I mean."

"In a way," she acknowledges, turning back to her work. Maybe it's something she doesn't want to know. I remember she's deaf, and move so that she sees me, and can better read my lips. I want to get this exactly right with no room for interpretation.

"You don't need to do that," she says, turning away again.

"But you told Sally you were deaf. Jake said so, too. Don't you read lips?"

"I hear you, just not with my ears. Some people I can hear that way, some people I can't. But you're one of us. I hear you just fine."

So here's the thing: Anyone who doesn't know what it's like to be an outsider can't understand what it means to hear *you're one of us*. It makes everything shift inside of you, like all the effort life takes is worth it.

"Ana?" Bea urges, impatient.

"Um…Um…" I stammer. I want to say this just right, because Ana is not just some nice old lady in trouble, she's *my* nice old lady in trouble.

Just take a deep breath and go for it, chickenshit.

"So there was a fight with Helene last night. Everything was torn up in Ana's room."

Bea doesn't say anything, but she goes a bit pale.

"They moved her to the unit for the worst-off residents and put an IV in her. She's out cold. They said she'd be in that room for good. And," I add after taking a big gulp of air, "her medicine bag is gone. I looked everywhere."

"I see," Bea finally says. "I didn't feel her when I woke up this morning."

I wait, but she doesn't say more. In fact, she seems calm. Too calm. *This is your sister!* I scream to the thin air. If she hears me, she doesn't say.

"We have to get her out of there!" I insist out loud.

"No," she says, resolute. "That's not up to us."

"We have to!" Now I *am* screaming, flailing myself around the room. "It's all my fault, and I can't leave her there. *We* can't leave her there!"

"Sit down, child. I'll explain."

I'll do anything she says, even if she calls me "child" ten times a day for the rest of my life, so long as she tells me how we can fix this.

She pulls up a chair for us both. "It's not your fault. Ana does not do anything, or allow anything to be done to her, without intending it. She has never once been anyone else's victim. Never in her whole life. She surely is not one now, however bad it looks."

"She's cuffed," I spit. "By the wrists. To her bed!"

"If Ana has been moved, or cuffed, or drugged, you can be sure it was planned. By her and her alone. She's smarter than you and me and both of the boys put together. Smarter than any human alive, maybe. That's part of her gift, having a brain that can do some truly amazing things. I don't know for sure what she's up to. But my guess, given she gave you so much of her Earth Magic, is that she's decided to work on higher planes, and she decided whatever they are feeding her through her veins would help. Being so far gone, it might also keep Helene from learning anything she should not know about you and Michael."

"But then it IS my fault! And Michael's, too! How can we let her live like that for our sake? It's not fair. Michael should go back home if that is the cost of his being here."

It hurts me to say that, but it's how I feel. It really is.

"No, it is not fair. I know it's not. But Helene could destroy so much, for so many, for so long to come. She's more than proven what she's willing to do to be sure the family meets her expectations. But sending Michael home, now that we know he is awakening to his gifts, won't do a thing. Magic is on the move, child. There is no stopping that."

"You talk like Magic has a mind of its own," I accuse, hearing my bitterness. Magic should be helping, shouldn't it?

Shouldn't it???

"It does have a mind of its own. We are only the conduits of Magic, and each of us has but a small portion in any given lifetime. Even the Keeper of Magic has little, compared to all that there is. So you see, there is no guarantee Magic will move in the direction we intend, no matter how clearly we intend it. When that happens, it is better to learn where it is going and adjust our course accordingly. In the meantime, Ana is wise to protect us all from Helene. It's a gift she's offering us. A sacrifice, yes, but a worthy one."

"But what can we do? I can't let her just lay there so lifeless."

She takes my hand in hers, that white-hot lightning immediately radiating between us. "The spirit of Magic is a powerful force. It moves in cycles that are attuned to a greater nature than we can ever fully know or understand. But we can listen and learn. Each day, each moment, listening for the whispers, the signs, the signals, the omens—anything we can pick up on, to understand what Magic wants."

Somehow, as if through her hands, I feel what she is talking about. It is moving in cycles in my hands, like a wave that crests and retreats, both crashing on and then pulling at the shoreline.

It's shifting something in me.

Not my determination, but maybe my ability to be more patient.

"Magic does not bend to the smaller needs of the individual family," she continues, practically feeding my palms with energy, "even if it is the last Clann standing. Helene will do all she can to manipulate Magic to her will—especially in this, the eighty-eighth year of Ana and myself. But Magic has a say, too, and for this, we are most grateful."

"What's so special about your eighty-eighth year?" I ask, feeling like I could live forever on the ocean running between our hands. It almost, almost, almost feels like Mom felt.

"Not now. Some things are better learned over time, as you increase your tolerance for the mystery and learn to be with what is."

She's starting to sound like some new age guru, yet I'm just sitting here, soaking it all up.

"I have to do *something*."

"For now, you learn the ways of Magic. That, and strictly abide by this one rule: For as long as I am here in this house, Michael must stay at a distance from me, and now, especially, from Ana, too. You will be my connection to him. Everyone must go quiet so that I can teach you as quickly and efficiently as possible. Even Jake must be put on notice not to practice Magic and to stay at a distance from you. You can be sure he'll not be pleased about that."

"I bet," I say, wondering if he'll be more upset about the Magic or me. Then again, who am I kidding? Magic would win by a mile. "But I still don't get it. Why would Helene want to hurt her own family?"

Bea looks at me with what might be the kindest eyes I can imagine. "It is difficult to grasp, isn't it? Both Magic and families are, and always will be, complex. Maybe just think of this as a time of great shift. While it is shifting, if we can keep the opposing forces of Helene at bay, we stand the best chance to turn it toward our intended dreaming."

More words I don't understand. Dreaming, now, too? "But I thought you and Ana disagreed on the danger?"

"My dear," she interrupts, finally letting go of my tingling hands, "my twin and I disagree on a good many things. But on this we are unified. Make no mistake; Helene is trouble and a powerful Magic is hers to command right now. We are all working against it. Even you, though you cannot understand your role yet."

My heart crashes along with my energy. This is the last thing I want Ana and Bea to agree on. "But you'll teach me and Michael, right?"

"I'll teach you, and," her voice lowers as her eyes drill directly into my own, "whatever you do with Michael will be your own business. If you catch my meaning."

I do. Chills run up and down me, making me feel just a little bit alive again. Michael was right. She can't break her promise not to teach him, but there's a loophole, and I'm it. If she teaches me, and I teach him, it all works.

"But what if I do it wrong? Show him how something works, or say it the wrong way? What if…"

"Trust yourself, Mayden," she interrupts. "You have not fallen onto this path accidentally. However it may seem to you, you are no novice here. Your connection to this Magic is lifetimes old. All I am here to do is help you remember what you have always known. There is far more to you and your place with us than we can say. At least for now."

"Really?" I want to believe it, more than anything.

"We trust the wisdom you carry, child. We trust you. Now you must trust us. And yourself."

I don't know what to say. It's a big thing, to be trusted. A seriously big thing. I'm not sure I ever have been. I mean, ignored? Yes. Assumed I'm doing fine on my own? Sure. But trusted? No. I don't think so.

It occurs to me, maybe for the first time ever, that trust is at least part of what makes you a family. I'm not used to it, and I'm not sure I'll be worthy of it. But it means the world to me that they are giving me a shot.

Chapter 17

I don't like thinking about my mother. I mean, deep thinking about her. I think about her all the time in that far-off, *I once had a mother who adored me* way. I just don't think about what happened or why.

But seeing Ana that way today, how can I help it? Ana will be the second officially dead person I have known, and her last days will be pure hell if I don't do something about it. If there's one thing I have learned, you can't just sit there, waiting and hoping. Dead is done—a hard, cold wall that you can do absolutely nothing about after the fact.

I gather more small sticks for the fire. We don't have a huge fire pit like Bea's, but our chiminea is working fine. It's a football field away from the house and down a hill that ends in a long border of trees, so no one will see the glow.

This assumes Michael is coming, which is a big assumption. I told him I'd meet him out here at the bench, but then Dad and his Navy friends cornered him right after Bea's amazing frittata. With the exclusive brandy brought out as a treat for the good old boys, it didn't look like they'd be breaking up the party anytime soon.

I don't have much experience making a fire, but a book of matches and some old newspaper did the trick to get it started. Oh, right, and the whispered request that Magic help me out with the element of fire. Bea would be upset if I hadn't learned at least that much today. How much real wood a small fire uses is something I'll have to figure out, though.

Along with ten billion other things.

As the fire grows, I practice breathing through my feet. You never know when you're going to need more of that power I used on Mrs. Hamilton. I stare into the flames, amazed that the sticks are already becoming coals, burning red. It's beautiful, but that only makes me feel bad because, honestly, I've never paid much attention to fire before today. I mean, fire was just fire, right? Now it's an element that seems to matter in my life, at least according to my new teachers. Makes you wonder what else is sitting right there in front of you that you've never really seen.

For the third time since I lit the fire, Ana's ashen face appears superimposed over the flames, as if in answer to my inner question. It's almost like she's here with me. Like she's traveling, just as Bea said.

Exceptionally wishful thinking, Julie Mayden.

Yeah, I know better. She's drugged up and pinned down in a terrible place. Like with Mom, there are some things even Magic can't touch.

Bea's face does not appear through the flames, but she is ever dancing in the back of my mind. My brain is trying to figure her out, put her in a box, but she just won't go. For one thing, she changes every three minutes. One minute I like her, the next I'm afraid of her, and the next I swear she is my own GranBea. Ana said she was a mix of good and bad and that seems pretty accurate to what I've seen so far. I know I want to learn from her because her power is palpable. But even that doesn't outweigh my loyalty to Ana if push comes to shove.

Maybe Bea is right that Ana chose to be tied down and drugged. But what if she's wrong? That nurse saying that place was Ana's last stop— Bea didn't hear how that sounded. She didn't hear the jail door slamming shut. Not like I did.

Ana's face is in a steady flicker in the fire now. Her sharp features are the texture of wood that is burnt to a crisp. She's probably going to look like that when she dies.

I can't imagine what a dead person looks like. I never saw my mother. They wouldn't let me. It's morbid to think about, so I try to shake it off. It doesn't seem to want to shake. I'd almost swear Mom has been around lately, watching all this. It's beyond wishful thinking, but comforting all the same.

I try to think about all the good, and the Magic to come, but I can't. Even if it's not this week or even this year, Ana is going to die. And these last days of hers will be spent in the only hell I know for sure exists. That is, unless I do something about it.

The fire pops, her face morphs, I jump, and something snaps inside of me.

Like that, I know. For sure. I'm going to do it. I'm going to get Ana out of there.

Michael will have to help me because it's partly his fault, too. We are in this together. We'll get her out of there together.

I peer into the fire, hoping Ana will help me figure out how to get the supposedly uber-good Michael to do something bad. I'll probably have to be a little extra bad myself. As if the idea is appealing to Ana, her smile grows. It seems to egg me on.

But would she encourage me to lie? Because I'll have to. To Michael. To everyone.

Michael doesn't know if what I tell him is coming from Bea or not, so I can say whatever I want. I'll be blowing up the trust just extended to me by Bea if I don't teach him the right things. But this is for Ana. I can only hope the end justifies the means.

I pull my sweater tighter around me, in part because the summer night air is getting chilly and in part because the fire spits and crackles in a creepy kind of reply to my scheming, like it's agreeing with me. Like it likes the plan.

Unless I'm imagining it. Which I might be.

I don't know exactly what the plan of escape should entail, but getting Michael on board with it is the first step. It will go something like this:

Ana is dying because of you.

Can you live with that?

I'm breaking her out.

Are you with me, or are you going to let her die in there?

Die. In THERE?

I'll make sure to punctuate with intensity. I'll use the fire in my gut. I'll crack the bread bowl that is his skull, so he sees it my way. Then we'll plan it all together.

"Hey," I hear a voice say from behind me, soft and low. My heart skips a beat. Fear? Excitement? Something else?

Who knows these days? It's all blending together.

"Did Dad bore you to death?" I ask casually, trying not to let my heartbeat make my voice all wonky. It's a good thing my face, now flushing full red with the shame of scheming, will be obscured by the firelight.

"No, it was okay. Guy stuff is all. Nice fire."

"It was hard. I lit a match."

"Sometimes that's more than enough," he says, like it means something. I don't catch his drift, but I'm not going to admit it. I want him to help me, so I need him to like me. Well, I'd also like him to like me. But that is beside the point right now.

"I saw Ana today," I lead.

"When can I see her?"

"It's not good." I wait, injecting dramatic effect into my face.

"What? Why? What's wrong?"

Another pause. "Bea said everyone has to stay separate. No one in the immediate family can see each other." I use "immediate family" because I've just gained some kind of lifetimes-old status in the family according to Bea, and I'm not about to deny it. I'm one of them, she said. Maybe not the inner circle, but I'll take what I can get.

"It gets worse. They took Ana down. Totally non-coherent. Handcuffed to the bed. Moved her to a heavily monitored section of the Village, so no walks, ever. Certainly no talks."

"Why?" he sounds panicked, which makes me feel bad, but not bad enough to stop with my plan.

"Bea says it isn't safe for her at any level of consciousness. Not with you around."

I turn away so he doesn't see me wince.

"It's because of me?" Shoot an arrow through his voice, and it would sound like that. Like there's a hole in the middle of his throat.

Now, I wait. I wait for his goodness to rise. He'll have to do something. Just like I have to do something.

"This is serious," he says, reaching out and turning my face toward him as if this will allow him to see a different story. In any other situation, it might be a romantic gesture. Right now, he just wants to know the truth.

Fortunately, it's all true. I don't have to fake my concern at all. "I saw her," I say, letting my pain show through my sad, tightened face. "She was knocked out cold. Like she was in a coma. It was bad, Michael. Really bad. I think it was Helene."

"She can't do this!" he practically yells.

I shush him. "I know. It's too much to ask of her, especially when she's just doing it for your sake." God, I'm disgustingly good at this. "There is good news, though. Bea came right out and confirmed that I can teach you whatever she teaches me, assuming she doesn't officially know about it."

"But at what cost?" he asks, starting to pace. "Ana's sanity? I don't think I can live with that."

"Yeah," I say, forcing myself to wait. I hope he understands. Someday.

"What do we do?" he finally asks, like I could say anything, and he's totally on board.

"I don't know." That's one hundred percent truth, and it feels good to tell it.

"I don't either."

"We're going to have to figure this out together."

"We can," he says, though the confidence sounds forced. "Which reminds me, I solved the problem with the spoon spinning. I know why it didn't work."

"Why?" I ask, biding my time. We'll get back to Ana after it sinks in a bit. With her face still hovering over the fire, offering a different expression with each flick of the flame, it's not like I'm going to forget.

"It's the bag she gave me to wear when I'm around her. None of my Magic works when it's on. But take it off, and it's all back."

Makes total sense. "How did you figure it out?"

"The way I figure everything out. I just leave my rational mind and go off looking for an answer somewhere in the ethers. I don't try too hard, just sort of put it out there. Playing sports is great for that—you get into the zone, let your body move without thinking, and then an idea comes out of nowhere. That's where I got the idea to eat only organic. I was wondering how to get better at Magic. I took the question out to the soccer field. Then all of a sudden, a ball came flying at me and in the split second between when I saw it coming and when it hit me, I understood that junk food was getting in the way. The ball nearly knocked me out. But when I got up, I knew I'd never risk eating junk again."

"So you stopped eating nachos and pizza and stuff, just like that?" Talk about sacrificing for your art.

"It wasn't hard at all. In fact, it was like I couldn't eat the junk anymore."

"Do you think you could use that method to figure out how to get Ana out of the Village? I mean, if I told you everything I can, taught you everything they teach me, and you got into the zone? Do you think something could come to you, just like that?"

"I'll try. But you should try, too. Anyone can do it. You set yourself up, then wait until it lands on you. You can attempt to make it up, but it isn't the same as something coming to you. The things that come to you are always better."

I doubt just anyone can do it, but I'll try anything for Ana. In the meantime, I'll start with plain old logic. "I know my way around the nursing home, but you can't get anyone out of the building from where she is now. I was thinking she could shapeshift time again, but she'd have to be conscious to do it, so no luck there. But maybe we could get Bea to teach us?"

I look deep into the fire, still seeing Ana. I can almost imagine her nodding in approval. "Maybe we could get Magic on our side. Bea and Ana have both said that Magic has a will of its own."

Michael smiles, but looks sad. "You already know a lot more than I do about Magic, and both of them, too. What they think. How they think."

"They don't always agree, so it's kind of hard to know for sure what's what. Then you throw Jake's ideas in? It's pretty much a total mind screw."

"Jake. So do you like him?"

"I don't know. I haven't thought about it."

Another lie. Someday, probably soon, I'm going to feel extra guilty about all this. Someday, I'll reach back into my memories and find the exact point when I screwed everything up, and everyone over. But that's not my priority right now. Right now, it's Ana.

Michael doesn't reply. Instead, he takes a turn at poking the fire.

Immediately, Ana's face disappears. Part of me is angry with him for messing it up, because I need her. Another part is glad because that means her spirit is, at least in some ways, only mine.

"You have to wonder what all this is about, don't you?" I ask, half to myself, half to Michael.

"It's about the three of us," a deep voice says. It's coming from the woods. I jump what seems like a hundred feet up. I can't see a figure, but I know the voice.

"Jake?" I ask.

Michael starts to turn toward it, but before he can, we hear, "I can't come near."

It is Jake. I hear him, but also feel him. "Got it. What are you doing here?"

"I want Ana out of there, too," he says, his voice seeming to ricochet off the trees. I can hardly breathe for the excitement I feel rushing through me, hearing those words. My body gets those tingles from the top of my head to the soles of my feet. There's something else, too. Some kind of understanding that circulates between us. No words are spoken, but it's as if we don't need any.

Like with me and Scottie when we mind-meld, I think.

"So we are a team, then?" Jake asks after a long pause.

I look to Michael, but he doesn't respond. He just keeps poking at the fire. How deep does this rift between them go?

"Yes," I say, agreeing for both of us, "we have to be."

"Good," Jake replies, "because we always have been. Together, we can do anything."

Chapter 18

"**M**ayden? Hello? Hey!" Michael is shouting. I'm confused. I'm standing right in front of the fire and see it has gone out.

When, exactly, did that happen?

"Where's Jake?" I ask.

"Jake?" Michael counters, sounding anxious.

"He was just here," I say, trying to figure out how much time it takes a full-blown fire to die down, and, thus, how much time I'm missing.

"Maybe not?" he asks. I look at him like he's crazy, but then why is my head swirling like a huge school of fish in a blender?

"He said we are a team, *like always*, whatever that means. He said the three of us had to work together to get Ana out."

Now I'm really getting worried. Because if Michael didn't hear what I heard...

"Are you all right?" Michael asks again, looking me in one eye, then the other, like a doctor checking for trouble.

I pull away. I'm fine. I think.

"I guess. I don't know." I hear my own voice. It sounds strange. "I mean, Jake was talking to us from right over there in the woods, right?"

"You heard him?" Michael asks, sounding worried, which worries me.

"But the fire was going strong just a minute ago. And now, clearly..."

"It's not," he fills in.

"I don't feel so good. Dizzy. Not quite to puking but, fair warning, I'm edging up on it."

If that doesn't put a guy off you, I don't know what will.

Michael immediately moves to my side, taking me by the elbow and waist, lending me some of his Quinn Clann juju, which, I have to admit, feels pretty nice right about now. He moves me to the bench and sits me down. I feel for his hand, and that flash of connection between us comes shooting through again.

It helps, so I lean into it.

"We have to tell GranBea," he insists.

"No need," she shouts from a distance, all out of breath.

"Do you hear her?" I whisper to Michael, not trusting myself right now.

"I do," he assures.

She comes into view from over the hill, moving quickly. I have this flash of imagination that she came trotting over here like a wild animal, changing back to her human form just in time. I have no idea if this is true, but the picture came easily. Either way, having her here makes my stomach feel better.

"You there," she says with urgency, pointing a finger toward Michael, "put your medicine bag on and step well away. Mayden, stay where you are."

"Okay," I say, even as Michael moves from beside me. "What happened?"

"Someone, or something, used Jake's image. He sensed it." She's bent over me and breathing heavily, back in her dirty rags and looking very much like she's eighty-eight. "He was falling off to sleep when his projection was called upon. He's well trained, so he knows when something is happening, especially at a distance. He told me right off, which is what you must do any time there is such an odd occurrence— if you want me to keep you safe. You understand?"

I try to piece together what I'm hearing. Jake was not here? Yes, I get that. But Jake's image was? Really? And they expect that might happen again?

"You have to expect anything and everything," she insists. "Now tell me, what was going on here before Jake arrived?"

It doesn't take me a second to remember my plotting to break out Ana and guilt Michael into joining me. "I think I might have messed up a bit," I offer apologetically.

"What happened, GranBea?" Michael says from quite a safe distance.

"It's not your mess up, girlie. This is my fault. I invoked the fire for you, but I never warned you to stay away from the element of fire for at least seventy-two hours. Basic rule of Magic. I could kick myself. I never thought you'd have a way to start a fire in this fancy backyard, but I should have warned you, just in case. Even a cigarette match could have been trouble. Not that you smoke. You don't smoke, do you? No, I can see you don't. I'm just not used to someone who doesn't know about Magic. But you can be sure mistakes like that won't happen again."

"What's wrong with going near fire?" I ask, wanting specifics, especially if she's forgetting what I do and don't need to know.

"Nothing wrong with it, in and of itself," she says, finally standing straight and breathing more evenly. "But the kind of Magic we did today lingers, like lighter fluid on your fingers. We taught you to breathe in Magic, and you know what bellows will do to fire! I suspect you were practicing the breathing before it happened, too?"

"I thought you told me to, to build up my Magical strength?"

"Quite right," Bea agrees, "in most circumstances. But between the air out here and the fire, you can conjure up quite a bit of trouble without knowing what to do with it. Or what it opens you to. I ought to have started your lessons with self-protection. It's just not clear where to begin when someone is so very new."

Protection is what Ana suggested, I recall, but I think that's more than obvious by now.

"So what happened?" Michael asks.

"Now," Bea says, her voice loud and clear, and every word enunciated, "I am glad to be talking to you, Mayden, but it is good I found you alone."

The meaning in her unspoken words comes to me easily. What she is saying is that she's not only not teaching Michael, she's not even willing to acknowledge his presence when she's teaching.

I look at him and see his hopeful face fall. It's killing him that they'll teach me, someone who is not even legitimate family, and not him.

"So what happened?" I repeat Michael's question for him, but also for me. It's thrown me that Jake was here, but then not here, or at least not him.

"That depends," she insists, "on what happened when he was supposedly here."

"Not much," I fudge, hoping I won't have to confess all the ugly little details.

"Out with it!" she insists, not even the tiniest bit patient. "You must tell me what happened in your vision. I have to know everything to decipher what the true message was."

"That was a vision?" I ask, excited.

A vision? I had a vision? That has to mean something.

"Don't be overly impressed with yourself, girlie. It's Magic's doing, not yours."

124

I feel a small bit of deflation but hang on to the fact that at least it happened to me.

"Well, you see," I answer, buying time as I decide how much detail I have to go into. Crap, I might as well just spill it. This stuff is too complicated for anything but straight up truth. "You might not like this, well, for sure you won't like this, but…"

She growls. I don't have to ask why.

"I was looking at the fire and breathing in the earth like you said. It got a little weird because I kept seeing Ana's face over the fire. I thought it was just my imagination."

"Just your imagination! I suppose you think your dreams are not real either? That your creative thought is better left in kindergarten, along with your crayons? Well, I'll be un-teaching you that before anything else. Gracious, the list of fundamentals we must cover is outrageous. What else?"

"Michael came, and we talked about the reason he couldn't spin the spoons, and he told me about how…"

"You're missing something important. I feel it."

"So, yeah, I was being a little sly about getting Michael to help me, well, with a plan I had." I take a deep breath for bravery. "It was to get Ana out of the home without your permission. I knew I needed his help, and so I was sort of, I don't know, making him feel like it was his fault so he would help me."

I turn to Michael to see yet another layer of disappointment register on his face. "I'm sorry, Michael. Really."

"We're alone, aren't we?" Bea insists. I catch her drift again. Michael shouldn't be here, and so we'll just pretend he isn't. Might as well just give me another knife to stick in his back.

"Totally alone," I lie. Makes you wonder what lies are okay and what lies aren't. "It's not like me to plot behind someone's back. For sure not yours, Bea. It seems like a stupid idea now."

"I appreciate your honesty," she says, as if she really does.

Michael says nothing, but I can feel his sense of betrayal.

Great way to start a relationship, Julie. Just brilliant.

"Then Jake showed up," I continue, but only because I have to. "I heard his voice from off over there in the woods. He said he wanted Ana out too, and that he and Michael and I would team up. He said that we had been a team before. And then it was like I skipped time or something. The fire was going strong when Jake got here, but then all of a sudden I was standing there and it was nearly out. That's pretty much it."

"Nothing else?" she demands.

"One thing," I suddenly remember, hoping this helps with Michael. "Michael figured out why his magic didn't work."

I look at him and point towards his bag. He touches it to his chest and I can see he gets it.

Bea nods again and again, saying nothing, like she doesn't even care that Michael knows. God, this family is hard to figure out.

"Was it a vision?" I finally ask.

She doesn't answer for a long while. When she finally does, she ignores my question. "So then, Magic has spoken its wishes. It wants Ana out of there, and it wants you, Michael, and Jake to work together to make it happen. It's impossible given what we all know, but Magic doesn't worry much about the impossible, nor does it help with the many details. Clues are about all we can hope for. So we will—all of us—think on it and decide upon a plan. For now, though, I'm more concerned about you, Mayden."

Ugh. "Because...?"

"Because Magic has made it clear it wants to communicate through you. You had the vision—and who knows when it started, perhaps even before Michael arrived. Ana's face in the fire could have clued you in, but how would you know that?

So it *was* a vision!

"It may seem you had the idea to betray us, but it is more likely the idea was not your own. I know it is not in your nature to intentionally betray or misguide another." She says the last bit louder as if making sure Michael doesn't miss that part.

"Magic? Communicate through me?" I feel the blood rush out of my face.

"It is a powerful thing and a great responsibility. I must tell you now, though, the cost of resisting what Magic wants is high."

"How did I know that?" I half joke. I mean, at some point, you just have to laugh at the insanity of it all. I look at Michael, though, and can almost feel his envy. I get it. I'm learning what he should be learning and doing what he should be doing. I try to say I'm sorry with my eyes.

"There is a lot you will just know moving forward," Bea says, sounding resolved. "You will learn in a variety of ways, not only the way you learned tonight. Through visions, yes. But also through all manner of strange occurrences. Magic will no doubt be trying to determine how to best work through you. I can help you with anything, so long as Magic does not want you to try to betray me again."

"I don't want to betray you ever! How can we be a family if we can't trust each other?"

"Magic is either the glue that will hold us together or the force that will rip us apart."

"But what does that mean?" I beg to know.

"Magic has found you and chosen you. It has made it clear it will speak its wishes through you. There is nothing any of the rest of us can do about it, but stay alert and act wisely."

"Okay, but then, why me? I mean, I want to learn. I really do. But this is important, and I'm already managing to screw up."

"Easy," she answers wistfully. "Because you are a beautiful young woman. Even with our extensive Clann, every other viable candidate has been beyond Magic's interest for many years."

"Now *that's* seriously creepy," I admit.

"It's not as you are thinking," she assures. "Magic is also female. It seeks to have a mirror to look into, so to speak. A beautiful, young, feminine face to imagine as its own."

"Mine?" I ask, incredulous. When has anyone—ever—wanted me for my face?

"Yours," Bea says, again smiling that toothless smile, almost like she knows something about this from personal experience.

Chapter 19

All I want to do is sleep, I think, as Scottie stretches two paws across my chest and pummels me gently. I purr back, still over the moon that she is healthy.

Which, of course, makes me think of Ana.

It's been almost a week, and I'm no more sure of how to get her out of there than I was when I first saw her tied down.

"It's my day off," I explain to Scottie. Actually, it's Bea's day off, which makes it my day off. Which means I'll have some time to myself.

Finally.

A week's education in Magic should be counted as a year. It's utterly exhausting, if only because it is so fascinating, exciting, and terrifying all at once. We must have gone through five dozen Magical food recipes already. I wouldn't say I'm getting good at cooking *or* Magic, not by any stretch of the imagination. But at least I'm starting to understand the unspoken language well enough to participate intelligently.

Intelligence. The word does not quite, exactly apply when it comes to Magic. There's a whole lot of leaping from logic going on.

But you get used to it. Sort of.

I realize this is the first morning I've slept late since a week ago last Sunday—the day I met Michael. Bea was only supposed to be here for the dinner meal, but she told Dad she had extra time on her hands, and it didn't matter that she was only paid for the dinner menu. He wasn't about to complain, especially when every single meal makes you want to run ten miles, just so that you can eat again sooner.

For the record, Dad, Sally and I have all lost weight this week. If that isn't Magic, I don't know what is. As expected, Bea-as-Finola has now reached goddess status with the parents.

Isn't that right, Scottie? I mind-meld.

I think the real reason Bea changed her mind, though, was what happened at the fire. She doesn't want anything to get started with me and not have her nearby. *Too much Magic to learn,* is what she said when I suggested this was the reason. But honestly, I don't care what her motives are. I've long given up on making sense of anything, let alone all of it put together. I just try to cram as much as I can into my brain with the intention of sorting it out later.

Scottie finds a bit of bare flesh on my one exposed calf to knead her paws into. I turn back over and reach down to draw her to my face, nuzzling her soft belly. Her getting well is still the best thing to come from meeting the whole Magical crew, and I'm never going to forget it.

For this alone, I'd have worked as her personal slave every day this summer.

The schedule isn't terrible, I argue with myself. Early breakfast with Bea and Michael, even with Michael keeping his distance, is always fun. There is tons of laughter at every little thing, except on those occasions when Michael gets all bent about being directly ignored by Bea. Anyway, it's amazing how fun doesn't seem like such a big deal until it is part of your daily life. Now that I know what I've been missing, I know I'm going to have a hard time when all this is over.

Then we have another, more formal breakfast with Dad and Sally. It's amazing how Bea shapeshifts from a haggish Magic teacher to a real chef the minute they show up. Her funny, irreverent, and graceful leaping seems to get tucked away inside her hair net and from then on, it's all business. The only time she breaks from this is when I mess up in a task in front of others. She has no problem telling me all about it, which Wife #4 just loves. Both Sally and Dad seem to have decided the education I'm getting is the very best thing that could have happened to me this summer.

If only…if only…*if only* they knew.

Then it's off to see Ana, though there has been no real change in her level of consciousness. They don't tie her down anymore, because really, there is no reason to. She's gone, flown off to who knows where, with zero light in her eyes. It hurts that there's absolutely no recognition that I'm there. Even so, I never miss a day. Anyway, it's good for the Village staff to see me in her new wing on a regular basis because none of us have forgotten what we will need to do.

We just don't know how to go about it. Do we wait until she is better? Will she ever be better? Bea says Magic will show us the path forward, if we give it time. That's easier to accept when I'm not looking down on Ana's comatose body. They don't have to look at her like that every day.

I do.

We'll know when we are shown by either Magic or Ana, is all Bea will say about it. I've argued that nothing can be up to Ana in the state she's in, but Bea insists I underestimate her sister.

I'll be honest: I hang on to that possibility like life itself.

On my way home, I try to spend a half-hour of ordinary life with Rod, but that is only marginally more effective than talking to Ana. I heard Dad mention the divorce on the phone with Rod's dad just yesterday, so I guess it's officially public. I remember how it especially sucks the first week or two after, or anytime you run into someone you haven't seen in a while who just heard the news. While Rod would never admit it, I think he likes that I check in on him. Old friends mean something, even if you can't do much beyond hang out. Soon enough he'll be fully out of danger and on with his life. Until then, I'll keep keeping tabs.

For me, though, our visits also serve as a reality check. Am I still sane? Can I hold a real conversation with non-magical people?

Yep. So far, so good.

After Rod, I come back and learn about lunch Magic, which is definitely different from breakfast Magic and dinner Magic. *Soup and sandwiches are about life,* Bea said the other day, though I had no idea what that means. Sometimes it's just best to wait until she expands upon her little nuggets of wisdom, even if it's an excruciatingly long wait. After lunch, she heads home for an hour, then returns to start dinner, and before long Michael is in the doorway, slumped down with a bag of cashews and bean sprouts, stuffing himself as if he has not eaten for days. I tried to tell him he can splurge a little, both with the workouts he's getting through soccer and his GranBea's Magic, but he is determined to have his body in prime condition for anything they are willing to teach him. Meanwhile, I'm gorging on anything and everything, striking while the Magic is hot.

Then it's dinner, which Michael always manages to be late for, and our after-dinner talks once Bea has left. Some nights he can barely keep his eyes open, but he wants to learn everything I can pass on. Mostly I give him the short notes, because there's way, way too much. And anyway, cooking Magic doesn't easily translate. You have to feel the ingredients, to smell them and talk to them, to find out what wants to happen next.

I don't mention all that to Michael. It's hard enough for him as it is.

A door slamming down the hall pulls me from the rehashing of my new life. Another fight between Dad and Sally must be in full swing. I pull up my silky summer sheets to hide. Bea says it's the heat from the fire working on more than Sally's waistline. It makes her cranky, the same way it would if she were on a strict diet. I asked if there wasn't something we could do about that, but Bea just shrugged, as if to say *you can't have your cake and eat it, too.* I also asked why I wasn't cranky, and she just laughed and pointed to the bag of chips I happened to have in my hand at the time. I guess I'm keeping ahead of the flames.

If you ask me, though, I think it's just that Dad and Sally are reaching that time in all his relationships when things go to crap. So far, they have all gone by pretty much the same schedule: A year or so of sticky-gooey-all-out love, a big wedding and new house (yes, Dad actually carried each bride over the threshold), twenty-some months of increasing distance, then boom, out of nowhere, it's over. All of them have gone that way, give or take a few months. Except for my mom. She was different. That was nine long years of what my Aunt Mia says was real love, even if they couldn't keep it together. I think Dad just decided never to risk his heart again. She had already left him before she was killed, but that didn't make it any easier.

Mom.

Just the thought brings guilt. Some days, I haven't thought about much at all. I don't know if that's supposed to be progress. I only know it seems wrong. Or different. Or something. Then other days, it's like she is right here, with me, closer than ever.

Utterly confusing. Again.

Anyway, as much as I don't overly enjoy Wife #4, I hope they aren't going to get a divorce. I don't like the idea of getting a new set of rules, plus all that comes with it—moving, redecorating, the works.

Besides, it just can't be good for Dad.

"Okay, Scottie, I have to get going," I say, lifting her off me and putting my feet on the ground. I swear I'm sore from head to toe. You wouldn't think cooking would be any great strain, but it is. You are constantly standing, reaching, lifting, pouring, and all kinds of things you never think about until you've done it for hours on end. Add Magic and working with all the elements—including Bea insisting we actually create a makeshift brick oven on the back deck so she could bake her favorite garlic and onion flatbread, and so I could learn about fire—and then on top of that add how much you have to think and remember about what goes with what and what never goes with what.

It's exhausting just to think about it all.

I head to the shower, where I think about all of this yet again, albeit from at least five other angles, then grab some breakfast alone (I think

Michael is as glad for the day to sleep in as I am), and head over to Ana's. I text Rod when I park at the Village, just to let him know I'm not swinging by today, but his cell is turned off. I leave a message. It's short, sweet, and a little less snarky than I might have normally left, but not so nice that he thinks I feel sorry for him. I do, but it won't help if it looks that way. He's got his pride. You have to admire him for that.

Standing at the Village buzzer, I think back just a week and a half ago, when I was coming to take Ana for our big walk.

Everything is so different now.

I'm so different now.

It's like I live in a whole new world. I'm not even wearing my army jacket, just a t-shirt and shorts, and my hair hasn't been intentionally crazy for days. I try to tell myself it's not about Jake and Michael, but it doesn't work. It is completely and totally about Jake and Michael. Maybe just a bit more about Jake than Michael, but the final verdict is still out on that.

The ladies at the desk buzz me through and have me sign in without a comment. No strange looks. One of them even smiles in a way that looks genuine. I guess that's the thing about not standing out. You don't stand out. It's a little bit of a bummer until I remember that learning Magic has made me truly different, so maybe I don't have to rely so much on just looking different. I think I'll have to think on that more, but later. Now, it's time for Ana.

Each step up the stairway is slower than the last. It takes all I've got to go in each day and see her so vacant. Not even a head bob. I have to brace myself, just to handle it.

"Julie!" Dr. Garcia says, surprising me as we meet. "It's good that you get your exercise by taking the stairs. One day, you'll be older like me and very glad you did."

I don't know what to say, in part because she spooked me (no one but me ever takes the stairs), and in part because I can't imagine how she calls herself older when she works here. She could probably still get a boyfriend, even, if she wanted to.

"I'll bet you're here to see Mrs. Quinn again. You do her good, that's clear."

"Why?" I ask, probably a little too sarcastic. At least I don't add *Because she doesn't need to be held down by cuffs anymore?*

"Didn't you hear? She's up again. Back to her old self, jabbering away!"

Oh, oh, oh the joy that rushes through my every cell!

Before I know it, before it even fully lands in my awareness, I've taken the stairs two steps at a time, raced down the empty hallway, and nearly slid into Ana's room.

It's true! Ana! Ana!

My Ana is up and smiling!

With my next heaving breath, I thank every god and goddess that ever existed, because I have been praying to them all.

"Ana," I whisper after a quick check to the bathroom. "We're alone. Can you hear me?"

Her head bobs enthusiastically: "Mayden, Mayden, Mayden, Mayden."

She's back!

She's *here*!

"Oh, Ana!" I get on my knees and put my head in her lap.

Pure. Total. Relief.

She strokes my hair. "Shh, Shh, Shh, Shh."

This is all I need. All I want.

But no, wait. I have to get her out of here while I can.

How, though? Immediately, Dr. Garcia comes to mind. She said I was good for Ana. It all clicks, without even really thinking about it. I say I'll be right back, race to find Dr. Garcia, and ask her if I can take Ana out for some fresh air. "It's been too long, and it helps her so much," I plead.

Dr. Garcia ponders just long enough for me to remember that I have Magic to work with.

I call upon the power in my belly, just as I've been taught. It's not okay to use it to outright manipulate someone, Bea has insisted, but if things are on the fence, it's okay to flood someone with what I'm feeling, so they can better understand my wishes.

I send *Please! Please! Please!* and *Safe! Safe! Safe!* toward the doctor's stomach. I send it hard. It doesn't take long before Dr. Garcia's smile grows and I have the holiest of holy grails!

Permission granted!

Suddenly, blessedly, amazingly, my world has once again righted itself. I take off, hearing Dr. Garcia call after me not to run down the hall, the way she did when I was a little kid. I try to slow down, but there's no way.

I am just. Too. Freaking. Happy!

Chapter 20

I'm not going to risk taking Ana deep into the woods, as much as I know we would both love it. She's already invoked her ancestors as we wheeled out, and I know she's just waiting until we are out of earshot to start talking. Just thinking about it makes my heart leap. I honestly thought she might never leave that room again. I stop when we have gone as far out as we can get and still be on a paved sidewalk. I only wish I had her medicine bag.

"You have been learning!" she says excitedly, looking me over and smiling proudly. Totally clear and present. Like she didn't just spend a week out in la-la land.

"Trying. About your medicine bag."

"I know exactly where it is."

"You do?"

"In my old room. I'll need you to get it."

Her words hit me in the gut. "It's not there, Ana. I'm sorry. I looked everywhere. The room was cleaned and sterilized top to bottom before I could get there. But I did get you some drugstore glasses."

I pull out the glasses, which I've been carrying with me everywhere, and she takes them, seemingly pleased.

"They are perfect! Thank you! Now, the medicine bag is at the very back of the top side table drawer," she insists.

"I checked all the drawers," I say, crushed to have to tell her. What can it mean when you lose your medicine bag?

"You'll find it there," she assures, her eyes dancing behind the lenses. So awake and so alive! It's hard to imagine her as I saw her yesterday, and the day before, and the day before that. "Or have you forgotten that we have Magic?"

Her words make me laugh out loud.

Isn't that what Bea asks me half a dozen times every single day? *Have you forgotten Magic?* Seems to be her most common phrase, normally coming anytime I use the word *can't.* You'd think I'd learn, but no, I always go back to thinking things are what they have been for the past sixteen years of my life. And that's just not true anymore. I often want to argue that you can't expect people to change in an instant, but I don't dare. Bea is fun, but also slightly terrifying with that Black Panther energy always ready to pounce. You don't want to mess with it for no good reason.

"I'll find it, even if it takes every ounce of Magic I've learned."

"Of course you will! Now, tell me everything." She is already moving her attention to look around and marvel at all the stuff she can see. It's like she can't get enough of nature while she has it. I don't mind sharing her attention. She deserves this, and so much more. Again, I feel a surge in my heart.

Pure. Happiness.

I cannot wait to tell Bea and Michael, assuming they don't already sense it.

"I don't know where to start," I reply.

"Tell me about what you have learned. I can see Bea is teaching you. Your confidence level has risen greatly and you are more at peace. That much change, occurring that quickly, can only be the work of Magic!"

I look into the woods, imagining how alive everything must look to someone who has been knocked out cold for a week. Actually, I can't. But it does make you appreciate it all more.

"Magic has changed me," I say, only now looking at it that way. "But it seems like the more I learn, the more there is to learn. And everything comes in little pieces that don't fit together."

"Not yet. But that doesn't mean not ever. It is true that the more you know, the more you realize all that you don't know. Perhaps it is better said like this: What you assume is learning, is more like becoming. I see you are becoming magical. In a world where there are so many limitations within the framework of time, space and energy, to become magical is to have more resources, and therefore, more confidence."

"Becoming magical," I whisper, because it's too much to say at full volume. Like that would be admitting something I'm not quite ready to.

"This is a good lesson in and of itself. The more you think you understand, the less open for knowledge you become. Some of the most brilliant and accomplished academics stop learning, thinking they already know everything. Stay in awe of Magic, and you will learn all you need to. For what it's worth, I believe you are right on track."

I nod, thinking this is what I miss from Ana. Bea is smart and a great teacher of Magic. But Ana is wise, and she gives me confidence. I need that, and with Ana, I'm not afraid to admit it.

"Can I ask you something?" I dare.

"Of course," she replies, sounding surprised I have to ask. "Anything."

"Magic came to me one night."

"May goodness prevail!"

"It changed everything around me. I mean, the whole world I was seeing wasn't real for a few moments. I still don't understand what happened. Bea called it a vision."

"May well be," she nods, though she sounds noncommittal.

"I saw your face in the fire. Michael was there, for real I mean, and then Jake came, but not really. All I heard was his voice. Michael didn't hear it, though. Then later, Bea came, and she said the part with Jake didn't happen. She said it was Magic and that it wants to speak through me. But I want to know what you think. Were you there? Or even just aware of it when it happened?"

Ana sucks in air. It's not quite a gasp, but it is clear she's not taking what I have said lightly. So it must be news to her.

"It hasn't happened since," I continue, "but Bea says it could anytime. She's been around me as much as possible, and keeping me completely busy. I think it might be so that Magic doesn't do something without her around."

In a split second, I realize it could be happening now.

But is it?

Feeling the ground beneath us, seeing the deep wrinkles in Ana's face. It's not some ashen shadow. She's the real deal this time.

Thank. God.

"Bea is right to stick close," Ana says firmly. "Not that you must worry about Magic. If you have been selected as a vehicle of communication, you will be protected by Magic herself, in more ways than you can know. But you are very early into your education, making it all the more dangerous. Magic must feel a great urgency, to appear so obviously, and so soon."

I wait for her to continue, but she doesn't. She seems to be considering it all. I can't blame her, given her image was used by Magic. But the more she is silent, the more worried I get. I mean, if something is big for Ana, it's got to be really big for me.

"What IS Magic, anyway?" I finally ask, if only to break the silence. "Is it really female? Or even like a person at all? I thought it was a force or something."

She evaluates for a while before replying, like she doesn't know how far to go with me.

I silently beg her to go all the way. Tell me everything. Everything. Please.

"Magic is most certainly not a person," she begins, hesitant. "You are right about that. It is something far greater than could be contained in one human life form. Even our Keeper holds only a small amount of what is available to our Clann. And, of course, there are countless clans at work at any given point in time. I suppose a force would be closer to the truth, but that is not quite correct, either. Let me think of an image to help you."

With this, I see her eyes glaze off, almost as if she's gone into her drug-induced la-la again. But this time, I see it differently. She's not gone, and definitely not gone against her own will. The realization hits me—Ana really does leave on purpose! So maybe Bea was right. Maybe Ana did take herself down this week. And then brought herself right back up when she was ready.

Relief practically descends on me.

I think I may be breathing full breaths for the first time since I saw her in those cuffs.

"Ah! I see it now," Ana says, back as quickly as she'd left. "Let's think of the force of Magic as a great chandelier. Beautiful, elaborate, decadent even. With many crystals, each hanging one from another, and all connected. The great power of the universe runs through the entire fixture. Each crystal is a specific form and style that serves as a conduit of Magic's light. But not only our Magic. The Magic inherent in all religions, all forms of goodness, and all of the darker energies, too. All manner of things carrying the power of the universe out into the world. Our Magic, which is to say that of the Quinn Clann, is but one rarified crystal on that great plugged-in appliance that leads straight from the One source out into the world."

As if her image is dangling in front of my own eyes, I get it.

Strong. Elegant. Beautiful. Complex. Functional. Electric. Flowing.

This, *this* is Magic? It's so much bigger than I thought.

"And it's a woman?" I have to ask.

"Not all of Magic. Our Clann happens to be of a feminine line, and that is very important to us, but that is not the only form. All things must have their opposite, at least until you reach the ultimate Source. I think of our Clann's Magic as a woman who is elegant, strong-willed and supple. But don't take that literally. Interpreting Magic on the literal plane is where everyone goes wrong."

I find myself now imagining the Clann as a beautiful lady, dancing in a long, blue, sparkly, and backless dress. It's so real, it feels nearly like a vision.

I look to Ana, my eyes full of utter amazement.

Ana smiles back at me, her own eyes shining joyful through her glasses. "I see Magic is talking to you in pictures, too! You received an image as well, and you didn't even have to leave here to find it. Wonderful."

I love hearing Ana say *wonderful*.

It's wonderful, in and of itself.

"Just don't think that image is all of it," she warns gently. "Magic is more fluid than that. Here's a piece of advice I wish someone had told me early on: Magic doesn't want to be understood. The minute you claim to understand, or even begin to think you do, you will be in for a few hard lessons."

"So a feminine crystal from a great chandelier is just a way to think of Magic, but not really what it really is? And when we forget how big it is and think we understand, we are at risk of having to learn new lessons that take us back into the mystery?"

I have no idea where that came from. It just popped out of my mouth, like I actually know what I'm talking about.

"Oh my dear Mayden. We have chosen well in choosing you, haven't we? Or did we choose you at all? Perhaps Magic chose you. Or, also possible, that you chose yourself before you were born, and we could not deny the force you set in motion when you did so. From what I am seeing in you, it might have come to be through any which way."

I don't know anything about who chose what, but I feel there is truth somewhere in what she is saying. That, more than anything, is what Bea has been teaching me. To feel things in order to know them. That's what all the blindfolded cooking is for. And learning a spice's scent, and taste, and feel, long before learning its name.

"One more thing?" I ask.

"Many more things, if you like!"

"You talked about good and bad. And just now, you mentioned darkness. Helene certainly seems dark. Does Magic care which way it goes?"

"Another mystery! I can say that, for twelve hundred years, the Quinn Clann has always asked that goodness prevail. While it is possible this could shift direction, such as with our current Keeper of Magic, I find it hard to imagine at this late date. I think we all find it hard to imagine."

I find it hard to imagine, too. So hard, it makes me want to do something about it. I have no idea what, but the feeling is real.

"Now, if you were given a vision that night, surely it was something important. What did you see?"

Again I'm hesitant because it makes it look like I'm not respectful of my teachers. But I have to tell the truth. I've learned that much. "Jake and Michael and I were thinking of ways to get you out of here. In the vision, that is. But Bea had already said no to the idea. So we were plotting a way around her."

"Naughty children!" she says with a tsk-tsk, but thankfully, there's lightness and humor in her voice.

"It was my idea, but we were going to work as a team. Jake said we had been a team before, but he didn't say when before, or anything more about it."

"And you? Did it feel like something you had felt before?"

Truthfully, I haven't said what I think to Bea or Michael, let alone Jake. I'm not even sure I know what I think. But I have this feeling...

Ana raises her eyebrows, like she has heard my thoughts again.

"I think it might be like it would be if it were from the past, only not from the past. From the future. Like we will work together in such a big way, someday, that the feeling could reach back to us. Sort of like something wants to show us the way and pull us along."

She just stares at me, eyes widened.

"I don't know," I quickly add. "It's a strange idea. I can't really say. Maybe it was in the past that we knew each other."

"Don't do that," she insists sharply. Her eyes bore harshly into mine, then soften. "Not ever. Don't give away what you know, even if you only have an inkling, because you don't understand it or you think someone who supposedly knows more will have a different opinion."

"But I could be wrong, and that could lead to mistakes."

"Yes. But it is more likely you will be at least a little bit right. Following that small piece of truth will then lead you to a greater truth. Surely that is a better path than giving away what you know."

"But you and Bea and Jake know so much more than me! And Michael, even though he hasn't been formally taught, has so much natural talent. If I go off in my own thinking, isn't that dangerous? Or disrespectful or something?"

"Bless you for how sincerely you care about respecting us, Miss Mayden. But these are matters that go beyond respecting another. They are your core truths. While I fully agree that we of the Quinn Clann may have more education and experience than you, each and every person has access to their own knowing, and that must not be compromised. Stay open to being taught, of course. But remember that teaching is meant to lead you to your knowing, not someone else's."

"It's all so confusing," I say, not wanting to complain, but also wanting, even needing, to get it right.

"That, you must let go of! And the sooner, the better!"

"What?" I ask, the confusion compounding.

"Getting it right!"

You would think I'd get used to these people knowing what I didn't say out loud. But I haven't. Not yet, anyway.

"An artist is not right. An artist is one who finds a perspective, then offers an interpretation. Magic is an art form. Think of it this way—with so many truths, and so many facets of the chandelier, there can be no single right way. That is not the nature of things. There is only what you know, interpreted through your view and your gifts. Sometimes, your truth will be in harmony with others. Other times it won't. Even so, insisting that you be right every time, for all people, in all situations? It's impossible. Besides that, it will drive you mad to try. Surely you can see that."

Not only can I see it, I can feel it.

"Exactly," she says, nodding her approval to yet another unspoken thought. "Now, let us turn our attention to you and the boys getting me out of here. That is what Magic wants, is it not?"

"Yes. Totally."

"Good, then. We must see how much strength you have garnered for such a great task. Here," she puts up a pinky finger and puts her elbow on her wheelchair arm, "finger wrestle me."

What? Seriously? That is just soooo out in left field. "You're kidding, right?"

There is no way I'm finger-wrestling an eighty-eight-year-old mostly-invalid, out in the woods, especially after the week she just had. I cock an eyebrow at her.

"Not in the least. I need to see how much Magic has taken hold of you."

Insanity. Pure insanity.

But apparently not to her. I offer her my finger and position myself to make an honest attempt. Even so, I have a feeling I won't win.

Sometimes it sucks to know what you know.

Chapter 21

I am once again in iffy territory.

Ana is tucked away in her room at the Village, her glasses safely in my pocket, and her medicine bag (yes, it was right where she said) in her new dresser drawer. Bea is shopping, Michael is at soccer camp, and I'm here right where I am probably not supposed to be, on the dock across from Bea's land, flirting with Jake.

Well, not *flirting*, flirting. More like toying with a connection across fifty feet of water, praying that doesn't officially break the rules about getting too close to a family member without Bea knowing about it. Not that I'm sure she doesn't. She seems to know everything she wants to know.

Yep, it's all as murky as the water between the pier where I sit and the land across the water where Jake is pacing. I saw the flash of him here a few days ago in a dream and decided to take my chances on him noticing me if I sat here long enough. It took all of ninety seconds, at best, for him to appear. Which makes me think it was him I saw crouching low through the bushes that first day, either as man or spotted leopard.

Fortunately, today he's a guy.

He's not so far away that we could not hear each other if we talked loud enough. Even so, we haven't said a word. I get the feeling he's following orders, and I don't want to mess that up. I dangle my feet over the edge of the pier, trying to act casual. Only nothing with Jake is casual, even with fifty feet between us.

Finally, I can't take it any longer. "Bea's shopping."

Jake nods, but doesn't speak.

"I shouldn't come over there, I guess?" My hope is showing up here is like when Bea talks to me about Michael, even when Michael's in the room. Like we're skirting around the letter of the law, but it's okay, so long as we don't cross whatever invisible line is out there.

He nods again, staring with wide eyes, and without blinking, as if trying to get his thought into my brain as deep as it will go.

Which is pretty deep.

An idea strikes me. "Fifty questions? All yes or no?"

He nods, smiling, but does not sit. The sun is behind me, and he has to squint, but I can see him just fine. Jeans and a t-shirt never looked so good. It throws me, so now I can't think of any question that's a simple yes or no.

Okay, wait, here's one: "Can you read my mind?"

He looks at me intently, without moving.

Yes.

Only he doesn't say it. I just hear it. Or know it. Or something.

Crap.

If we do it this way, it's going to drive me crazy later, because just like my little mind-melds with Scottie, there's no way to truly know you said what you think you said and heard what you think you heard.

Say "yes" out loud, I think but don't say, just to confirm.

"Yes," he says out loud.

Ugh! I think I'd rather go back to not knowing if what he says is real or not. Reading minds is dangerous territory, given a few of the choice thoughts I've had about him.

Start short, easy, he silently instructs, his face set and firm, like he's dead serious about all this.

Short and easy? I guess that blows my plan to have him tell me all he knows about Helene.

Helene, he repeats, frowning.

Oh how lovely. He not only knows what I intend to say, but everything else? How do you guard your mind, especially with where mine tends to go when looking at him?

Sucks to be you, he sends, then laughs out loud. It's more gruff than Michael's laugh, not that I'm trying to compare them or anything.

I like them both, I realize.

Both laughs, I quickly make sure to think. Really, this is such dangerous territory.

Thanks, I intentionally send back, hoping sarcasm translates. I look around to see if anyone might be watching our non-verbal conversation. It's got to look like insanity meets insanity.

Nope. Not another soul in sight.

Helene's bad news, he sends across the water.

"Why?" I say out loud, already forgetting the rules. *I mean, how?*

Messes with your mind, he sends.

Now I laugh out loud. *Like everyone in your family doesn't?*

Screws with your mind. Hard. On purpose.

How? I repeat, despite knowing this is the exact opposite of a yes or no question.

He cocks his head, like he's trying to figure out how to explain it in simple enough terms. It's amazing how much you can read on someone's face when you're really looking. I pride myself on noticing body language that others don't seem to, especially facial cues. This not-talking thing with Jake will most certainly use all of my skills.

Hard to describe.

Try, I urge.

He thinks more. *Scans your brain for self-doubt.*

Crap.

Then uses it against you.

Crap. Crap. Crap.

You don't know it's her. You think it's you. Your own thoughts.

Lovely. Just lovely. *Using Magic?*

This time, he nods with eyes exaggerating, all wide and darting around. He doesn't have to send the thought that she's batshit crazy. His face says it all.

How did she get so powerful?

Complex answer.

Try. I mean, if someone is going to use Magic to mess with your head, you're going to want at least a few details, right?

Next question, he sends.

Okay. Ana or Bea? Who can I trust?

Depends.

I refine my question: *Does Ana lie?* Somehow I can't imagine it.

Pass.

Does Bea lie? I can totally imagine that.

He laughs. *Tricky.*

That could mean a lot of things, I think but do not say, or send. At least intentionally.

Next question.

I realize I have a dozen or more now, but they all boil down to one, so I brave it.

Why me?

Another day, he sends, suddenly starting to turn away.

What? Already? I'm only a few questions in!

"Wait," I say out loud. I want him to stay, even if all I can do is look at him. But I can't think about that. Not with him right here, listening in on my thoughts.

We can't hide from each other, he sends, turning back toward me, but looking like he might go at any moment.

Not trying to hide, I defend, sending the thought with an extra push.

I'll protect you.

Okay, that was out of left field.

"I'm not safe?" I say out loud, forgetting again.

Relative to the situation.

Says nothing. Explain.

Protection. It's my job. I'm a protector. Using Magic. He sends each part separately, almost like he's enunciating. His face is as sincere as I've seen it yet. The feeling is that he wants me to understand this above all.

"What do you protect?" I say again out loud, this time intentionally. I want to be clear on this part.

Whatever. Whoever. You.

You'll protect me? It seems too big to say out loud, not to mention too much to hope for.

Only if you want me to.

I want, I send back before I can even think about thinking about it.

He nods like it's a done deal. *I have a question.*

Shoot.

How is Michael? His face is all scrunched up, like he doesn't even like talking about him.

He's a good guy, I assure, semi-noncommittal.

"Do you like him?" Jake says, this time out loud.

Not like you, I think, and send, before I can stop myself.

Jake smiles, showing those perfectly beautiful teeth.

See you in our dreams, sweetheart, he sends. At least that's what I think he sent. He was turning away again as he sent it and the wind seemed to somehow cut him off a bit.

I want to say something, or send something, because I have seen him in my dreams. I only remember flashes, but it's definitely him. But if he is seeing me, too?

It doesn't matter. He's gone.

I stand and walk the plank back to my ordinary life. Or at least more ordinary life. Actually, no, even that's not true. Ordinary has completely abandoned me, except in tiny, bite-size nuggets, like when Dad or Rod appears for a cameo.

It's all so crazy, Julie Mayden, I send to no one but myself.

Even crazier how much you like it this way, Julie Mayden sends back.

Chapter 22

Something isn't right.

I can't say what for sure. On one level, I'm having a typical breakfast in the dining room with the family and Michael. On another level, it's not. I just don't get *how* it's not.

I've been on the lookout for Magic's antics ever since the fire, if only because Bea has insisted I be ready for it to show up anytime, anywhere. Finally, I have a sense it's up to something. But for the life of me, I can't pinpoint what.

It isn't Bea, even though she is banging around in the kitchen, upset about something. I don't think she realizes how loud she is when she's not paying attention. One of the hazards of being deaf, I guess. It isn't Dad, who is sitting here reading the newspaper as he does every morning, or Sally, who is eating a huge bowl of cheesy grits in stone silence—I'm guessing she and Dad had another fight. It could be Michael, who should have left for practice an hour ago, and hasn't said a word as to why he's hanging around. But if it is him, there are no other clues to go on.

Then again, maybe it's just me. Or wishful thinking. Or something.

"I have an idea," Dad says, laying down his newspaper.

"Don't hurt yourself," I joke.

"I mean it," he says, a little stilted, but not without all humor. "We'll need your help, Michael."

"We?" Sally asks. So this must be news to her, too.

"Your Grandmother Helene will be coming back at the end of the week, right?" he asks Michael.

Crap. Immediately my gut churns.

"Yes, sir."

"Did you know it's her birthday?"

"I did," he replies, then swallows hard. You can see his strangely slim Adam's apple bob. It's probably the only slightly unattractive feature he has, which is why I look for it. It helps me remember he's not completely perfect in the looks department.

"I was thinking, we should have a party for her, here," Dad says, looking from Michael to me and back to Michael. "Julie could learn something about catering since she's taken so well to the kitchen."

Okay, I really, *really* don't like this. "Catering? Me?"

"We'll hire out the majority of it. But the organizational aspects would be an invaluable education for you. Sally has learned a great deal from being on the organizational end of so many of our parties."

I wonder if he knows how patronizing that sounds, even to someone who's not overly fond of Wife #4.

"I'll be glad to help," she offers, not exactly excited, but not begrudging the work, either.

Just shoot me now.

Maybe this is why something felt strange. I'm going to have to meet Helene, face-to-face. The Clann's top nemesis, or so they all say, and now I have to throw her a party.

"Are you sure that's a good idea, sir?" Michael asks.

"A party is always a good idea!" Dad bellows. "We'll make it an early afternoon affair. Food, balloons, even dress up the gazebo with summer flowers, the way Sally likes. Who doesn't appreciate a party?"

"I don't know, Dad," I say in a totally deadpan voice, preparing to drop the only bomb I can think of. "Do you think old people like birthday parties? Doesn't it just remind them of how soon they'll be dying?"

"Good God, Julie! I sure hope you don't say that to her. We want Helene to like you."

Right, I think. Meeting her without instinctually hissing is already going to be a stretch the size of the Grand Canyon. Playing the game so that she likes me? That would require a leap into another universe.

"Why do you care if she likes me?" Voice even, shaking hands hidden.

Yes, I can do this.

"Because we're business partners. And you like Michael, and Michael likes you."

Oh. Come. On.

"What does that have to do with anything?" Hidden hands wringing. Face totally red.

"Honey," Sally interrupts, "you sound like you're trying to arrange a marriage or something."

Michael's face has gone red, too.

"Dad, I..."

"What's wrong with families getting to know each other?" he defends, without listening to me. As usual.

"In fact," he continues, "I think we should surprise Helene. You two could go out and get her mother, Mrs. Quinn. She's better than ever, I hear. That would be a great surprise after all this time. Helene has no idea how good you are with her, Julie."

Michael looks at me: *Is he serious?*

I look at Michael: *I think so.*

"You two could manage to pull the surprise off, couldn't you? I'm sure with the right incentive we could get Finola to help plan the menu. A grand finale to her trial with you, Michael."

It's insane.

Or is it?

The mental dominoes are clicking.

"So you want Michael and me to take Mrs. Quinn out of the Village without her daughter knowing, for a surprise party here?"

All of a sudden, it's too good to be true, especially when I hear myself say it out loud.

"I think it's a brilliant idea!" Dad insists.

I look again to Michael, who is clearly as alarmed as I am.

And then, the smile.

He's getting it.

I have to admit—though I hate it, I love it.

"I think it's a great idea, too, sir," Michael says slowly.

I wonder about Bea and notice her loud banging pots getting louder in the background. It's like she's been listening and might not be quite as pleased about the idea as we all are.

"I don't know," I say, trying to make it sound like I'm less than enthused because it is sure to make Dad and Sally insist.

But then, suddenly, oddly, I notice what's wrong.

It's the clock.

The clock on the mantle chimes every fifteen minutes and has a ticker so loud it could drive you insane. It's ticking, only way, way too slow. I glance back at Dad and notice his eyes are sort of weird, as if vacant behind the surface.

I look at Sally's. Same.

And Michael's. Yep.

I get the wrong kind of chills. The bad chills. The very, very, *very* bad chills.

Again I notice Bea making a clattering in the kitchen, and I turn to look, but she's not in the kitchen.

I am.

I'm right here, sitting at the island in front of her.

She's banging a stainless steel pot right next to my ear.

Loud.

"Come on back, girlie" she yells, clanging and clanging away. "Come on, all the way back."

"What? Stop!" I reach out to grab the large metal spoon she's hammering into the pot. "That's loud!"

"'What' is right," she replies, standing over me like a mother hen. "What happened? Where'd you go?"

Suddenly, I feel sick. Puking sick. I push past her and get to the trash can just in time to upchuck, losing it right there in front of her. From behind me, I hear her sigh.

"It'll be all right now," she assures. I'm glad she thinks so.

When I'm spent, I rinse my mouth with water at the sink and then slowly, carefully return to sit at the island.

I keep my head down, but I can feel Bea watching over me. I appreciate it. I really do.

Finally, the dizziness in my head dissolves. The spinning stops.

I listen for the clock in the dining room. It seems to be ticking normally again.

"Magic grabbed you, did she?" Bea asks, more to confirm than as a wide-open question.

"I think so." My body is covered in chills, and I see the hair on Bea's arms standing straight up.

"I could see it coming over you even before you went all the way out. Held on to your feet to make sure you didn't go too far. When that didn't work, I got the pot and started hitting it."

"How long was it?" I ask, looking at the kitchen clock, then out at the afternoon sun. "Four o'clock? It was breakfast, I mean, where I just was."

I don't know how to explain it. Can you lose most of a day with Magic?

"You don't remember cooking with me here all day today?" Bea asks, more alarmed than I am comfortable with.

"No. Did I eat breakfast with my dad and Sally and Michael?"

She shakes her head. "They all left early. You ate with me, in here. We made a bowl of cheesy grits."

Now her eyes go wide. "Oh my. My, my, my! That must have been it. I love it when Magic goes to work like that."

"Work?" I have to ask, though I do feel exhausted.

"Remember when I instructed you to blend in a question while you stirred the pot?"

"No," I reply, terse. Like I didn't just say I don't remember anything?

I'm feeling totally cranked all of a sudden, but you just don't get cranked with Bea. Not if you're smart. Even so, I can't think of a way to take the snark back.

"Well, I do! You asked about how to get Ana out of that place she's in. You stirred the question into your cheesy grits. You added hot peppers, and then I put in a little something extra to help you along."

"What did you put in?" I ask, my eyes squinting in accusation.

"Aw, nothing much, a little…" she winces, "…bit of poison. But just a little."

She poisoned me? Bea, my teacher, my mentor?

No, I can't go there.

"How long ago was that?" I ask.

"Good point. Let's see now, that would have been nine hours ago. Exactly."

"Is that significant?" I ask, not sure why, except that she's been teaching me all along that I have to listen to the questions that come up, and the questions behind the questions.

She nods vigorously. "Oh, yes, always. Nine hours and you put in nine peppers. Nine times nine is eighty-one, which is an eight plus a one, which added together equals nine. That's three nines, which is nothing short of a spell. Goddess, we might as well have asked for you to be abducted, now that I think of it."

"Abducted?" I barely eke out. "Aren't you supposed to be careful with me?"

Sure, I don't want to piss her off. But I also don't want to be upchucking baby aliens I picked up in the stratosphere.

She shrugs, looking slightly offended. "If you don't want to learn."

"I want to learn. I just want to be safe."

Bea gives a harrumph. "Not possible. You can protect yourself from darkness, sure enough. But safety from the Magic that is leading you? No. Not possible. You'll lose ground as sure as gain it in the process. If you're not up for that, I say get out now."

"Can I get out?" Not that I want to. But I wouldn't mind knowing if I have the option.

"No, not really. It's too late. You signed up, girlie. You're in."

That's what I thought.

My head is spinning again. I'm tempted to move toward the toilet, assuming I can make it that far, but I don't want to leave the comforting stability of the chair. *You signed up, girlie* rings in my ears. Bea is watching me like a hawk, like at any moment she might need to grab her wooden spoon and pan again.

"Breathe," she instructs, her voice sterm. "Nine times."

I do.

It works.

"I think I'm okay."

"Good then, let's unravel this and find out what Magic wants now. Where did it take you?"

"To the dining room. You'd think it would be more exciting, really."

"It's plenty exciting. What did you learn?"

"Nothing. We were just having breakfast. Oh wait, Dad was saying we should have a birthday party for Helene. Here."

Thank God *that* was just a vision.

"A party? You sure?"

"And he wanted Ana to come as a surprise. Michael and I both seemed to be in favor of it, even though we know we can't get everyone everyone together like that."

Bea begins to think with her feet. As in, literally. She moves from the sink to the door and back, pacing the way she does anytime she's trying to work something through. A complex recipe. Whether or not it's hot or sweet that's called for. How to slow down the rise of the temperature gauge without adjusting the flame.

"Magic must want us all together," she mumbles, not to me, "but why now, with such risk? It makes no sense, especially this early in our eighty-eighth year. We've barely met you. Hardly had any training time at all."

Even if she's not really talking to me, I'm glad to listen. These are good clues to what is going on in her head, which is normally a total mystery. I file away the eighty-eighth year tidbit the way I do so many of her tiny little info bombs. I remember Ana said something about them being eighty-eight, too. Someday, maybe, the tiny bits will add up to something.

I'm not counting on it, but a girlie can hope.

"We were planning to wait till the end of the year," she mutters on. "Till the very end of the year."

More tidbits. More pacing.

Suddenly, she looks up at me. "What else have you got? Anything? Something unusual, maybe?"

I wrack my brain. But it was all so ordinary. I shake my head no.

"What made you come out of it?" she grills.

"Nothing special. I just noticed the clock was ticking extra slow, and their eyes were all weird, and then you seemed to be mad about something, banging the pots in the kitchen. But that might have been your real banging."

"No, no, we must consider all the clues. I was thought to be angry about it. And yet you and Michael were in favor of it. What about Sally?"

"She was all for it. Oh, wait, I forgot, it was like Dad had this agenda, wanting to do this so we could get the families all buddy-buddy, and Sally was saying it sounded like he was arranging a marriage."

"Ha!" she nearly leaps. "We do know Magic would love that, don't we?"

"Me and Michael?" I ask, utterly horrified at the thought just laid right out there.

"One of the boys, anyway," she says, shrugging.

"But when I told you Ana said I'd have to choose between them, you said that was nonsense."

"If I recall, and I do, I said it was poppycock. But that was about her going on about good and bad. I didn't say anything about the boys. Couldn't, not with Jake so close."

"What's wrong with Jake so close?"

Tidbits, please.

"Everything! He'd start fighting for you, tooth and nail, right now, if he knew the competition was on already."

"Is it?" I don't mention that I know nothing about a competition. She doesn't know what Ana's told me and vice versa. I'll take any advantage I can get.

I'm very *not* good that way.

"Most definitely! Michael is here, taking up all your time, wooing you."

Michael is not wooing me, but I'm not going to argue.

The more I talk, the less Bea will.

"Clearly, Magic is growing more interested in your future life with Michael. If you don't believe me, believe your own vision. Magic was matchmaking, no uncertainty there."

"I'm sixteen!" I finally explode. "What if I don't want to have a future life until like, way, way into the future?"

I mean, all I want is a boyfriend. Or even just a date once in a while. And anyway, I like Jake as much as I like Michael, maybe more. I can't throw him out because Magic has an agenda.

"You put a lot of restrictions on Magic," Bea argues.

"It's my *life!*" I say, standing, and realizing I'm still a little woozy.

"Not exactly. Not entirely. Not only yours, shall we say. You signed on the dotted line with Ana. You told me so."

"This is insane!" I yell, pivoting to find myself looking right smack dab at a sweaty, grass-stained, and nonetheless gorgeous Michael.

No. Not now. Please.

"What's insane this time?" he asks, half-laughing, making sure to keep his distance from his GranBea. The question sounds innocent enough, so I don't think he heard the thing about marriage.

Thank. Freaking. God.

"Ask her," I insist, knowing full well she won't speak to him directly, even if he does.

Bea looks at him blinking, innocent, like he's not even there, then turns back to me. "Magic wants us to figure out how to manage having everyone in this house at once. So we'll have a party, won't we Mayden?"

"Who's everyone?" he asks me, his eyes narrow.

"You, me and Jake. Plus Dad, Sally, Ana, Bea. Oh, yes, and Helene."

"Holy sh..." he starts, then looks at Bea and stops.

"Exactly," I say, satisfied that at least someone understands how impossible this is.

"But I can't even be near GranBea," he says directly to me. He's too good at playing all the games she requires even though you can tell he hates it. I keep wondering if that is something to like about him or not.

"Exactly," I say again.

"One thing you'll learn," Bea says, still directing her voice toward me, but extra loud so her meaning can be understood even across the room, "is that more often than not, Magic will turn things upside down to get what she wants. Our job is to take the message given, decipher the clues as best we can, feel down into our guts to know what is true and possible, be cautious to our own prejudices and wishful thinking, and then move forward with a plan."

Suddenly I'm wishing for Algebra, where even the missing elements of an equation make some kind of sense once you figure know all the rules.

Perhaps you can put your head together with Michael when you see him, and come back with such a plan. Tomorrow would be soon enough for me."

She looks at me fully satisfied, like she's laid it all out, and there's not a thing we can do to argue it.

I look to Michael with a *soooo?* question mark on my face.

"If you see her," he says direct to me, "you should tell GranBea I think a party with Helene and Ana is a great idea."

Seriously? But I guess I shouldn't be surprised. He liked the idea in the vision, too.

"Maybe you and I could talk about it over dinner, say, tomorrow night?" he asks me. "I'd go tonight, but I've got some thinking to do."

"Sure, she can go out on a date with you," Bea offers, for once directly to Michael, the glee ringing in her voice. I can almost see her brain firing up, imagining me walking down some hundred-years-old church aisle, meeting my Prince Michael at the end of it.

"Sure, great," I accept. "It will give me all day tomorrow to go through the very long list of questions I want to ask your GranBea."

Bea lets out a harrumph, but doesn't argue.

For once.

Chapter 23

"I have questions," I declare to Bea, far more of a demand than a request. I shove a handwritten list to her across the kitchen island. Now that I have more of a heads-up on what I'm getting into with the family, I want to know it all. My plan is to get her to answer each question in detail, and then take the exact same questions over to the Village and present them to Ana. From there, I'll compare answers, noting where the twins agree and where they don't. Any disparities in opinion, I'll mark as open for interpretation. Hopefully, the plan is sheer genius. Otherwise, I'll just be driving the crazy nails deeper into my skull.

"As I have mine," Bea replies.

Only she doesn't have a list, just this hard, serious look in her eyes.

Michael stands in the doorway, knowing full well what is on my list because I ran it by him at the guesthouse earlier this morning. He agreed all the items were worthy, but naturally was most interested in question #5: *Why won't the family teach Michael the ways of Magic before his eighteenth birthday, even when he is already learning on his own?* We both agree that it's way beyond time for him to be given a decent reason.

I want to be sure to get to that one at least, because I can see the whole teaching-once-removed thing is eating away at him. I could literally feel him wrestling with how he was going to handle it all last night. His frustration was so strong, it felt like it shot out a mile in every direction. I'm guessing there are now pace marks in the guesthouse carpet. I'm honestly afraid of whatever decisions he came to.

It doesn't feel good.

At. All.

In fact, it feels like the answer to question #5 might be needed to tip some internal scale he's weighing. He didn't say any of this to me directly, probably because he knew he didn't need to. We've gotten close enough to know we are on the same page most of the time. I'm not sure I'd go so far as to say we'll always have each other's backs, but it's certainly heading in that direction.

Bea reads, frowns, smiles, and then frowns again as she continues to pore over the list.

I dare a look at Michael. He's silently resigned, or resolved, or something. Who knows, maybe he's just exhausted.

I can tell when Bea gets to #5. Her expression freezes. "We'll get to these later," she says, firm and final. Her meaning is easy for me to translate: We'll talk only after Michael is gone.

I look back toward him just in time to see he has turned, lifting his backpack over his shoulder as he leaves. I mean, it's not like he can't translate just as well as me.

"You have to tell him something," I insist to Bea, as soon as he is clearly out of earshot. She turns away as if she can be truly deaf to any conversations she does not want to have.

"We'll start with my questions," she says, pulling out the saucepan, garlic, butter, and onions.

Sadly, I have no power in this. Bea calls the shots here, plain and simple. I guess in eighty-eight years she's earned the right to do things her way. Or maybe I'm just thankful she's giving up her life to teaching a total novice—probably not the easiest thing she's done in the last few decades.

The onions and butter start to fill the house with a stunning aroma. It's crazy how that one simple combination of food wakes up all your senses. It's seductive. It also makes my will more pliable. I'm beginning to think Bea does it on purpose.

I brace myself, willing my senses to ignore her to the best of my ability.

This butter cannot lull me. These onions will not sway me.

We have questions to get to, on both sides. Clear headed, I await her list. But she's taking her time, and now adding a ridiculous amount of paprika.

Not. Good.

I'm hoping she has easier questions than mine, but I'm not banking on it. Thus far, she's asked almost nothing about my life, my school, my family. All the basics that most anyone asks and I do my best not to answer. Today, I have a feeling I won't get away with it.

You have to wonder, is there such a thing as precognitive dread?

"Tell me about yourself, Mayden. Your life. Your school. Your family."

Sometimes I amaze myself. I really do.

"What's to tell?" I reply, intentionally casual, getting up to put away last night's dinner dishes. "I'm going to be a junior in high school. Dad is with Wife #4. Scottie is my best friend. I have a few other friends I don't see very often, but we are loyal to each other. Oh, yes, and I am potentially in line to be a Keeper of Magic for the Quinn Clann, a feminine tradition which goes back twelve hundred years."

I'm hoping the last line pulls us into another conversation. Or at least that it moves into her barking at me for my insolence. I'm not banking on it, but it's worth a shot. Anyway, if she wants me to go into detail about the other stuff, she'll have to probe.

"Tell me about wife number one," she probes.

Immediately my gut feels like it's been hit by a hard, flying baseball bat—fast and impossible to avoid. I want to form the words "you mean my mom?" in reply, just to confirm that is, in fact, what she means. But my throat is too tight. No words get through. My eyes also start to tear up.

The truth is, we don't talk about Mom in this house. We haven't in any of the houses that came after our home together, back when it was Mommy, Daddy, and me. We don't even admit to thinking about her here. She's the reverse of a ghost, a hole that takes up space in the house, yet with nothing in it.

"I know some of the story," Bea prods, as if that might make it easier. But how does she know? Who told her? Who could have told her? And if no one told her, that's more than creepy. That's over-the-top scary, at least for me. Because somewhere, Mom might be a real ghost, right? And if anyone would know about that stuff, the Quinn family would. "I'd like to hear it from you, though."

I feel pinned, a butterfly suddenly chloroformed and put on display.

I'm trying, I swear, but no words will come.

It's all stuck, the way it's been since I was little.

"You were four when she left," Bea begins for me, turning off the stove, taking the water glasses out of my hands and leading me, sitting us both on the stools at the island. It's the heart-to-heart I've never had with anyone but Aunt Mia, Mom's sister, and only then when we were safely tucked away in San Francisco, where no one else knows me. It feels wrong to talk about it here, not to mention with someone new.

But Bea's hand is now warmly electric: I can't seem to resist. My throat clears, too.

Oh, I get it. She is using Magic on me. Resistance is increasingly impossible.

But maybe I don't want to resist. Maybe it's time to talk about Mom, here in my own house, in my city.

Yeah, Bea is definitely using Magic. I would never, ever think that on my own.

"Mom was beautiful." These are words that I have never said aloud, even once. It's frightening to hear them come out of my own mouth.

"Yes," Bea coaxes me on. She seems to have honey in her voice. There's also a pulling sensation in her hands, like she's drawing it out of me. Despite myself, I go straight to the center of it all, ready to tell her everything, things even Mia doesn't know. My knees bang involuntarily against the island, like they might after a jolt in the electric chair.

"She said we'd have every four days together," I say, not so much talking as hearing myself talk. I sound young. Very young. "Every four days, just her and me. Daddy would get three days, then we would have four. The divorce didn't mean she wasn't my mommy. She would always be my mommy. She said that. I was only four, but I remember."

"Yes," my elderly magician coaxes, not letting go and not letting up.

I think I'm going to cry, or maybe I already am.

"I counted the days. One, two, three. Day four she was supposed to come. She was going to get me in the afternoon. I was packed. I was ready. But she wasn't coming. She was dying."

My own words shock me.

"She was dying," I repeat, just to hear it again.

"Tell me," she encourages, her voice like hot tea with honey.

"I only learned in bits and pieces what happened, almost all of it from Aunt Mia, and only when I got older." I hear myself sound older now. More like me. "I get one week each year with my aunt. I love our weeks because she looks like my mom did, so when I'm with her, it feels like my mom is a little bit alive again. I think that's why it's only one week. Dad doesn't like how I am when I come back."

I swear, I have never said any of these words out loud. Certainly never together all at once.

"What happened?"

"Mom was with a woman. I mean, *with* her. She left my dad for her. Her name was Genevieve. Mia said Mom really loved her, and that Genevieve really loved Mom. She was married, though, too. I don't know if they were divorcing, like Mom and Dad, but her husband found them."

Here it comes. Here it comes.

"He shot them. Both of them. It was on Day Four. Day Four was the day she died. In the morning. While I was packing to go see her."

"Yes," Bea says, her hands sending Magic that is steady, even, and sure.

My tears are spilling over now, but mixed in with the pain is a sense of gratitude for the listening, and whatever it is that is flowing through our hands.

It's the same thing that she used to cure Scottie, I bet.

I don't want her to say anything. Definitely not to try to make it better. But I do want her to know it all. It feels right, like this has to happen if I'm going to move from my family to hers. "Dad got full custody, but there was a court case because Mom came from a lot of money, and somehow, even though she died after they were separated, Dad was set up to get a big hunk of it. Aunt Mia told Dad she wouldn't fight him over it, so long as I got to spend one week every year with her."

I shrug, trying not to show my bitterness. But it's there, along with a dark, musty, metallic taste in my mouth. What I don't say—what I still can't say out loud—is that from where I stand, Dad sold me at the price of one week a year in exchange for spending Mom's money on idiots like Sally. It's probably not the whole story, but even if it's not, I blame him for not talking about it. For not explaining it all. For not helping me make sense of the most senseless thing in my life. That's what you're supposed to do as a parent, right? You're not supposed to pretend it never happened.

Bea allows me to sit here, lost in my thoughts, but it's not awkward. It's sort of nice.

I don't know how long it is before she lets go of my hands, but when she does, the Magic wanes. When it's gone, I feel oddly clear, as if a big wind just blew through my body, opening it up and clearing it out.

"You'll use this pain in your Magic," Bea assures me. "We all do. Which leads me to the next question on my list."

I try to shake my brain free of everything it is thinking. But for sure I'll return to it. It will be different now, having said so much out loud.

Better, I hope.

"It's a big question," she warns, "but one you'll have to answer sooner than you think. Best to try it out on me first."

"Okay," I say, standing to get back to the dishes. Whatever Bea cleared in me, it worked on my whole body. I feel light. Like life is easier. Not easy, but easier. Which is a lot.

"What will you do with the Magic you are given," she asks, sounding almost formal, "should you succeed in becoming the Keeper of Magic for the Quinn Clann?"

Seriously? I think my head just might explode.

I hardly know how to jump from the conversation about Mom to any other topic, but this one is particularly impossible. How could I possibly know what I'll do with Magic? I don't even know what it does. Or what it's for.

"How do I know? I'm sixteen." *And kinda new at this,* I do not add.

"Sixteen is plenty old to know what you care about. As the Keeper of Magic, you'll have a power unlike any you have seen or imagined. If it is to be yours, it must be yours for a reason. Magic will insist that you have a plan, an idea at least. That's what you'll need to present as you make your formal challenge, or you will never be confirmed."

Formal challenge? Confirmed? She makes it sound like I'm going to need a platform to run on for Student Council. "I don't know. Why do I need to know now, anyway?"

"Because it will inform the direction the Magic will take. And because what you offer the world during your time as Keeper matters to the entire Clann. Your intention is part of the decision that will be used to help you win the role as Keeper...or to block your way. We know it is a reality that you could change your direction once you win the role, as Helene surely did. But it is our duty to know and weigh your heart to the best of our ability."

The whole idea lands both hard and with a shock, like a meteor from outer space suddenly appeared in the backyard. Pretty much all my life I thought I would be a follower. Not a leader, someone who decides and directs. But Ana said much the same when she told me about the potential for the Clann dying. If I am to lead, I guess it's only natural that they would want to know what direction I'll take it in.

"What you create with Magic will naturally be different from what anyone else would," she continues, sounding more like Ana every second. "It's essential that you understand that and consider carefully what your time as Keeper will accomplish. This will also inform us all about who will be your best helpmeet." She turns to crank up the stove flames, and I notice they seem to match the rising burn in my face.

Helpmeet again? I mean, what kind of outdated thinking is that? Now they're thinking Michael or Jake is supposed to help me as Keeper of Magic, too? And what is this *us all* business? Am I going to choose a boyfriend by committee, and only then after Magic has a say?

Bea goes about her cooking, no doubt intentionally leaving me to think about what she's just said. Despite myself, despite that it's just wrong to think of Jake and Michael this way, I think of Jake and Michael this way.

Jake first. He's like Bea—real and only simple on the surface. Raw and powerful. And a protector, he said. I don't have any idea how it all works, but my guess is any Keeper of Magic could use that. But then there's Michael. He knows his way in the world. He can play the games, like with Dad's Navy buddies. That's the stuff I would have zero patience for, so again, I could see it as hugely helpful.

My thoughts land the only place they can: As Keeper of Magic, should I get the job, I would totally, completely, and absolutely need them both.

Chapter 24

"Thanks for coming," Michael says to me from across the restaurant table, sounding way too formal. We're not at North Waters, which could be good. Or bad. "I wanted to talk to you alone."

Immediately, my gut takes a dive.

I didn't expect that this was for fun, but now it feels like serious business. I honestly don't have any idea what it is he's going to say next. I only know that, all day, I had a feeling I wasn't going to like it.

In fact, that I'm going to hate it.

It's good we are at the farthest corner table, out of earshot of anyone here unless a waiter comes over, which none have so far. Maybe he doesn't want anyone to see me make a big fuss. Not that I'm the type to, but still. Already I feel tears starting to form behind my eyes, which is just so ridiculous. I have to tell Bea that whatever she did with my heart in the kitchen, she needs to undo it. I was a wreck over every little thing today.

"You're leaving early," I blurt out, having no idea where it came from. Just one of those things I know the second that I know it, and there it is, coming out of my mouth.

Michael nods. "Right after the party. I'm wasting my time with this family."

Wasting his time? How can he say that? How can he even think it?

"What? Why?" The word breaks up as it comes out of my choked throat. I can't help it. The tears start dripping, one after the other, in tiny plops from my cheek. I blink and blink, but they just won't stop. Of all the things he could have said, this is the last thing I saw coming.

But then, maybe I just didn't want to see.

"They won't teach me," he says, reaching out to hold my hand. If he thinks this will make me feel better, he's flat out mistaken. I can feel what I'll be missing. Him.

They are doing what they can, I want to say.

"I'm getting only a fraction of what they're teaching you. That is not enough."

I notice there is no bitterness in his voice, not even anger. Just sadness. This has been killing him, for sure. I mean, I knew that. But I didn't think it would come to anything like this.

I look at his hand as he holds mine. Why is he holding it, just to let go? Is it me? Could I have done something better? Showed him more? Explained more clearly?

"I need to go where I will be taught directly, even if it's through a different tradition."

Little teardrops keep falling, wetting my starched white napkin.

Why? Why does it mean so much to me to have him here? To have him learning alongside me? He doesn't have to marry me. He doesn't even have to like me.

"Haven't I helped?" I manage.

"You have. But I deserve better than secondhand. There's hardly any real power coming through. You know that as well as I do. It's like reading a book to learn the living art of Magic. I need more. I need to be practicing. I need a teacher."

"Give them some time," I beg.

"I can't. I won't. I've found someone who is willing to teach me right now. Up in Maine, at least until I head back to Europe for school. If Helene tries to stop me, I'll hide out and not go back to school at all. I've stashed away enough money to live for a decade on my own. And I promise you, I know how to hide. I've been practicing that for years."

He's going. I can hear it, but I can also feel it. I also feel that he'll be gone a long time.

Damn this knowing. Damn. Damn. *Damn.*

"Who is he? Your new teacher?" Somehow I know he's a he. That feels like it could be a problem, too. We are, after all, a feminine tradition.

Well, not *we.* But more we than *not we.*

"He's a shaman. Native born and raised. He takes just a few students every year. Someone told me about him, and I got in contact. He said he knew about me before I called, that he heard it from the Spirit world. He knew things about me that he couldn't have known."

I recall Ana telling me about the chandelier and all the different facets of Magic. But it doesn't seem right that Michael should leave the family and learn another way. I look up at him, my heart physically hurting as it bangs against the walls of my chest. I keep looking around for some sign this isn't real, that I'm in a vision, that this is Magic's cruel joke. But there is no slowly ticking clock. In fact, if I had to bet on it, I'd bet Magic is not pleased about this either. All I can do is look at Michael and try not to let out a huge, heaving sob.

"Say something," he pleads, as if it matters to him what I think.

"What will you tell Bea?"

"I don't know. If the shaman has real powers—and trust me, I'm not accepting that he does until he proves it—and he really has seen me coming, then she probably already knows about it, at least on some level. I've learned to hide myself from Helene, but GranBea's trickier."

"How can you do this?" I burst out. All at once, I feel the betrayal, the way I imagine Bea and Ana will. Jake, too, for that matter. "How can you just leave your tradition, your family, your Clann, when they're doing their best to keep the line alive? The Magic of the Clann is threatened, Michael, and now you're making it even more risky."

"They don't need me to keep the line going." This time, bitterness creeps into his voice. "They have you. And Jake. You can only marry one person."

"What if I don't want Jake?" I ask, even though at this moment, I am aware that I'm lying. Crazy-making, this knowing things. Now that I do, for sure, I shouldn't lead Michael on. But I have to try everything I can.

"I saw him last night," Michael admits. "I felt for him, and contacted him from across the water. I know I'm not supposed to, but I had to risk it."

"What did he say?"

"I can tell you this: He's nuts for you. I'm sure the two of you together is lifetimes old, just like I'm sure he fell in love the minute he saw you. So did I, in my own way."

There is no protecting my heart now. It feels like it's being crushed, like it's being thrown in a huge trash truck and someone has turned on the smasher.

It hasn't hurt anything close to this bad since Mom.

"Then how can you leave?" I beg to know.

He can't go. He just can't. Not to go to some stranger to teach him ways that are not our ways. Why is he doing this to all of us? To me?

"Here's how it will go if I stay: Jake will fight for you, and he will win, and the two of you will get together, as you should. There will be no place of leadership for me in the family, even when I turn eighteen."

"This is crazy," I say, finally removing my hand. "We don't even know what is going on. We don't know what love has to do with this.

Or choosing you or Jake, or any of that."

"Seems you know something about it."

"Well, they told me some stuff, but how do we *know*? Why can't we all just learn together? And leave all the relationship stuff for some other time? It's all happening too fast."

"Sometimes you just know, right?" he asks, challenging me to be honest with him.

"But things change all the time, so how can you know for sure? For today *and* tomorrow? Maybe you are the one for me and I just don't know it yet. Because I think, I mean, I might have fallen in love with you, too."

As my brother, my friend, even my soul mate, if there is such a thing as a soul mate of a different kind.

Michael sighs, stands, and comes around to me, taking both of my hands so that I stand with him. Just like that, as if we were alone and not in a public restaurant, he pulls me close to him. So close I can feel the warmth of his chest. He leans in, almost kissing me.

A part of me is thinking, this is it: This will be the first time I've been kissed for real. My face is wet with tears, and people are probably looking. But those things don't matter. That's not why another part of me is saying *no, no, this is not right.*

"You love me?" he asks.

I nod, honest.

"But you do not *love* me," he says, as if he knows.

I look into his eyes and nod again, slow but definitive.

"Trust me," he whispers, "Jake is the one for you."

Without warning, and without a kiss, he releases me and guides me back to sit in my chair.

"I'm sorry," I say, feeling gutted for him, "Maybe you can't choose who you love like that."

"Don't worry. I know all about that." He gives me a small, sad smile. Maybe the saddest I have ever seen on a guy.

"How? Do you love someone?" That, at least, would be some relief.

"It's different for me."

"How?" I press.

He looks directly into me, but I feel his hesitance. He seems to be weighing what he will or won't say next. It takes him forever.

"I'm gay," he finally says.

Two words, clear as a bell.

Shivers. Chills. *Truth.*

How did I not see that?

Or did I, and I was just too caught up in my own boyfriend saga to see it?

Because now it makes total sense. Now it seems utterly clear. Now I get it.

"So you see how there is no place for me in our Clann? Not with a feminine tradition. Jake laid it all out for me last night. Patriarchy or matriarchy, makes no difference for me. Marriage and magical offspring are requirements I will never meet."

He takes a deep breath.

I realize I'm holding mine.

"So now you'll go with Jake and perpetuate the family line, and I will wish you well with that. Because I love you, too. But because there is no place for a gay man, I'll leave. I need my own Clann, one where I can be true to myself and who I am."

"But there has to be a place for you! You're a Quinn! No one will care about you being gay. They'll be glad for you. It makes it easier. Don't you see?"

"They will care," he says, resolute. "You can see how hard they're fighting for the matriarchy to continue. They come from another time. So I'm going to learn Magic where they will teach me just because I am me. The natives have long honored the two-spirits, the gays and lesbians, the transgender. That's my kind of Clann."

I don't know what to say. I've never thought of it that way. I never thought of any of this. "How did I miss this with you? I feel like an idiot."

"Don't worry about it. I told you, I'm good at hiding. It's funny, though," he says, sounding like there's a rock in his throat, "all these years Helene has worked so hard to make sure I'm the one to carry on her legacy, and she never once considered this possibility. I knew I liked boys when I was six years old. She could have seen it if she wanted to, but she didn't even think to look."

It's just too much to take in.

I should say something, but I can't.

I hate it, but he's right. Completely.

"Okay," he says, shifting to a firm, almost business-like voice, "so I'm here till after the party. I'll play along with whatever you cook up, but then I'm gone. I have to ask you not to out me. Please. I don't want them to think I'm leaving because I'm ashamed of who I am. Because I'm not."

"You shouldn't be. And, absolutly, I won't say anything."

"Hope you don't mind, I'm going to skip dinner. I'm not very hungry anymore. Besides, it looks like someone is waiting to talk to you."

"Wait, you're going? Now? You and I have to…"

"I'll send her in," he interrupts, leaving me. Leaving us.

I want to say something, anything, to make this better. To get him to change his mind about leaving. Something that could make this work for him. For all of us.

But nothing comes.

Nothing at all.

Chapter 25

I'm stunned, unable to comprehend what just happened. Things are going so fast. Too fast. I want to turn and look at who could have found me here—no one but Bea knew where Michael and I were going tonight—but my face is a wreck.

I wonder if I'll ever stop crying, now that the bottle's been uncorked.

"Do you mind if I sit?" I hear a voice from behind me say. It's a woman's voice. Strange, smooth, with a slight hiss. She comes around the table to within my view even before I can turn. She's lightning quick and agile like Bea.

Definitely has Magic.

I nod and examine her as she sits. Her hair is black, her small eyes dark with a tint of red in them. Strangest eyes I've ever seen, but she feels okay. In fact, her presence is comforting for reasons I cannot explain.

I'm trying to ask who she is, but the words just won't come. It's like my voice has an on/off switch lately, and I can't always access it.

"You look like that was no fun," she says sympathetically.

I nod again, taking my already wet napkin to my face. She hands me hers, which was Michael's, and I start to cry even more. I try not to think about the fact that he just left me here and will leave us all soon.

Pretty much impossible.

"I'm sure you are wondering who I am," she says, smiling through the thinnest lips, "and why I have joined you."

I look around, listen for a clock ticking at half time, or a vision of Ana the next table over. Everything feels weird, but it's a different weird than when Magic comes and changes things.

This time, I realize it's her. She's what's weird.

As in extra weird, even for the family.

"I should introduce myself, then, though we have already met."

"We have?" I finally squeeze out.

"At Bea's house, in the woods." I wrack my brain for anyone besides Jake and Bea, but the three of us were alone.

"So this," she laughs, sounding a bit nervous, "is the part that is going to be hard to accept."

Despite my misery, I have to laugh. Exactly how much insanity do they all expect me to live with?

"I'm Python."

If that is supposed to mean something, it doesn't register.

"I was on the porch when we met. Bea nearly ran me over with her rocking chair, and you were kind enough to ask her to watch out."

It takes a moment to compute. This woman is Python, as in the snake on Bea's porch.

"You're a shapeshifter."

Incredible. Impossible. Amazing.

"I am."

"And you shapeshift into a snake?"

I could see it. Really, I could. Even so...

"Not exactly, but close enough."

"No, not close enough," I say, surprising myself with my sharp tone. "Not today. Today, I need *exactly*."

"Sure," she says, upbeat and friendly, not at all like a snake. "You know how Bea and Jake shapeshift into an animal every so often?"

"Theoretically," I confirm.

"Well, I go the other way. I'm a snake, and I shapeshift into a person every so often."

"Am I on some bizarre reality TV show and nobody told me?"

"Very similar, but different. More real than reality, if you know what I mean."

"Oh, sure. I know just what you mean."

Not. A. Clue.

Looking into those tiny snake eyes, I begin to feel the parts of me that have broken off with Michael's news start to return. "Why are you here?"

"While I am not officially of the Quinn Clann, I am an honorary member, and I've been brought on as one of your teachers. I teach change."

"Change? As in actual *lessons*?"

She nods vigorously, though it's kind of wavy and not just up and down, so that it makes you a little nauseated if you watch too long. "We snakes are the champions of change. We shed our skin and start over many times in one life. We also know what it is to feel raw and move forward anyway. Much as you are feeling these days, hmm?"

"Much," I spit. She doesn't deserve my sarcasm, but I'm up to my eyeballs in change. If she's bringing more, she needs to take a number.

"I understand. It's very difficult with all you've been through. But things are going to go even faster very soon. Much faster than you think. With Michael leaving, we have to get on with your education as quickly as possible."

"You know about that? Does that mean Bea knows, too?"

"She knows. He's been in touch with another magician. That doesn't go without notice in a family of Magic."

"I thought his new teacher was a shaman."

"Same difference, for our purposes."

I wonder if she knows the biggest reason he's going, but quickly turn my mind from it, just in case she doesn't. I'm not going to out him, intentionally or otherwise. Not a chance.

"I find it hard to imagine things going faster," I admit.

"I understand, but it will. Soon. You'll need my help, so, here I am."

I'd walk into her metaphorically open arms, but it takes me just a little longer to warm up, especially to a snake.

"I have no choice about the speed?" I ask, on the off chance the Great Chandelier wants to give me even a tiny bit of a break.

"Not really."

I sigh. "What can you help me with?"

"Adjusting, for one thing."

God, I feel I have to pull every bit of information out of her. "*To…?*"

"Everything. Who you are. Why you were chosen. Jake."

"Jake?"

"It's no easy thing, loving a shapeshifter."

"I never said I loved him," I immediately defend. "And by the way, just because this all works out for the family—Michael leaving so Jake is the clear choice—I'm not so sure I'm on board with all of it. The whole masculine/feminine line thing, it's rather outdated, isn't it?"

I work very, very hard not to think about Michael, and, in fact, think of everything else I can. My last day of geometry class, if Rod will be okay, three kinds of butter, how the hole in the back screen door will soon be big enough for Scottie to crawl out of.

"But the Quinn Clann is a feminine line," she argues. "It's who you are. It's who you have always been."

"But you said you teach change. What if it's time to change?"

"Well, yes, but not like that. We don't need to worry about any of that now. If you do not love Jake, there's time. Children will not be expected right away."

"Children?" I nearly yell. "How fast, exactly, does this have to move?"

Because, you know, I am just not going there. Just. Not.

Not. Not. Not.

"Oh, no, nothing like that! You've still got your confirmation qualifying, then if you succeed, your full training, which could go quickly, or take up to a full year. In that time, Jake will have to prove himself to you. To all of us. No, no, there is plenty of time before children."

This woman is offering me more details than Bea or Ana has in a week, so let's skip the kids thing and get some real information. "Full training?"

"Yes, yes, then the Grand Challenge, the outcome of which there is no way to predict, so all this could be moot."

"Bea never said anything about a Grand Challenge."

"Oh, I see. Well, then," she backtracks, "perhaps we should let her explain it, when the time is right."

"I would love it if you would explain it right now."

"We should go now," Python suggests.

"Where?" I sigh, though I hear my voice trailing off, like I'm not really here.

At least not all of me.

It's Magic this time. I'm sure of it.

Only this time, instead of other things changing around me, I'm the one changing. Floating off in a thousand bits and pieces, my whole body coming apart.

"Very good, Mayden! A powerful start," I hear Python say, a hollow echo to her voice.

"What's happening?" I ask, my own voice airy and thin. Thinner than a snake's skin.

"Don't worry, no one will notice," she says.

I look out toward the others in the restaurant. I hadn't even considered worrying about what this must look like, but it doesn't matter anyway. There is no one to see. In fact, there is no restaurant to see. There's nothing to see.

Nothing.

"Think of this as the in-between place," she echoes. "Yes, yes, you're getting it. They told me you would be quick."

I begin to look around, in and through the darkness, trying to see my hands, or feet, or anything.

"Don't bother trying to look at yourself here," she instructs.

"Why not?"

"Because it can be frightening."

"Why?" I don't feel frightened at all. I feel wonderful. Light. Like there are no troubles, could be no troubles, not in the whole wide world.

"It's not until it hits you," she warns.

"What hits me?" I sound far off, even to myself.

"That you are nowhere."

Her meaning comes clearer and clearer until I realize just how true this is.

I'm nowhere.

Absolutely *nowhere.*

It is quickly terrifying, like when the bottom drops out from under you on those super-high rides at the amusement park.

"Yes, yes, that is exactly it. You are doing wonderful. You are almost as good as dead, now."

Like that's supposed to help? I think, then lose the thought.

Lose everything.

Everything.

Chapter 26

If you ever have the chance to be nowhere, I highly recommend it.

Yes, it's frightening at first. Terrifying, for a moment there. But then you adjust, and it's like nothing you have ever known. Like being up with the stars on the darkest night, when they're just popping, only you don't see them, you feel them. And you can move like you have no weight at all. A tiny tap of your not-there toe and you reel in feather-light somersaults. You don't think about how heavy you are when you're in a body, being somewhere. But in comparison, it's crazy how much we lug around every day.

Time is different, too. It doesn't matter. Not like you forgot your watch, but like you can't imagine why anyone would ever wear one in the first place. I understand now why the clock slowed when Magic came calling. Why keep track of time in the first place? We are timeless. Like the weight of our body, dealing with time just makes everything harder. This, then that, then that, and then yesterday, and the day before. It's all so much to keep track of when you think about it. These are burdens that don't exist outside of time.

Perhaps best of all, you don't worry. Not about anything. What can hurt you if you're nothing? *Almost as good as dead,* Python said, and she was right. Everything that can hurt you has floated off. Once the dying is done, you're golden.

Yes, that's it. Exactly. You're golden. Like those tiny flakes they put on statues to gild them. Light, airy gold.

How wonderful it feels to float and float and then float more.

Only, then it ended. I guess it had to.

Python warned me, from somewhere in the darkness, that it might be hard to come back. She said not to be alarmed if I was sad, given a lot of shapeshifters get a little depressed after their first experience out.

I suppose it's because you see how good things are when you're not in your body. But she said any problems with reentry simply had to be endured because, with shapeshifting, you have to go through the nothing phase to turn into something else.

I heard every word she said. But honestly? I didn't care.

It was said in nothingness. Even words are weightless there.

Then I came back, more suddenly than I left. Not to the restaurant, though. To my own bed, some thirteen hours later, according to the clock on my phone. Scottie was here waiting and only a little surprised at my sudden arrival.

A little depressing was a total understatement. I must have cried for an hour. Over Rod's parents' divorce. Over Michael leaving. Over Ana saying it might be the end of the line for the Quinn Clann. Over evil people like Helene.

Over humanity as a whole, really.

Now I look out my bedroom window at the summer rain pelting the flowers and wonder about this world. Why is it so heavy, anyway?

"I love you, you know that, right?" I ask Scottie, pulling her close. She only nuzzles and purrs, but it helps.

"Julie?" Dad calls from the other side of my bedroom door.

Talk about heavy. "Yeah," I reply, though I'd rather not.

If I can't be nowhere, can I at least be not here?

"Can I come in?" His voice is all happy, only not the authentic kind.

Ugh. We are in for a talk. A human talk. A heavy human talk. I hear his hand jiggling on the door handle. Really, there's no stopping him.

"Sure."

He lets himself in. Golfing clothes? Not a good sign. He only goes golfing on workdays when something is wrong. Add to it that it's raining again, and things must be bad.

"Can we talk?" he asks, coming over to sit next to me. I scoot over to make room. He reaches for my hair and pushes it out of my eyes like he did when I was little.

Another bad sign. I don't know how I know, but I know…this is not going to be good.

"What's wrong?"

"Nothing's wrong," he replies, over-frowning. "I was just wondering how you are."

"I'm fine." I mean, it's not like I'm going to tell him I've been out exploring nothingness and returning to somethingness just plain sucks.

"That's good." He's inspecting his fingernails, then the ruffle on my pillow.

"Whatever it is, Dad, just say it."

"You're right. There is something. It's Sally and me."

Didn't I see this one coming? Didn't I?

"We're thinking of a trial separation."

"No," I say, pulling Scottie even closer. You can't tilt all my worlds in one summer. It's just not survivable.

"I thought you didn't like her." He looks truly surprised.

"I don't. But I'm not going to like the next one you bring home, either."

"It's not been that bad. Has it?"

"Yes, it has. But that's not the point." I feel strangely free to speak my mind. Maybe it was the freedom of nothingness, or the impact of Michael leaving, or one of the ten thousand other things I've faced lately.

Whatever it is, I have an incredibly low tolerance for bullshit right now.

"What is the point?" He asks it like he's the kid and I'm the adult. Like I know how things are and what he should do. It's an unfair, even cruel, thing to do to your kid—making them the adult. But, it is what it is. If he needs to hear it from someone, and I'm the one here, then so be it.

"You can't collect wives, Dad," I say, sitting up straight. "You're getting too old for that. You have to think of more than, I don't know, whatever it is you think of when you make life decisions that are totally unstable."

Man, I am missing weightlessness.

"It's more complicated than that," he argues, though there is no conviction in his voice. I think he really does want someone to tell him what to do when it comes to things like this. I wonder if my mom did that before she fell in love with a woman and asked for a divorce.

"Is it?" I mentally start considering how Magic could help me. Or Dad, rather. I mean, haven't I been practicing for something just like this? Like when I don't know what to say or do, but something needs to be said and done?

No angels start singing, but I do think of something to say. Or rather, I just start saying it and hear myself talking. "Remember how you wouldn't let me quit tennis lessons last year? How you made me practice, even though I said I hated it? You said I wouldn't know if I liked it or not if I didn't get past the hard parts. That you don't know if you like something until you get good at it? Do you remember that?"

"Marriage isn't a sport, Julie."

"Exactly. It's way, way more serious. It's a relationship. A commitment. And you're not good at it. You quit all the time, probably right when you get to the hard parts. So maybe you haven't gone past the hard parts to find what enduring love is. I hear that is why people get married. You know. For love. For long term. Not for sport."

Dad looks at me like he knows I'm right, but also like he's tired. No, not tired. Weary.

Welcome to the club.

"Good advice. I'll think about it."

"I hope so," I say, meaning it.

"How are you doing, anyway?" he asks, which pretty much floors me. I guess it shouldn't. When he's up, he assumes everyone is and goes his merry way. But when he's down, he assumes we all are, too. Or maybe he'd just like to feel needed today.

"I want a party," I blurt out. At least, it was my voice that spoke it. I don't recall any advance thought.

"For your birthday?" he asks, looking confused because that's several months away.

"No, for Michael," I say. Whew, yes, once again my own voice and thoughts. "Well, really for his grandmother."

"Helene?"

"It's her birthday at the end of this week, and he'd like to surprise her. I'll do all the work to get it ready. Maybe we could even have her mom come. I take her out all the time now, and it would be such a great surprise."

I force myself to wait. To not add things like how he could likely network if he invited all his contacts and stuff like that. Convincing him to do something he doesn't want to never works. I can only hope the initial idea has enough merit to carry it through.

Dad ponders, then nods. "Okay. Can you get Finola to help you handle the food details? I'll ask the grounds staff to tidy up the lawn. How many people do you think?"

"Everyone you can think of," I suggest. I mean, the more diffuse, the better, right?

"I can think of a lot," he says in warning.

"Fifty? A hundred?"

"I could get a hundred here pretty easily. If Sally makes the list, two hundred."

"A hundred would probably be good." Diffuse is one thing. Drowning is another.

"I'll tell Finola. And Michael. Thanks, Dad."

He gets up to leave, then turns back. "You've never even met

Helene, have you?"

"No, but I'm sure she's nice."

"Helene? Nice? As a grandmother, maybe." He doesn't say it, but I'm guessing that nice isn't the word he'd have come up with. "So does this mean you like Michael?" There's a kind of lilt in his voice and one eyebrow raised.

"Not *like* like, but yeah, I like him." It's a sad, huge understatement, but anything more would be too hard to explain.

"But not *like* like?" he seeks to confirm.

"More like a brother," I say, which for some crazy reason makes me think of Jake and how I don't only think of him as a brother.

So easily distracted. So very, very easily, Julie Mayden.

"It's going to happen someday, though, isn't it? You're going to find a guy you do like and then leave home, and all this parenting stuff will be over."

"More likely college will be your first real rival," I try to assure.

"Even so, you'll be gone. Who will keep me from making the big mistakes?"

"We can only hope that by then you'll have grown up enough to do that yourself," I say, smirking.

"You've turned into a pretty cool kid, you know that? Something very magical about you."

Blow me away. There is no way he knows the compliment he just gave me. It feels good. Especially from him. Which must mean something, even if I don't know exactly what.

"Go play golf in the rain," I insist. "You'll feel better."

He leaves, shutting the door behind him.

Snake. On the back of the door.

Somehow, I immediately get that it's Python. "What are you doing here? And how did you get in?"

Python doesn't say anything, being a snake, but Scottie is instantly going hissy-nuts. I grab her just as Python slithers down to the door handle, then drops to the floor. Poor Scottie is totally freaking, clawing and spitting, and pulling to get at her.

I move to open my sliding glass door, put Scottie out into her covered kitty house, then turn back to see Python, the woman, standing next to my bed.

"How are you getting along?" she asks, like nothing odd just happened.

I have to admit, I'm almost used to all this.

Almost.

Her question is not a casual hello. She's checking in on me after coming back to the hell of somethingness from the pure joy of nothingness. "It's hard, like you said."

"Nothing is really something, isn't it?"

With just those words, I'm suddenly remembering nothingness full force, like a hit to my lungs, so beautiful it's hard to breathe.

"You did good. Excellent in fact, especially for your first time!"

"I did?" I mean really, how would I know?

Python laughs a thin laugh, moving to lean on the edge of my desk, or more like curl up at the edge of it. Strange body shapes this woman gets into. Either she's great at yoga or well on her way to severe osteoporosis.

Or she's a snake.

Because that's totally possible.

Sigh.

"You got there, and you got back, both on your own, and on your first try. That is extraordinary!"

I wonder about the alternative, but don't ask. "I don't know if I could do it again, though. I mean, if I tried."

"It's a bit like getting a running start at first. Think of it like a storm that is coming. You ask for it, then feel it coming, and then you just put yourself in the way of the wind instead of taking cover. The more you do it, the easier it gets. And sometimes it just comes for you. I can feel it coming on half a day ahead of the shift, sometimes. My skin crawls."

"Sounds uncomfortable," I say, resisting the urge to ask if a snake's skin doesn't always crawl. Also wondering if you really can ask for a storm, or if it was just a metaphor.

"A little. But also exciting, don't you think?"

"Seriously exciting," I say, grinning. Magic is like a hellacious roller coaster ride. It makes you want to puke, yet the moment the ride is done, you're immediately ready to stand in line to go again.

"May I ask you something?" Python asks. "Do you want all of this? Magic, that is."

She doesn't ask it in a challenging way, it's just a question. Still, it makes me nervous. I don't know her yet. Not like I know Ana and Bea. "It's a lot to get used to. A lot to learn. And I don't know what to think about the shapeshifting part. I mean, really, who would? And what good is it, other than that you can hang from a door if you're a snake? Which, granted, is pretty awesome."

"You're right. Doing all this just for fun would be preposterous. It is too hard a path, too high a price to pay. You do it because it is who you are. Because not doing it is painful. It would be limiting yourself when you know there is more. For those of us who are called, ignoring the path would feel like you missed the whole point of your life."

The price to pay. I'm still wondering on that. But missing the whole point of your life hits home big time. "Ana's said things like that. She puts it in different ways, and everyone keeps asking if I'm up for it, even though I keep saying I am. It's like she has to keep making sure I'm totally in. But I am. Every day, I'm more and more in. It's like it comes from a part of me I don't know yet, but I want to know. *Have* to know."

"You've said it perfectly," she agrees. "And here is a secret for you. The part of you that will understand someday is the part that is making the choices for you now, even before you realize it. It probably doesn't make sense to you yet, but I assure you, someday it will."

She's right about that. But I feel her words are true, even if they don't make sense. Like I can see the future, and it's just waiting for me to catch up so I can understand what I'm seeing.

"It will be good in the end, though, right? Not just crazy-making forever?"

"Oh yes, yes indeed! More than good. If you are meant for it, it will be wonderful."

"Nothingness was amazing. That's for sure."

"Just wait until it shifts past nothing and takes you on to something again," she offers with a kind of snake hiss that would be ultra creepy if it wasn't totally fantastic.

"I can't wait," I admit, because I really, *really* can't.

Chapter 27

"This is impossible!" I nearly scream at Bea, handing her the stuck jar of artichoke hearts like everything—every single last thing on earth—is her fault.

She takes it, opening it easily. "Use your belly fire next time."

"To open a jar?" I ask, rolling my eyes. That's pushing it, I know. But it's a pushing-it kind of day.

"To do anything," she replies, not fed up just yet. Maybe she even understands. "That's where your energy gets stored. Call on it and send it to your hands. Easy."

Easy. Easy. Everything for them is so *easy!*

"That's not what's bothering you."

"You're right." I slop the artichoke hearts into the iron skillet. They sizzle and spit, like I want to. "It's the hundred people coming. Like I know how to throw a party for a hundred people. The last party I had anything to do with was a laser tag adventure for a dozen kids, and all I had to do was show up and let them sing me happy frigging tenth birthday." (For the record, I hated it.)

I turn up the heat, feeling her watching me, knowing I'm doing it wrong.

"That'll burn," she warns me, but not too strongly, like if I want to burn my magical creations, why should she care? Same thing with the party. If we fail, no big deal. And if Helene hates the living guts out of me for throwing it and reminding her she's one year closer to death?

Oh. Well.

I turn the knob down twenty percent, but only because she's right. I'm getting reasonably good at the underlying principles behind most frying, sautéing, broiling, and baking. Still, as Bea is fond of saying, when you're working in the realm of Magic, your mood risks everything.

"Did you call about the tables?" she badgers.

"Yes. And the silverware and the punch bowl, and the delivery of everything, and the invitations, and the hired help, and…"

"All I asked about were the tables." She sounds like she's starting to get annoyed. Which is good, because I'm up for a fight. And bad, because if we get into one, I will lose so fast you wouldn't even know there was a contest. I'm sure of that. Just like I'm sure Helene is going to have my head on a platter if I do even the tiniest little thing wrong. Probably even if I don't.

"Sorry," I mumble, the same way I did this morning at breakfast with Dad and Sally. I wasn't any more sorry then than I am now, and with them it got even worse, because it led to Sally attempting to jack us all up with that hyped-up happiness guru crap. She asked me what I wanted in life so she could visualize it with me.

I think it's her way of saying she appreciates my talk with Dad. He's all into her again, which might have had something to do with my request for help from Magic. Or not. Anyway, I couldn't tell her what I really want, which is to figure out what I'm supposed to tell Ana and Bea and the whole Clann about what I'll do if and when I become Keeper of Magic.

I said I didn't know, but Sally pushed, so I tried to think.

I could have answered what I would have said a month ago, or even three weeks ago: A boyfriend. But I'm afraid to want that right now. Or, I could have said I want Ana out of that hellhole Dad calls a nursing home without staging a totally insane party where no one is going to be happily surprised. Or, I could have said I want Michael to stay here and be my best friend and brother forever. Or, I could have said I want to know why everyone is so morbidly afraid of the dark and scary Helene Quinn—even me, who has never met her—and what in heaven's name I'm going to do when everyone who has been hiding out for years gets together under the gazebo in my own backyard. Or, I could have said that I want to shapeshift into something wild, even if it takes me five thousand years to learn how. Or, last but certainly not least, I could have told her that I want to be a member of Bea and Ana's Clann more than I want to breathe.

Naturally, I didn't say any of that. Instead, I offered a thoroughly sarcastic *breakfast in peace?*

Hence, the *sorry*, which was forced upon me by Dad.

Suffice to say, they were not amused.

"Apology accepted," Bea says in a way that makes me think she actually *is* amused. Maybe she knows how unlikely an apology from a teen is, or maybe she just appreciates the humble pie it takes to offer one. Or, maybe she knows that I'm so uptight because all the things I want are simply not the things I'm going to get. At least not anytime soon.

Lots of highly uncertain *or's* in my life these days.

I could just ask outright: What's the deal with Helene? Why are we inviting her here if you've made sure to stay off her radar for so long? Will she like me, and what if she doesn't? But I don't want to ask Bea. I want to ask Ana. And later today, when all these party details are moderately under control, I plan to.

I add a few pinches of several expected spices, but offer up no specific intention. Bea didn't make it a task, so it's probably just a plain old lunch. Between stirs, I set the table. It's just us two every day, but most days Bea has me practice creating a whole meal, from grocery list to fancy plating to the proper containment of leftovers. Honestly, I'm glad for every moment of it. Even with the weight of a hundred people on my shoulders, I'm aware these lessons are going to end with the party. I take in every detail she offers like it's my last chance. Especially with Michael leaving, it actually might be.

"She isn't going to hate you," she assures.

"Who?" I ask, though I know already. She talks about what you are thinking about more often than not. Even so, I want to hear her say it. I want to hear how the word *Helene* comes out of her mouth.

"Helene?" I ask, forcing the name into the room.

"It's best not to speak of her directly. She has feelers out there, looking for any signs and signals we might give."

Feelers? I'm not sure I want to know more. But here I go, asking: "How do you know she won't hate me?"

"She's not one to waste that much energy on someone with no power. You'll annoy her, to be sure. But that's a far cry from hate. Save that for when you challenge her to become Keeper of Magic."

Doesn't that just make a girl feel reassured?

I go to the fridge to get some extra goodies for the sauce, grab the two-quart pan and some water from the instant hot water tap, then step into the laundry room to get the hand-rolled pasta we made earlier, which is now drying on a small rack. I can't float around from room to room the way Bea does, but I notice there's far more grace in my feet than there was even a week ago.

"Don't go so fast," she scolds me from the kitchen. "You can't do Magic if you're not paying attention."

"It's just lunch for us," I argue.

"I would not assume anything at this point," she says in that mysterious I-know-something-but-you-don't way of hers.

Okay, so this isn't just lunch for us. What else it is, I don't know. And I won't until she tells me. But I can take a hint. That much I have learned. I go slower because, graceful or not, I'm not stupid.

"You can be afraid of her, or you can work on your power," she says.

I grab a handful of sundried tomatoes to give the sauce a little extra pop. "So she can be impressed, feel I'm worth her time, and then really hate me? I don't think so. Besides, how much more power can I get in a few days?"

"A lot," I hear a different voice say from the kitchen.

Jake!

Chills and more chills. If this is our *more* for lunch, I'm totally in. I come back to the kitchen slowly so as not to appear too eager. It's Jake all right, in a baby blue button-down and jeans. Tennis shoes, too, like a real person, not just a dreamed-up fantasy.

He cleans up good, I think, then immediately try to pull the thought back. If he can read me across a river, he can read me far too well in the same room. I try to slow my breathing and act normal.

"Hi, Jake." I force my voice to sound even. It cooperates. Mostly.

"Hi, Mayden," he returns, just as calm and steady. His voice always has this low grumble to it, so that it's not hard to remember there's a spotted leopard somewhere in there.

"Took your time getting here," Bea chastises. "I called hours ago."

"The nature police were out," he replies, not taking his eyes off me. "I had to make sure the house stayed hidden."

"So you *do* hide the house!" I say, though once again I'm immediately reminded how crazy that sounds. Bea looks at me like I'm a little slow. Or a lot. Like obviously they hide the house. Like how else could they live there without getting kicked off of government land?

But then Jake smiles, and I smile, and I hardly remember what we were talking about.

Great.

"Watch your fire," my teacher warns. I jump, realizing the artichokes are starting to burn for real. I toss them into the pasta sauce quickly, begging them to shake the edge off the bitter black parts. Not likely, but with Magic, anything is possible.

"Why'd you call, GranBea?" Jake asks, coming to take a look into my saucepan.

My face goes red for no good reason. Actually, it feels like my whole body is burning.

"Can I taste?"

He intentionally touches my fingers as he takes the wooden spoon. His unique current runs between us. A divine something meets…I don't know.

I don't know anything.

"Hot," I say, both in warning about the sauce and in response to his touch.

Jake laughs. I blush. It's all incredibly plebian.

"You're gaining power!"

I nod, shrug, sort of bob my head, not unlike Ana does when she's pretending to be out of it. I notice how he smells like he brought the fire pit with him, all earth and smoke.

Is that romantic? I'm not sure if it's romantic. It might be romantic. Or not. Or…

He takes another taste and seems to roll it around in his mouth a bit. "No really, that's good. I can feel the Magic in it. You're a natural."

I can't help it, I flash him my own set of ortho-adjusted teeth.

"I called," Bea interrupts, "so you could explain to Mayden here about the next steps in shapeshifting. I learned so long ago, I forget what you need to know. I'm scuttling off now. I think I can leave you two to lunch."

With that, she is gone. She left so fast, I have to look around to see if Jake and I are here, or if Magic is playing tricks.

I don't want to make a mistake. Not this time.

"I'm here," he says out loud. "I can feel it when Magic uses me, like that night in your backyard with Michael. It's not like that now."

"Do you think Bea all of a sudden forgot how to teach shapeshifting?"

"No way," he says, laughing easily. "She's the one teaching me. I think she just wanted us to spend some time together. You know, for *some* reason."

I don't know what to say to that, or how much he knows about Ana and Bea's plans for us, or what Michael said or didn't say to him when they met, so I just get on with serving our meal. He watches, wearing what Dad calls the stupid smile. Really, you can see it on anyone when they're attracted to someone else. It's obvious.

I'd smile the same smile right now, if it wasn't for the food. If I had known I was cooking for Jake, I'd have been less of a jerk when working with the main ingredients. How many times has Bea said that what you feel when you cook makes the meal? I'm sorry he's going to eat frustration, sarcasm, and grump.

"Maybe you should give me your perspective on shapeshifting," I suggest once we sit down.

"What can I say? It's hard. Sometimes it hurts. But it's awesome. Python told me she's gotten you to nowhere. That's really good. You have no idea how fast they're letting you learn this stuff. It took me years to get as far as you've gone."

I'm beyond excited to hear it but not sure I should show it. If Michael is hurt by my learning, Jake could be sensitive about it, too.

"What do you think I'll shapeshift into? I mean, I know everyone is different. Do you think I'll be a spotted leopard, like you?"

"You're too nice to be a leopard."

"I'm not always nice." I remember what Ana said about how Jake isn't always good. If he's not, he probably doesn't want a girlfriend that is. I try not to think about being bad together because of the whole thinking-without-talking thing we did at the beach, but I will definitely return to the idea later. And anyway, why is a leopard not nice?

"If you say so," he says, though he hardly sounds convinced.

We start to eat (thank you, thank you, artichokes for not tasting even one bit burnt!), but the communication doesn't stop.

Have you seen me in your dreams? he sends.

It takes me a minute to get on board with the non-talking talking.

Have you seen me in your dreams? he sends again, before I can answer.

Flashes.

Do you love Michael?

As a brother.

Only a brother?

Only a brother.

Do you remember me yet?

Not sure what you mean.

Don't forget what you know about me.

Like what?

He stares, intent. *Like I'm on your side. I'm your protector. Remember that, even when it gets bad.*

Will it get bad?

He nods, then speaks out loud. "You'll feel betrayed. By all of us. Remember I said that here, today. That I knew about it. But also that it doesn't matter. It's only because we have to. We would never want to."

Betrayed? That's something I haven't thought of. Maybe I heard it wrong.

Betrayed?

Yes. Sorry.

I don't know how to process that. Not a clue.

But you're on my side, right?

Always.

With that, we go off into a kind of timeless silence, which only a quiet type like me can appreciate. It's comfortable, and I sense he likes it, too. I'm not sure how long it lasts, but it appears we ate during it because my food is 100% gone.

Do you remember me? he asks again.

How could I remember you? I just met you.

From forever.

I don't know what that means, and it's corny as hell, but I get the shivers in a whole new way. Despite myself, I can't answer. I should. In fact, I should know exactly what to do right now. But I don't.

He stands to leave, touching my hand, sending crazy volts through me.

I want to ask how you remember someone from forever. And if we were speaking, or if this has just been some hugely awkward lunch. But I don't, because I don't actually want to know. I just want to feel what I'm feeling.

It might be stupid, but I've heard love can be like that sometimes. I don't know. I only know I want to find out.

Chapter 28

"**D**oes this mean I have a boyfriend?" I wonder aloud in the car, though I am driving alone.

"Maybe. Maybe not." I answer myself.

Maybe I imagined it. Maybe we didn't mind-meld at all. But maybe we did. Anyway, I keep thinking about him. Jake. My boyfriend? Maybe.

I hadn't remembered much about the dreams he has been appearing in until he brought it up, but since then there's been this avalanche of memories. He's been visiting at night ever since we met. I just didn't realize it was him. Or realize I was dreaming. Or something.

But now I know, and one thing is for sure—I most definitely have a boyfriend in my dreams.

But Magic, please, dreaming is totally not enough.

It makes me wonder how fast you can go from strangers to love. I mean legitimate love. Not just stupid smile love. Ana will know. She'll know about the whole betrayal thing, too. My feeling is that it's about Helene. But I could be wrong. I'm too close this time to assume I'm accurate—another thing Bea droned on about again and again and again. When you're too close to something, or you want it too much, your radar for knowing things can go all wacky on you.

Best not to trust yourself, Bea said.

You have to trust yourself, Ana said.

Thus, I know nothing.

I arrive at the Village and make sure I have the list of questions I had for Bea with me. I may not get any more of them answered (like, zero), but I have to at least make the attempt. There's only so much time today, unless Ana is up for some serious shapeshifting of the clock. Anyway, no doubt I'll leave with more questions on the list, not less. That's how it always goes when it comes to Magic.

We also have to talk about the party. What, exactly, are we going to do with all of us there together? How do we handle Helene finding her there? Will there be some big reveal? This is the last time I'll see Ana before that happens, so I need a solid, workable, sane plan for when all hell breaks loose.

Not that you can actually plan for something like that.

Just the thought of bringing Ana to my house makes me crazy excited. She's going to get out of this place for a whole afternoon. It will probably be the best thing that's happened to her in the last eighteen months.

Unless it all blows up, I warn myself.

The idea practically crashes into me and my heart revs up for what must be the tenth time today. Please let that be a simple fear and not my knowing acting up.

I see someone else ahead of me at the door and quickly make my way through behind them without the buzzer police noticing. I use the back stairs and don't run into anyone, but for some reason Ana's door is closed.

In the middle of the day?

Not. Good.

It takes no time at all to see what I have been intuitively dreading. Ana in the last place I want to see her, flat in bed. She's totally knocked out. Not comatose, like before, and I don't think she's out there floating by choice. I know this look. She's on pain medication.

A lot of it.

Ana, I say in mind-meld, not daring to speak even after checking the bathroom. She gives no answer. This can't be happening. Not two days before the party.

No, no, no and why, why, why?

Ana, I have to talk to you. Can you come around?

No response, but I hear the door open behind me. It's Dr. Garcia, I know even before turning to see her.

"Mrs. Quinn fell last night," she says softly as she reaches to take Ana's pulse. She makes a face like it's bad, but I've been around this place long enough to know that if she had broken real bones in a fall, she'd be in the hospital right now. So we've got that in our favor, at least.

"She wanted to practice standing. We told her no, but she tried anyway."

The angry heat rises in my face. Tell Ana no? Don't they know who she is? Do they think they can treat her like just another body here, waiting to die? I'd say all of this, but I'm too furious to speak, pacing back and forth to keep my mouth shut.

All I know for sure is that I have to get her to the party, now more than ever.

Dr. Garcia puts a patronizing hand on my shoulder. "Things like this happen at this age," she says.

Like I don't know that? Like I don't know anything?

I find my voice, suddenly desperate: "But our surprise party for her daughter is the day after tomorrow. You gave us permission to take her out for the afternoon."

"I'm not so sure about that now," she says, carefully watching my face for reaction. "We'll see, though, okay? If the swelling clears up, and the pain can be managed, she won't need so much medication. But I'll warn you, after a fall like that, she'll be weak."

You're forgetting Magic, I think, *but I'm not.*

The doctor hesitates, then adds, "We have both seen this before, haven't we? Many, many times. Life expectancy after a fall is never very long. You know that."

"That's not what's happening," I insist.

"Why don't you sit with her a while? It might do her some good. And you, too."

It's all I can do not to rip her lungs out of her chest. Instead, I clench my jaw until she leaves. I don't want her pathetic words. I want her help. But what can she do?

I'm the one who has to do something. This is what I've been trained for. I know Magic. I know who Ana is. And most of all, who I am.

"I'm not forgetting Magic, Ana. Not this time."

Some kind of fierceness rises inside me, strange and new. I feel confident in what I've learned and become. I am here at this exact moment for a reason. I came today, not tomorrow, and not right before the party, because today is the day I am needed.

Ana gave me her power, right? That red-hot burning in my hands? Why? So I can give it back to her. That much I know that I know that I know.

Bea taught me that anything that needs strength can get it direct from my hands. I just have to let the energy in my gut come up and through them.

I stare at my hands, feeling a definite strength grow inside me. It feels something like excitement, only more physical. Like my whole body is gearing up, getting ready to do this.

Maybe I don't have enough of what Ana needs. Maybe I'm a novice next to all the others. But what kind of magician would I be if I didn't do all I could?

The decision to attempt healing Ana is a done deal. But how, exactly, do I go about it? The only healing I've ever seen was on Scottie. Nothing Bea did was obvious to me. I ponder, letting the energy grow and move inside me. I wonder, how strong is strong enough, but not too strong? I have to be careful. I mean, if I could break a bowl with my anger, what could happen to Ana if I send all this through my hands?

"Magic," I whisper, imagining a feminine form, all sparkly and floating high above me. "Show me what to do."

Chills run through my body, but no visions appear.

No magical knowing.

No whispered words from afar.

No flow.

I do not spontaneously leave into nothingness, where I might find some great elixir to return with. Nothing is happening. Am I blocked? I can almost hear Bea's words to Michael that first day in the kitchen: "A smart Magician learns what is blocking him and how to dissipate the interruption."

So maybe I am blocked? But, by what?

It comes to me quickly: My anger. I'm still boiling deep down at Dr. Garcia. My body tingles in *yes*.

So, I will have to get rid of that first. I remember Bea's lessons about it on a particularly rough day. Doing it exactly as I was taught, I take several deep breaths, connecting myself to the ground below, through the floor, and through the other floors beneath us, all the way to the center of the earth below. I get an image of hot flowing lava, the kind that can spark a fire in a split second, and allow my anger to flow into that, going up in flames immediately on contact. I imagine the ashes flowing away from me, with more lava from deep, deep below the earth's surface.

All the details of why I'm angry fade away. I'm just angry. Boiling. Feeling it all.

Don't lose yourself in it, Bea instructed, *but don't pretend it away, either. Feel it good and honest, until it's gone.*

I nod, though there's no one to see.

I will myself to wait in the heat of the fire until I see the energy that was anger turn into pure lines of power. I hook into it, just as I was taught, and then bring it back inside me.

Usable energy, just as Bea promised.

It's like I can hear her. Like she's right here, showing me the way.

Okay, I'm ready.

Go to it, girlie.

I get no words of detailed instruction, though. No images.

My stomach grumbles, loud.

Seriously? I'm hungry? Right now?

It rumbles again, this time even louder, actually hurting.

Despite my best intentions, I find myself thinking of tomato soup and Challah bread with Dijon mustard and ooey-gooey melted cheese. I pull myself back from the sensations.

Focus, I instruct myself.

And then it comes to me: The power is in the food. And my power is in fire.

I know what to do! My own heart ablaze confirms it all.

Ever so gently, I put my hands on Ana's bad foot and think of anything and everything magical I have put on a plate since I began learning the ways of Magic. I call upon the healing powers in each and every ingredient I've gotten to know.

Flatbread with extra virgin olive oil, thyme, and lemon. Broiled.

Peppers stuffed with rice, olives, and peppercorns. Baked.

As I've been instructed, I use all my senses. I smell. I see. I taste. Everything in my imagination is invited in so that the essences can join me in the spaces between the atoms.

It's all just as Bea taught me, though I never imagined it would be anything like this. I guess that's why she always says you have to expect anything. Because you can't expect something like this. You just can't.

Grilled, farm-fresh summer squash on warm corn tortillas with drunken goat cheese.

Three-cheese risotto with a dash of chipotle and salt.

The images are so fresh, so alive in my memory, I'd swear I could smell them, even in this horribly sterile room. I wonder how long it's been since Ana's had a real meal here? Tasted a trio of crab, mango, and avocado melting in her mouth?

Too long. Far too long.

I feel the healing essence behind the ingredients moving through my hands into Ana's swollen foot and somehow know they are strengthening her.

Apple spiced hummus dip with warm pita chips.

Rice in grape leaves with lime and parsley.

Fresh honeycomb and fig marmalade on piping-hot biscuits.

Spring rolls with habanero chili sauce.

Hand-cut French fries with rosemary and roasted garlic.

Grilled eggplant in spicy marinara.

Au gratin potatoes with sharp white cheddar—no, wait, *Piedmont!*—*and truffle oil with a tiny sprinkle of sea salt.*

Tofu in tamari.

Mushroom ravioli in heavy cream sauce.

As each dish passes through my awareness, the feelings grow stronger between my hands and Ana's foot. She doesn't come around, but she does seem to relax, her breathing more peaceful and even.

Amazingly, my stomach starts to fill, without eating one ounce of real food.

I return to my cooking and conjuring as the dishes seem to flow from one to the next. I make myself enjoy the nurturing solace of a full stomach, noting that, as Bea has said repeatedly, not everyone is so lucky to have one.

Milk and fresh-from-the-oven oatmeal raisin cookies. What can't that cure?

Angel food cake with berries, because angels couldn't hurt right about now.

Pineapple-coconut sorbet alongside the bliss of a moist, tropical wind.

Dark chocolate banana bread pudding with white caramel and pecans.

I smell each dish, taste them, and then feel their power move through my hands, sending surges of nurturing healing into Ana. I watch as her breath deepens even more, into what appears to be a great sleep.

I feel an immediate urge to stop.

I get a full feeling, as if I've done what I could.

The Magic of the good, wholesome, delicious foods will do its work now.

I pull my hands back and see her foot seem to relax, just a bit.

Go home, says a voice that is mine, and yet more than mine.

I nod to myself, feeling a new understanding rise in me. Bea always insists that we have to act as if our intentions with Magic are already accomplished and that this is the greatest insurance policy for it being so. Not a guarantee, because we can't control the intentions of Magic, let alone the life force of the entire world and everyone in it. But if we have enough faith to proceed as if our wishes will be heard, why on earth shouldn't they be?

I get that now. I really do.

I quietly leave, realizing how amazing it is to be able to do Magic, and to know all that Bea has taught me. Now, we can only wait and see if it works.

Chapter 29

I've done the math, and I think I'm going to vomit.

It's not like the nerves didn't already have me in their grips. Now, on top of everything else, I realize there are a hundred folding chairs waiting for me outside on the lawn. Each one needs a fitted fabric cover from here in the laundry room, and not one is anywhere near ready to go. The covers are sealed in the kind of tough plastic it will practically take God to open.

According to the instructions, each chair cover needs to be carefully opened (*all rips or tears will constitute a purchase*), steamed to remove wrinkles (*detailed how-to provided online*), pulled tight over the seat frames (*detailed instructions provided online*), and tied into a standard square-knot bow on the back (as expected by now, *detailed instructions provided online*).

I've no time for one chair, let alone one hundred.

I'm thinking a bad job will take five minutes, a good job ten. Each. One hundred times the minimum five minutes, and I have five hundred minutes of work in chairs alone. I don't want to think about how many hours that is because when you add that to the other gazillion items on my list, each of which has its own five to fifteen to fifty minutes associated with it, it becomes utterly clear that I will not accomplish my tasks in the exactly three hours and seventeen minutes I have before people start arriving.

Had someone told me I needed to add labor to the delivery fee, we would be fine. But did anyone? Did anyone mention that when you order the fancy white linen covered folding chairs, assembly would be required? Did anyone say anything at all about wrinkles? No. Not Bea or Sally or the supplemental caterer or the party center's personal project manager which is assigned to each customer.

I guess they all forgot.

"You look stressed," Michael says, his leather duffle hanging over his shoulder, weighing him down.

Weighing me down.

I can't think about the fact that he's leaving as soon as the party is over. I just can't.

"I'll deal with it. Can you help me open these bags?" I ask, adding a truly desperate, "please?"

"Sure," he says, heaving off his bag, digging around in it, then pulling out a pocketknife. I immediately weigh the options of him accidentally cutting into a chair cover versus not getting the job done and choose to risk the potential slice and dice.

Take it out of my inheritance, if you must.

"Are you worried about today?" It's obvious, even out of the corner of my eye, that he is upset. I stop for a moment to look at him dead on.

I answer, then go back to revving up the steamer, which I did not even know we had until this very hour. "You're the one who sounds worried."

Maybe he's having second thoughts!

If he doesn't leave, things will be all right. Or at least a thousand times more right.

"I am worried," he confesses, "about you. I have bad news."

If I had time, I'd stop and nicely probe it out of him. But I don't. Not today. "Just tell me."

"Two things, best one first. I'm leaving early. In a few minutes. I'm afraid if I see them all together, I'll stay. And I can't stay."

"What? Wait. No. You can't. This is *your* grandmother's party, remember? What am I going to do with her? No. No way. I simply will never forgive you if you leave before this is over. Ever."

"That's the least of what I'm hoping you'll forgive."

Clearly, he wants to tell me the second thing. But after that, I'm just not up for it. "Please realize that I've only got two out of two billion good nerves left to help me today."

"I talked to Jake last night," he says, ignoring my plea. "I had to risk seeing him again before I go. It was good. But then he told me about today."

He doesn't sound worried. He sounds sick about it.

I make a split second executive decision. If it's not about his deciding to stay, I'm not up for hearing about whatever torture there is to come. Jake hinted at it, and anyway, I can feel it.

"Michael," I insist in such a way that there is absolutely zero wiggle room in what I am about to say, "do not, under any circumstances, for any reason, add to the hell I'm in right now. If something bad is going to happen, then it will just have to happen. I will totally, completely, utterly fall apart if I have anything else on my plate before this party starts."

"But…"

"Do. You. Understand?"

He nods reluctantly, seeming to want to press it, but respecting my choice. "But there's one thing you have to remember, later, when all this is over."

"What?" I snap, remembering Jake said there was one thing he wanted me to remember, too. Everybody's one thing is adding up pretty quickly.

"I didn't know," he says, mysteriously saying everything and nothing at once. "Everyone else, they knew. But I didn't. I only found out last night. I've been trying to decide what to say about it, but there isn't any way for me to do it and not…"

"Too much information!" I shout. "I got it. You didn't know. I'll remember that. Now, do me a favor and call Dr. Garcia to find out if Ana has permission to be released for the afternoon or if all of this is total wasted bullshit. The number is by the phone in the kitchen, and she said she'd tell me this morning."

"GranAna's coming."

"How do you know that?" I ask, immediately suspicious. How much, exactly, is going on behind my back?

Wait, no. I'll just take it as good news. I need some.

"GranBea arranged for a driver to pick her up, too."

"She's all right, then?" I ask, wondering if my healing worked, even a little. The queasy feeling in my stomach must be dedicated to her, at least in part, because hearing the news eases it up a bit. That, plus the relief of knowing both the call and picking Ana up can be taken off my To Do list.

"More than all right," he says with a slightly sarcastic tone, again like he knows something.

"That's great. I mean, we promised we would get her out of there, and now we will." I hear myself sounding like I'm trying to convince myself of something. Like this party really will be a good thing, just like we planned.

He doesn't answer.

I'm going to ignore that, too, for now. Later, I have a feeling I'll try to remember every single clue I'm avoiding at this moment. I glance at the clock, first to make sure it's ticking. It is, so no luck there. Second, to calculate the time gone by and the added time I'll have, now that Ana is taken care of. The math still doesn't work, but it's better.

"You don't have to steam those," Sally says as she rounds the corner of the laundry room, startled at the mess of plastic and linen, then looking at me like I'm crazy to be playing Cinderella at this late hour.

"You want to?" I ask her as I hand over a stubbornly wrinkled fabric thing that, Magic willing, one day will be a bow.

"There's a little zip tab here to open the package," she says, showing me this tiny sliver of plastic, something I ought to have seen, which will make the opening a thousand times easier. Those directions were probably online, too. "Then all we have to do is throw them in the dryer with a clean wet towel for about five minutes a load. Nice day like today, the rest of the wrinkles will work themselves out through the moisture and gravity on the chair. With our super-sized dryer, we'll be done in three loads, max. And yes, I'll be glad to help you. Leave the chairs to me. You have other things to be doing, right?"

Never, ever, in my life did I want to kiss the feet of someone more than I do right now. And it's Sally's feet, of all people. I hand her the whole mess. Someday, I'll say thanks for everything and really mean it.

Michael follows me into the kitchen. I still don't want to hear what he has to say. Even more, say what I have to—goodbye. But it seems it's now or never. He knows it, too, because he's looking everywhere but at me.

"You'll be back." It comes out more of a statement than a question, but really it's a question.

"If they'll have me," he says.

"They will. You have to know that. You're family."

I don't know how all this will play out, but I do know this: If this family won't have Michael, they surely won't have me.

"In the meantime, at the right moment, should it come up..." He pauses, and I take a minute to let him sort it out. You don't rush a goodbye like this, no matter how much you have to do. "I want you to know it's okay to tell them. That I'm gay, I mean. I decided I'd rather they know the whole truth than think I'm abandoning the family just because I'm upset about them not teaching me. Jake already knows everything. I told him last night. I told him I was leaving it to you to decide if, and when, the Grans are ready to know."

I nod my agreement. Who knows when the right time comes for something like that, but I'm glad he's not going to hide who he is from them.

No one should hide, no matter what the cost.

"Are you afraid of Helene and what she'll do if she finds out you're going to learn Magic from someone else?"

Michael just stares at me, looking really, really sad. "I'm not worried about me. I'm worried about you. Try to be ready for anything today."

"That's the only thing I can be ready for," I say, having no energy to laugh.

Michael smiles, looking all the more handsome, now that I love him. "You are good, Mayden, like Ana said. Better than you know. You'll do fine. I know you will. You have to." With that, he pulls me near and hugs me. Hard. Like it means what it does: We're friends, real and true. "I'll miss you."

I nod, unable to say the word *goodbye*. "Come back," I whisper. "Soon."

He doesn't answer, just lets go and returns to the laundry room for his bag. Which means he knows what I know. It won't be soon. I hear the door from the laundry to the back yard open and then slam shut. I take a deep breath and will myself to turn to my list of things to do, trying to think of anything but my new best friend, my almost brother, walking out that door.

Pastries, I suppose, are next.

Pastries and falling apart, not because the party might flop or Helene might hate me, but because the family is now divided, and I have no idea what to do about it.

Fortunately, time moves fast when there is way too much to do. I keep chanting *shapeshifting time, shapeshifting time, shapeshifting time*, but I'm not sure if it's working or not. We're only twenty minutes out when Bea finally bustles in. She looks nice, more dressed than I expected, though her polyester pantsuit looks like a throwback from the Seventies. She's even wearing bright red lipstick. I have a hard time imagining it's to impress the guest of honor, but you never know.

"Alrighty then, where are we?" she asks.

Together we run down the long list of things done, the things yet to do, and then start in on guidelines about which trays should be served when.

It seems all business, but there's something going on behind it. I can feel it. They taught me to feel it.

"I suppose it's time we talk about our guest of honor," she finally says, trying to sound casual, yet eyeing me nervously. I have never—not once—seen or even imagined Bea as someone who gets nervous. All this must be pointing to something big. From the feel of it, it's the Loch Ness monster-with-a-huge-ugly-head kind of big.

"Go for it," I say, bracing myself for anything. Anything at all.

"Well, then," she starts, "she will arrive just after the other guests. We've prepared the gazebo with the ninety-nine orchids. We also pulled out your father's chair from the upstairs hallway and put it under the shade there. That way people can approach her without her having to stand. We will do everything important on the gazebo itself."

"What is she, the queen?" I mock. Dad's big chair is this gothic church monster from a few hundred years ago, red velvet cushion and all.

"She'll have Jack and Sam with her," she goes on, "as well as Dorothy and Craig."

"And they are...?" I lead. Sally made the guest list and sent out all the invites. Another way she was a big help. I might have to rethink her role in my life. A little.

"Jack and Sam are her greyhounds. They are quite large, but well-trained, and only attack if commanded to. Dorothy and Craig are a different sort of hound. She calls them assistants. At least two of the four protect her round the clock."

I'm thinking this is something they might have been kind enough to tell me about before right now, if only so that I could have arranged for doggie bowls or a freshly shot moose or something. And did everyone just happen to forget that Scottie might be roaming around outside? Not anymore. She'll stay tight in my room until it's all over.

Which, it will be, eventually, right?

I mean, how long can a few hours last?

I start to wonder if the hounds are shapeshifters too, but pull myself back. Because really, I don't want to know.

"You should stay back until everyone has gone to the gazebo," Bea continues, excruciatingly cautious with her words. "Then, it will be your turn to approach. You must do so alone." The thought makes my heart stop. I swear, a full two or three beats' worth of nothing goes on in this body of mine.

"You're really going to treat her like royalty?" I attempt to hide my irrational but utter terror behind a thin, thin veil of disgust.

"In our Clann, the Keeper Of Magic is just that."

"So at what point do you think she'll figure out you're here? And Ana, and Jake, too? All of us together, the exact thing we've all been so careful about avoiding?"

Bea gives me another look, up and down, like the day we first met. Assessing me. I get the sense she is trying to see how much I can take. "She already knows," she says flatly.

What? *What!*

How? When? Why?

All along, I've been expecting the huge, explosive moment when she realizes everyone who has been hiding from her is in one place. The climax of her surprise. And she *already knows?*

Bea hesitates, looking like she's about to deliver fateful news. News that could change everything.

I get it. I'm about to learn that thing—that one thing—I was warned about from Jake and Michael. She hesitates again, then looks out the window, and not at me, as she speaks. "This isn't Helene's party." She looks back, no longer hiding from her truth. "It's yours. Helene is coming here for you. You are our guest of honor."

The chills of truth return. It doesn't seem to matter that I don't want them. That this time, they hurt as they run through me, lifting the hair off my arms.

"I don't get it," I respond, given Bea is just standing there.

She offers no details.

No explanations.

No loyalty.

"You wouldn't, child. It takes time for things like this to become clear, and even more time for them to sink in. We can only hope you will forgive us when at last they do."

Chapter 30

Ninety-nine orchids, one hundred linen-covered chairs, and twenty-four platters of food—all for me.

Who would have guessed?

Who *could* have guessed?

But there it is, there they are, waiting for me at the gazebo, complete with Dad's gothic chair just a few feet away. A hundred people, including Ana in her wheelchair, as lively as I've seen her, have made their way up as I watched from the kitchen window.

The dreaded Helene and her crew were last. I only saw her from the back, but her two hounds, which were as huge as hyenas, and her two assistants (one big black man, one bigger white woman, both looking like cops), flanked her closely. They've all been up there for a while now, theoretically chatting and eating, though it looks far more strained than that.

The only thing left to do is join them.

I've said that to myself a dozen times already, each time bargaining for five more minutes, the way you press a snooze button on an alarm you have no real intention of listening to. It's been way too long, but I'm no farther up that hill, now am I?

In the distance, I see Jake standing next to Ana and Bea, looking toward the window every so often. For a moment, I think maybe I'm stepping into an arranged marriage, but that doesn't feel true.

This is about becoming the Keeper of Magic. I'm sure of it.

I mentally walk myself through going up there alone. My heart is in my throat, pounding like a hammer against my vocal cords. I try to tell myself I ought to be happy, like a debutante at a ball. But then I remember I'm a wallflower. That I'm not who they hope I am. That I'm an outsider, and I have no clue in hell how to make pastries worthy of serving on paper plates, let alone the silver platters they went out on.

I can't help it. It does feel like a betrayal, just like Jake said.

And Michael tried to warn.

And I knew from the moment I woke up today, if I am completely, totally, one hundred percent honest with myself.

In spite of everything, I somehow start walking. Or maybe it's just my legs, knowing their destiny.

It's a few hundred yards, half of it uphill, from the kitchen door to the gazebo. I'm wearing a dress for the first time in a decade, if not more.

I wouldn't have, if I had known.

My shoes are reasonably stable, but there is a heel to them, and I'm not used to that. What are they, half-inch or full? I can't remember what the sales lady said. I just showed her the dress, told her we'd be outdoors, and she went right for this pair. She didn't even need to measure my feet. She just looked at them and declared them an eight. It was almost as if she knew my size-eight feet would be walking up this hill on an otherwise perfectly pleasant, sunny summer afternoon.

Why not? Everyone else did.

The scent of orchids wafts toward me, pungent, no doubt straining in the heat. I look up, directly into the light, thinking I ought to be hot. But I'm not. I'm cold.

So maybe I'm dead. Unlikely, but a girl can dream.

Or maybe it's the Magic. Maybe I'm not even here.

Maybe no one is here. Wouldn't that be nice? A good trick, for once.

After a formidable forever, I reach the crowd, which parts for me, just like in the movies. There, right there, front and center in Dad's Gothic chair, sits Helene.

It's not like you have to point her out. Who else besides Ana in her wheelchair is sitting?

Who else has two hounds and two hovering bodyguards?

Who else wields an ornate silver staff that looks like it was stolen from the Middle Ages?

Who else is everyone looking at, besides me? You can almost catch a rhythm to their heads, like a tennis match: Helene, then me, then back to Helene, then back to me.

I don't look the Keeper straight on, but it's not hard to see out of my peripheral vision. She's not what I expected. First off, she looks so much like Ana, tall and beautifully boned, that I can hardly imagine she's as bad as everyone says she is. You can see Michael in her, too. It makes me miss him all over again, coward that he is. Her hair is not gray and pulled into some sharp, tight bun like I expected. It's long and blonde, perfectly placed to frame her face. Clearly colored, but it's done well.

She's pulling it off. She's wearing a pencil skirt, nothing flowing or fancy, and a fitted jacket. The suit is dark gray with a pale blue oxford shirt tucked in exactly as much as it's supposed to be. She looks like she's just come from one meeting, on her way to another. Probably has.

So she'll just have me for lunch and be done with it.

Like Bea said, I'm not important enough to get worked up about.

Python-as-woman steps forward to offer me a steady arm when I finally reach the five short steps I have to climb. I take her hand, like I know what to do. Like I've always known what to do. I look around and see so many faces, most I don't know. But there's Ana and Bea, and Jake. And Python and Sally.

Wait, Sally? What must she think? And where's Dad?

Can't think about that now.

In the never-ending silence, I scan the faces staring at me. Surely there must be someone else I know out of all these people from Dad's work.

Oh, wait. I remember. This isn't Helene's party. It's mine. But then, who are these people?

As if sensing each other, our eyes lock at the same moment: Aunt Mia.

Aunt Mia? Here? But it's not our week.

And anyway, she never comes to my house. Not even once since Mom died.

I look at her and shake my head slowly. How can she be here? What does she know? She smiles back at me, like I should be happy. She excitedly mouths *wait and see.*

Like I have a choice.

"We'll begin," Bea says, stepping forward, obviously the head honcho something or other. No wonder she's all dressed up.

"May goodness prevail," the crowd says in unison.

Really? I mean, *really?*

Despite their good intentions, I feel Helene's less-than-welcoming energy on me so intently I want to puke. Maybe she does hate me, after all.

I look away, up into the sun. Why is it so cold?

"I, Bea Quinn, alongside my sister, Ana Quinn, past Keeper of Magic, do hereby call this meeting to order."

Really, truly, I may puke.

But a meeting is better, more manageable, right? No one expects you to have fun.

There is polite clapping from everyone except Helene and her goons. Even the dogs look seriously annoyed. I notice her wrinkled hands and how the bones of her fingers almost poke through the skin as they wrap tightly around the neck of her staff. It's like you can see the blue blood through her veins, slightly alien. Her first finger circles the top of the carved silver ball on top, going round and round like a nervous tic, though I doubt that's it.

Pissed off is more like it.

I want to steal a glance at Jake, who I am sure is staring at me, but I don't dare. We'll lock eyes, he'll start talking without talking, and I'll lose it.

I swear, I will totally, completely lose it.

"In this, our eighty-eighth year," Bea goes on, so formal she is almost not Bea at all, "we hereby exercise our right to challenge the Keeper of Magic."

The crowd takes a loud, collective deep breath. Helene stiffens in her seat. The dogs must sense it; they dip their heads and growl.

Seriously? Like they didn't all know? Why else did they come?

"We do believe that Magic has not been served well by our current Keeper, nor has it served our Clann and our world."

I want to look at Ana, because I know this must hurt her to hear this said about her own daughter, but I can't. She'd think I forgive her, and I don't. I can't. They could have told me. They *should* have told me. You don't lie to a sixteen-year-old who doesn't know shit about Magic. Not if you are any kind of good.

You could leave, Julie Mayden. You could just turn around right now.

"Therefore, we exercise our right, as is provided to anyone in their eighty-eighth year, to choose a challenger from among the fine. If successful in this challenge, we move that our nominee will immediately and irrevocably become the next Keeper of Magic, with all rights, responsibilities, and privileges therein."

I can barely hear what she is saying. My mind is so busy trying to make sense of it all. If they had just told me there was a ceremony, or even a meeting, I could have prepared. Why keep it from me?

They don't trust me.

That's it.

What else could it be?

"Have all five criteria been met?" Helene's shrill voice demands. At last I steal a look directly at her face. Not exactly the ice queen from storybooks. But closer to that than not. She feels me looking at her, I am sure of it, but does not look back. Probably thinks I'm not worthy of her direct attention.

A small, angry flame starts to burn in my gut. Who does she think she is?

"They have," Bea replies.

Sally starts to clap, but she's the only one, so she stops. It tells me all I need to know about her involvement. She may have been invited today, but she's no insider.

"First, the criterion of extended observation," Bea calls out.

Ana manages to get herself to stand up out of her wheelchair.

Ana? Standing? Despite myself, I move to help her, but am held back with the hand of some stranger. I get a flash image that this is what she was practicing when she fell the other day. I wonder how long she has known, or if she has always known, what today was really about.

Please, please, please don't let her have always known.

A lie like that could break me right now. It really could.

"I have observed the challenger indirectly for eighteen months," Ana offers in a formal tone, much like Bea's. "A full six months beyond what is required."

She sits again, struggling to get back down.

Do not cry, Julie Mayden.

Do. Not. Cry.

"Criterion met," Helene says, sounding bored.

"May goodness prevail," everyone speaks aloud, even Jake.

Of all the things I've seen and heard these past two weeks, this chanting in unison thing wins the prize for most wacky-creepy, hands down.

"Second," Bea states, "the criterion of early training. I, myself, can attest to this as her teacher. She has succeeded in all the prerequisites."

"May goodness prevail," the choir sings.

But will it? Can it, with liars like this?

I am stone-faced, more horrified with every second that passes, but I am determined to not let it show.

"Third, the criterion of potential interest from a suitor."

Jake clears his throat. "Criterion met."

I can't help it. Tears start rolling down my face. My first potential boyfriend is a check on their list? I don't look at him. I can't.

"Is there evidence of innate gifts?" Helene asks with a sneer, as if that would be practically impossible.

"Fourth criterion," Bea cries out, keeping order like she doesn't come from a dirty little shack in the woods. I'm a little shocked at my own ugly thoughts, but really, she deserves it.

Again, Ana struggles to stand. "Wisdom and insight are showing significant early evidence."

"You know early evidence is not enough!" Helene declares happily to her own mother. Her human goons chuckle.

"She has made the first leap in shapeshifting. Very early on, too," Python adds proudly.

"The first leap is hardly sufficient," Helene insists, not bothering to look up.

Honestly, this is all the evil she's got? I thought I'd be pinned to the roof of the gazebo, or something at least a little more fantastical by now. She's just sitting there, barely trying, far more annoying than powerful.

I watch as her finger circles her staff, like she's beyond bored.

"Healing gifts have been verified," Ana adds. "Just two days ago, a complete healing was conducted using the methods taught, through direct connection with Magic and the use of the creative imagination."

A few *oohs* and *ahhs* come alongside the unified, "May goodness prevail."

A test, Ana? Is that what that was?

I want to scream at her, insist my healing work was heartfelt, and beg her to stop all this. She might as well, because there is no way in hell I'm going to be anyone's Keeper now. But I don't say a word. There's more betrayal coming. I can sense it.

I have to know what it is so I can never, *ever* trust anyone again.

"Fifth criterion, proof of lineage through a family member," Bea states.

Well, there it is. Despite myself, despite all that I hate about what is happening, it still hurts to hear this, the one criterion I know I cannot meet.

From the crowd, Aunt Mia steps forward. "It was I who began the nomination process twelve years ago, at her mother's last request. And for the record, I am fourth removed from the suitor."

I can't breathe. I can't do anything.

Mom? Her last request?

This can't be happening. What am I supposed to think? How am I supposed to think?

You can't just spring that on someone. It's not fair!

A rush of ideas short circuit my brain, the dominoes both falling into place and flung in every direction. I mean, is Aunt Mia saying what I think she is? That I am a part of this family? By blood? Am I a real member of the Quinn Clann?

I look at her, my mother's sister, whom I have always trusted. She nominated me for this? When I was four years old? Because Mom wanted it?

"Fourth removed isn't far enough for the suitor!" Again Helene is gleeful.

"I apologize if I have offered a lack of clarity," Mia adds. "I am fourth-removed from the suitor. This makes the challenger fifth-removed."

"Fifth-removed meets the criterion of adequate family distance from the suitor," Bea confirms.

"May goodness prevail!" the crowd nearly shouts.

I can barely keep my knees locked. I'm going to fall.

Any moment now, just watch.

But I don't fall. I'm just standing here.

I need to think.

You can't just throw Mom in, like icing on the cake. You just can't.

They all lied to me. Even Aunt Mia. Why?

I hear it like a chant, over and over again in my head: *They lied. They lied. They lied.*

For years. For my whole life.

I gasp for breath and can't get enough.

I should have let Michael tell me. He would have warned me.

Not like Jake. Or Bea. Or even Ana. They could have. They should have.

They lied. They lied. They lied.

Bea puts a tall, ornately carved stick in front of herself, seemingly unaware that I am suffocating, folding in on myself. "I formally submit that all criteria have been met and move that we continue with the proceedings."

The Clann offers real applause this time.

Finally, Jake catches my eye. *This is the hard part, Mayden. Watch me.*

I look away. The hard part? And which part, exactly, has been easy? Was it learning Ana lied to me? Or that my mother was part of a twelve-hundred-year-old tradition of Magic that no one bothered to tell me about?

Helene stands, leaning heavily on her staff, her finger still circling, circling like a fixation she can't stop. "I concede that the five criteria for a challenge have been met. However, I must inquire. Does the challenger consent to the requirements of the training to come?" She turns to the crowd, looking every bit the politician. "Does she even know the requirements? It appears she doesn't know anything, poor dear."

There is silence. Not good, I'm sure. But then, who cares? At least she knows I'm the *poor dear* here.

But God, will she stop with that damn finger circling? I swear it will drive me mad.

Watch me, Jake sends, though I can barely hear him.

Don't listen. He lied.

"Additionally, is she prepared to state the ways in which she intends to bring Magic to the world?" Helene asks the crowd. "Seeing that you all feel I am not meeting the demands of my role adequately, surely you will expect a great deal of the next Keeper, especially one so young. I'd like to hear her plans now. Wouldn't you all?"

Jake sends thought after thought. I feel them, even through the cheers of the crowd, but I block each one before I can know what they are. I do recall, vaguely, that he warned me about this. About Helene. But he should have said more. A lot more. He should have told me everything and made me listen.

He lied. They all lied, lied, lied.

"The requirements in regards to training," Bea begins. "One. The challenger must share her vision for the future of the Clann should she become the Keeper of Magic, and the Clann must confirm this vision."

They did tell me about that part. But it's not like that helps me now.

"Two. Should the current Keeper of Magic be deemed unfit to choose her successor, and should there be any eighty-eight-year-old female Clann member to produce a challenger, then the criteria for a right and just challenge must be met and confirmed. Three. Once the criteria are satisfied, there shall commence a training period of not less than three months and not more than one year, until the challenger is sufficiently trained to enter into a wholly fair challenge with the current Keeper of Magic."

I don't care what the conditions are. I don't care about anything. *They lied.*

"Four. Should the challenger win this fight, the Keeper shall immediately and irrevocably shall lose her position and the challenger shall be inaugurated within twenty-four hours." Bea stops for a moment, looks at me, then continues. "Should the challenger lose, she shall forever be banished from the Clann, and the reigning Keeper of Magic shall be free to choose anyone from any Clann, at any time, to become her successor."

Banished? And when exactly were they going to tell me about that little loophole?

Liars! Liars! Liars!

"Now, inform her who her trainer will be," Helene insists to a completely quiet crowd. Even the birds have stopped chirping.

"Five. The challenger shall be trained by the current Keeper of Magic."

Everyone's holding their breath on that one, staring at me.

Are they freaking kidding me? Already I can't think, can't breathe, can't stand to be here with even one of them. And they want me to learn Magic from *Helene?*

"Is it so agreed, Julie Mayden?" Bea's face is a stone, but I can feel her begging me.

I'm guessing they want me to speak now? Like I get a choice in all of this? Well, finally.

"I'm supposed to train with her, to then challenge her?" I seek to confirm, my words coming out hard and bitter, pointing a finger directly at Helene.

Just saying it aloud tells me these people are so whacked.

Bea nods. "As is required, according to the tradition."

Look at me! Jake practically yells. It's so loud I can't ignore it.

Despite myself, I look. But when I do, he isn't even looking at me. He's looking at Helene.

Thanks. Some protector he's going to be. Then again, I've probably imagined all that.

I bore a hole into his head with my words: *Screw. You.*

I see Helene smile. She's got this, and she knows it.

God, will she stop with that damn finger?

Yes, yes, the finger, Jake sends, almost screams. *Look at what I'm looking at!*

This time I get it. I look at him. He's not looking at me or Helene. He's looking at the silver top of Helene's staff. In specific, at her finger circling the staff.

Suddenly, what he said at the beach rushes in—Helene screws with you, and makes you think it's you.

Your thoughts.

Your ideas.

I look at her, at Bea, at Ana, at Jake.

I look at Mia, who won't look at me.

Why?

Because she lied. And she hates me. Always has.

Not your thoughts, Jake insists without saying a word.

Now I really, *really* can't breathe.

I think I get it. I think I know what to rely on. Not anyone here. Not anyone anywhere.

Just Magic. Only Magic.

Magic, please, show me what to do.

Without a moment of forethought, I lunge for Helene's staff, grabbing it at the neck. The crowd gasps and a full rush of breath comes into me for the first time in forever, even as all four of her goons lunge at me.

In a split second, I look directly into Helene's eyes and know that all I have to do is not give in.

"Let go of my staff!" she screams. The dogs bare their teeth, needing to be held back by their collars.

"Let go of my mind!" I scream back, feeling my strength return full force.

Again without planning, I knock the staff out from under us both with a quick kick and...

And...

Everything stops.

All sound. All movement.

It's just me and her, and I won.

I won.

"What kind of creature have you chosen, Mother?" Helene asks, her voice deep with anger. "One who would harm the sacred staff of the Keeper? What a pitiful mistake."

I look around as if for the first time.

Not liars. Friends. Family.

"I see no reason to go on with this," Helene says, now addressing the crowd. "The challenger has refused to accept the condition of me as her teacher. I'm not even sure I could teach her, novice that she is. Who touches the Keeper's staff? No one would dare unless they were completely dense and wholly without honor."

"I remind you all," Bea cuts in, also addressing the crowd, "that the challenger has one moon and one sun before she must decide. A full twenty-four hours." She turns to me to add, "And I suggest she take it."

I look at her, and Ana and Sally and Aunt Mia, and something returns to me. Something like loyalty and friendship. Something like love. Even so, there's too much to consider. Too many implications. Too many variables.

I have to do what I do—retreat and think. Alone.

"I need time," I say, and turn to walk away.

No one argues. They even part to make my way easier.

If the few hundred yards from the house to the gazebo was hard, the return is nothing less than agonizing.

They are all watching me. I can feel their eyes on my back.

Only Jake is following, I sense. He could catch up, but doesn't.

In your own time, I feel him send. *I'll be close, but only if you need me.*

I don't reply, because I can't. I need my own thoughts. Not even his will be of help right now. I walk into the back kitchen door, away from their eyes, and then straight out the front.

Once out, I can think of only one thing to do. I take off my shoes and start to run. Slow at first, then faster, then as fast as I can.

I need nothingness, I wordlessly beg of Magic. *If you have any interest in me at all, give me nothingness.*

It isn't immediate, but as I run, it comes, like a strike of lightning.

I dissolve into in bits and pieces heading for nowhere.

It all drops away. The Clann. The world. Everything.

I am free.

Chapter 31

Who knows how long I'm *nowhere?*

Eventually, though, I find myself in a body. And yet not *my* body. There are not two feet on the ground, but four. I am no longer a teenage girl, but a massive complexity of muscle covered in thick, black hair.

Whatever I am, I am something else.

My thinking is clear and simple. I move, feeling grounded to the earth in a way I never have. The padding under each of my limbs makes contact with the sweet floor of the woods as I move, lithe and agile.

The solidity below me tells me all is well.

All is so very, very well.

Sniffing the wind, I understand things I have never known. Direction is a sense. Scent is information. Hearing is sorted into three categories: unimportant, food, and danger.

Simple. Easy. Clear.

I have never run so freely or for so long. The moon leaves, the sun arrives, and I wonder where it is that I'm supposed to be? Nothing comes to me. Perhaps there is, finally, no obligation. I run because it feels good to run. I move this way because I want to, then that way because it draws me.

No other reason. No reason needed.

I run and run until I can't anymore. Panting, I stop.

So easy. When you're tired, stop. When you've gone far enough, go no more.

The endless rush, the urge to feel my very soul fly free begins to dissipate. Other signals come, suggesting food, but I am too spent to follow my nature.

If I just lie down, here, for a moment…

"It's her!" I hear a voice say from a distance. My eyes won't open. So tired.

"Get a blanket. She's shivering. Here, help me get her near the fire."

"Thank God," another voice says. "Mayden? Mayden? It's Aunt Mia."

But how can Aunt Mia know me as Mayden? How can she be here at all?

My brain starts to fill with fog. Or maybe it's ideas. Thoughts. So many thoughts. Who knew thoughts were so heavy? I recapture myself as I was before. Things were clearer, then.

I sorted things out while running, almost without trying, or even knowing.

I understand now. I know who I am. I know who I am meant to be.

I'm exhausted, but I know a time limit has been set in motion. I hope it has not passed. I want to be the Keeper of Magic for my Clann.

Not want to be. *Must be.*

"Back off, all of you," Jake barks with authority, putting something around my shoulders. Jake is easy to place, but it takes a moment for the word "blanket" to register in my head. It's a blanket. Yes. My mind connects the image with the word. It makes sense. Oh, but what a price there is to pay, just for things to make sense. It's like cymbals crashing close to your ears.

I drift in and out, trying to remember where I am, and why I am here. I grab a moment's understanding, but it leaves me again.

"Only six hours," I hear someone say in a moment of coherence.

"I said back off!" Jake growls. It feels as if everyone retreats.

I like the sound of his voice.

Jake. My protector.

Simple. So very simple.

"You did great," Jake whispers, his voice a purr in my ears. He nuzzles my cheek, the animal in him connecting to the animal in me. Without thinking, I turn toward him, touching the corner of my mouth to his. He turns in toward me further.

My first kiss.

I like it.

But sleep. I need more sleep.

I fade off, Jake at my side, curling up next to me, keeping me warm. It seems to last forever.

"Two hours," I eventually hear a voice insist. I try to track it, and realize it's Bea's.

Take your time, I hear him say in the words with no words.

Jake?

Here. For you.

That was so messed up. I'm not sure if I am sending, or just thinking thoughts, but it seems to get through to him.

I did warn you.

You should have told me more. Made me listen.

I couldn't. But I've been here, right here the whole time. We all have been.

I'm an idiot. Everyone must think so.

No one thinks so. We've always known it would have to be like it was.

Why?

"I'd like to speak to that." It's Ana, obviously overhearing our unspoken conversation. I force my eyes open. She's wheeled up next to me, extending her hand.

I take it. I cannot imagine a world without Ana in it. No matter who she is or what she had to do. It is her name, along with Mother's, I would call upon for strength should I ever truly need it.

Still, she did lie. A lot. How can that be good?

"You could have told me," I croak out.

"And if we had? If we'd told you that you were selected as a young child, and that this was your mother's dying wish, what would you have done?"

"My head hurts," I say. Jake rubs my arm, gently, not too much.

"You might have taken the role for your mother's sake," she continues "to fulfill her wishes, and not your own. You are like that."

I hear people agreeing in the background. Not a hundred people, but more than just the few of us.

"This had to be your calling and your choice," she says. "No one else's. If you are to be the Keeper of Magic, that choice had to be made free and clear of any sense of obligation."

"It's true," I admit, "I would have done it for my mother, without question or thought."

Ana nods. She knew.

"So I'm a member of the Quinn Clann? Truly, by birth?" I think I just need to hear it again.

Maybe again and again.

"You are," Bea comes close to say. "And for all of our lies, you must know this: You are the only one we all felt confident in nominating as the next Keeper of Magic. The only one with any real and true chance of defeating Helene, especially with her as your teacher. Our faith in you has always been true."

I forgot the part about Helene as my teacher. "But how can I learn from her? If she's bad, and she teaches me, how will I stay true to what is good?"

"As a candle lights a room," Aunt Mia assures me.

For some reason, this makes me think of Michael. I wish he were here. He should be here. That much I became sure of, out there in the night. We are meant to be together. To work together, all three of us. I saw that future, as clear as anything I have ever seen.

"Under two hours," Bea repeats gently.

I look to Jake and feel the strength of his presence. Even if he can't run as the spotted leopard should, he has to know how wonderful it is to become your truest animal self.

I get better at shapeshifting every day, he assures me.

"What kind of animal was I?" I ask aloud. Black fur is all I can remember.

"Black Panther," Bea says proudly, "like me. We are cut from the same cloth, girlie. I couldn't be more happy about it."

You were beautiful, Jake sends, probably too shy to gush in front of them all. I catch it on the wind, like a breeze, refreshing me.

"About the challenge?" Bea says, obviously in a hurry.

"Do we have to go back to my house? See everyone? I shouldn't have been such a coward."

"You're no coward," Jake insists.

"No need to go anywhere," Bea assures. "There's enough of us here, now, to bear witness to your decision and decide upon it. If you are ready, we'll get out the pen, you'll make your declaration of intent, you'll sign your agreement, and it will be so. We can give you a little more time to formulate a proposal, if you need it. But only a little."

I look at her, then Ana, then Mia, then Jake. My family. My real family.

I don't need any more time. I'm clear on what I'll do as Keeper of Magic. It became clear when I was out there, running, at one with the earth and everything in it.

"I'll challenge Helene," I say.

Ana smiles and Bea cries. Who could have imagined she'd be the blubbering one?

"Thank you," Ana says. "We all thank you."

"You might not," I say, knowing what I have to say could blow it all, but that I have to say it anyway. "First you should hear what I'm going to do with the Magic."

"Yes, of course, we want to know!" Ana says.

I force myself to sit up. They all come closer, ready to listen. Dozens of them, I think.

"Maybe you don't," I warn, suddenly nervous again.

They look at me, waiting, as unsuspecting of what I'm going to say as I was of what they did back at the gazebo.

"As a member of the Quinn Clann," I start, trying to sound formal, given the occasion, "if I am the Keeper of Magic, I will be changing many of our oldest traditions."

I hear a series of gasps, and continue before I lose the nerve. "First, no one person will be the Keeper of Magic. That is too much power for only one. Things can go wrong. Look what happened with Helene."

No one speaks. I don't think they can.

"I will need both Michael and Jake at my side. And so, as Keeper, I will insist that three of us share the power and responsibility equally."

I don't dare look at anyone but Jake. "Jake is a potential suitor, yes. But he's no helpmeet. He's a man. Michael is, too. They both are leaders, in their own way, and they need a role that requires more than just doing whatever the female Keeper of Magic says. Besides, Magic herself showed me in my first vision that we had always been together. I was shown that for a reason."

"Michael will always have a place here," Ana insists.

"But a real place? A place of power?"

"If he wanted that," Bea argues, "he should have shown his desire to be a suitor!"

"No," I say, realizing this is the time. "He told me I could tell you something important, and there is no easy way to say it but to say it: Michael is gay. He will never love a woman, because he doesn't love women. He loves men. He's known that since he was a small boy. Even though I wish he were here to say it himself, he's not. He's gone because too much was kept from him and for too long. Without a place for him, a real place, I'm afraid we may never get him back."

Ana and Bea look flabbergasted, though I can't be sure about which part. That he's gay? That we may never get him back? You can see the understanding dawn on them, but nothing comes from Ana or Bea.

"Ana," I go on, "do you remember what happened with your father? How he wanted a place of leadership in the family, but there wasn't one, and how that ate away at him? And how he turned to his bad side because of it? We can't let that happen to Michael. He's too good. We need him too much."

Still nothing. Everyone is silent, maybe even holding their breaths.

Wheels are turning in all their brains, to be sure. But no words. And time is running out.

"So this is my intention. That three will rule equally, and no one will be kept out for any other reason but that they are undeserving of the role."

I wait and wait, but still, there is dead silence.

Jake is with me. I can feel that.

Aunt Mia is only worried because of Ana and Bea, but I know she'll be as proud as my mother would have been. She probably thinks this is for Mom, but really, it's for anyone who has no place—who cannot find home just because of who they are and who they love.

Ana looks to Bea and Bea back to Ana.

I can feel the stalemate in the air. We all can. It's twelve hundred years old.

Come on, Magic. Come on.

"This would be so very different for our Clann," Ana finally says.

"Yes, I know. But just as you have challenged me, so I challenge you, Ana Quinn and Bea Quinn. These are the times I was born to. They are the truths I have to follow. These are the times we live in now. Unless you don't want me to lead, I am sorry, but I give you no other choice."

"I don't know what to say!" Bea cries out.

"I do," I say, because I do. "You say *may goodness prevail*."

Again there is quiet, as if everyone must pick up the gauntlet I have thrown down.

"May goodness prevail," Jake says proudly, moving closer, showing his support with a hand on my hand.

"May goodness prevail," Aunt Mia repeats with tears in her eyes.

Ana looks at Bea, and Bea at Ana.

The sisters confer privately, silently, in ways I'm sure only twins can.

Finally, they turn to me. "May goodness prevail," they say in unison.

It is so strong, and so true, I swear I can see the goodness rise up on the wind and shoot out into the world. I can only hope Michael feels it, wherever he is.

"May goodness prevail," all the others say in joyous unison.

This time, it doesn't sound weird. It sounds exactly right.

Bea quickly moves to get a huge piece of paper, already filled out with a ton of legal mumbo jumbo, and a gargantuan pen.

"Tradition," Bea says to me, opening a bottle of ink that might be as old as she is.

I sign *Julie Mayden* at the bottom, but Bea doesn't look satisfied.

"Of the Quinn Clann. You have to write that," she insists.

Of the Quinn Clann I write in big, swooping letters, so big no one will ever question it.

Not even me.

Please visit MaydenChronicles.com to read the epilogue.

Acknowledgments

An indie artist relies on so many different people to make a book come to form. Most of all, I thank my husband Brian—who has always encouraged the time and energy I have put toward my writing. I am blessed beyond blessed to have my life held together by you.

Next, I send a warm and heartfelt thank you to my early readers of the first draft, which was first published in blog format at MaydenChronicles.com. This included blog followers, friends and a special group of elders from the Asbury Community in Solomons, Maryland who helped me understand what life might really be like for our character Ana. Your input and encouragement for the story kept it going all that first year and ultimately inspired my completing the final draft of book one.

Six years later, the ending was completely rewritten and several more drafts were completed. Early readers during this process included a secret Facebook group that included Lisa Jemus, Helena Loki Solorzano, William Frank Diedrich, Stephanie Johnson, Eve Unterkoffer, Shelley Schanzenbacher, Kirstin Asher, Jamie Dee Schiffer, Carin Currie, Kyle Lutz, Maggie J Hensley (and her entire classroom in Phoenix, AZ), Rachel Hubbard, Cathy Mesick, Alena Roney, Lucy MacKay, Nylah Bannister, Sabrina Hinkleman, Kaylee Brace, Catrina Noelle Ashton, Jennie Osterman, Cathleen Cowell, Julie Fletcher Cowell—I thank you all. In addition, I cannot thank sage reader Lelia Nebeker and meticulous editor Terry Nebeker enough. I am also indebted to my teenage interns, Ana Yacopino and Sheridan Connell, and my Irish team, John Rooney and Finola Howard.

Other Fiction By Robin Rice

A Hundred Ways To Sunday
Venus For A Day
Do-Overs: An Irish Story

About Robin Rice

An internationally published author of both fiction and non-fiction, Robin is also a social change artist and a mentor to high performance leaders. Her writing has been translated into three languages, and her social change efforts have been featured in major media in 30 + countries. In 2012, she created YourHolidayMom.com so that our LGBTQ youth could have a loving mother's support between Thanksgiving and New Year's Day. In 2014, Robin created the #StopTheBeautyMadness campaign at: StopTheBeautyMadness.com, offering a stark look at our beauty culture through 25 intense graphic ads. Her "50 One-Minute Meditations With Robin Rice" app is available for both Apple and Android devices. To learn more, visit RobinRice.com.

Made in the USA
Middletown, DE
06 August 2016